Alliance of Bonds and Storm

Book Two of the Sorrowborn Trilogy

April Davis

Kevin A Davis

Inkd
Publishing

For readers.
For Family, born and found; in all their wondrous colors,
preferences, and identities.
For Love

Alliance of Bonds and Storm

Contents

Introduction	ix
Chapter 1	1
Chapter 2	8
Chapter 3	15
Chapter 4	21
Chapter 5	30
Chapter 6	36
Chapter 7	42
Chapter 8	47
Chapter 9	53
Chapter 10	59
Chapter 11	68
Chapter 12	76
Chapter 13	84
Chapter 14	93
Chapter 15	103
Chapter 16	108
Chapter 17	114
Chapter 18	127
Chapter 19	132
Chapter 20	138
Chapter 21	146
Chapter 22	151
Chapter 23	156
Chapter 24	162
Chapter 25	165
Chapter 26	170
Chapter 27	176
Chapter 28	180
Chapter 29	186
Chapter 30	193

Chapter 31 202
Chapter 32 210
Chapter 33 219
Chapter 34 227
Chapter 35 236
Chapter 36 245
Chapter 37 253
Chapter 38 261

Afterword 279
Acknowledgments 281
About the Authors 283
Also by April Davis & Kevin A Davis 285
Also by Inkd Pub 287

Introduction

The Sorrowborn Trilogy is a character-driven YA Adventure Romance set in the area that once had been Georgia and the Carolinas.

Caitlyn and Dean have escaped Camp Sparta and hidden in the marsh at the north end of Lake Marion. However, nowhere is safe, and they must make some quick decisions.

TO COLUMBIA
ALLIANCE
SUMTER
IANDIL
CRYPTID
ZONE
CENTER
KISHARN
VINNIE
NORTH
MARSH
LAKE MARION
INTERSTATE
SAVANNAH
CHARTER
CAMP
SPARTA
SANTEE

Chapter One

The cool, early morning breeze of March in the Carolinas kept me from standing in the shallows of the water as Dean did. He wore only jeans rolled to the curves of his calves until they couldn't get any higher. Black hair waving, he cast one of the fishing lines with a ripple of muscles tanned from shoulder to waist. The cold never seemed to bother him, a benefit of his werewolf condition.

He reached back, offering me the pole. "Caitlyn?"

I blinked and jerked into motion to swap it with the one I held. "Sorry. Distracted."

Dean smiled and winked before he began reeling in the drifting line. Over the past three weeks, we'd found a balance between light flirtation and dangerous agony. He still couldn't control his emotions if we went too far beyond a kiss. Four times he'd shifted into his wolf form and run away, leaving me worried, unsatisfied, and in tears.

I tied off the pole and set it in the tripod of branches and mud where it would stay until we caught something or the bobber threatened to get tangled in river grass. Around a piece of ground six feet wide, the endless marsh jettied into a wide swath of a lazily drifting tributary that he found offered the best fish. We'd managed to stay fed and safe from soldiers and cryptids, though I smelled like a swamp and loathed cleaning with the brownish water. Lake Marion stretched south from where we stood, a never-ending expanse of deeper blue.

Tonight we'd take Dean's rowboat out for some night fishing. A single compound would be lit on the northeast shore of the lake, but they wouldn't bother us. We'd met two of them once, a couple who were out hunting. Three families and their cats had gathered together and built some protection against the cryptids that the Sorrow had brought. Dean had lied and told them we were traveling west. The woman had been nice enough to offer six pecans in the winter, which we'd rationed over three days.

I didn't miss Camp Sparta, but I missed the food — and Roxie. Shaking the thoughts away, I focused on Dean's arms.

"Not cold?" I asked. I'd taken to wearing his jacket. Werewolves evidently kept warmer even when they hadn't shifted. Still, he was standing in freezing water without shoes.

"No regrets." He checked his lure then stepped back on one foot to cast it out. "Except for this hole that is tapped out. With warmer weather, we might need to move our spot closer to the lake."

After weeks of only sneaking out of our hideout on the boat at night, I was ready. "Let's scout out a spot today. I can trail a line behind the boat as we go or something."

Even with his face away from me and mostly covered in black strands, I could see his expression tighten. He glanced at the trees surrounding us. Some were on bits of marsh; some stood in the water.

"C'mon. Call it a date. I'll bring candles," I coaxed.

"You don't *have* candles."

"Grump."

"Naive."

"That doesn't work. Grump is a title, naive is a description. You're horrible at this." I pulled my blonde ponytail back and retied the cord. "Please?"

He glanced at me, shrugged, and began reeling in his line. "No regrets."

I bounced on my toes, water oozing around my boots, then quickly grabbed my pole. I could reel it in at least. Pulse rising, I spun the tiny handle.

It took us twenty minutes to get back to our camp, which consisted of a lean-to on oak roots with a shred of plastic we'd found. It did nothing to stop a downpour. The stench of fish mingled with the heavier scent of our fire pit.

I considered taking off my boots, but we might end up out of the boat at some point. I let him slide it into the water, stowed our fishing gear alongside one of the oars, and climbed in.

Dean had worked out a path through the marsh to the lake, and our nightly trips had widened it. I had never traveled it in the daylight. Some of the leafless trees were testing shoots, but as we neared the broad expanse of water, the shore and horizon became defined.

"Keep an eye the lake. If anyone is out, they'll be there."

I dutifully watched the endless line of grass and tree trunks. Birds, raccoons, and squirrels dominated the woods here. As the tendrils of marsh thinned, the lake became the horizon to the south.

When the white campers of the compound came into view, I was surprised. "There." I gestured as he wove through two trees. "They've got boats?"

Two silver crafts slightly larger than ours were pulled into the grass. Two men stood on the shore facing another who sat at a picnic table, surrounded by four small trailers.

A truck and two ATVs were parked farther out. A shadow shifted as a dog moved at the feet of the man inside the compound. Beyond a wire fence, a winter forest rose up the incline.

"Soldiers." Dean spoke the word like a swear. They *had* been trying to kill him.

In each of the boats stood another figure. I could make out the weapons, even as Dean jostled us.

"They often check in on the people who are out here at the edge of the zone. I didn't know they came this far north." I sagged, knowing Dean would move our camp.

"Philanthropists." He was turning us around.

"What's that?" I asked.

"Kind people."

They weren't; we both knew that. The army did protect the citizens of Santee, and they patrolled the areas where rare groups like these families refused to leave. I didn't know what they'd do if they caught a traitor like me, but Dean they'd either kill or dissect for being a werewolf.

An echoing gunshot set the birds around us squawking and flapping out of the trees. The man inside the compound sprawled back over the table.

I saw the muzzle flash from the camper window when the closest soldier went down. The gunfire rumbled across the lake as flashes fired into the campers from the woods on the southern side. Dark uniformed soldiers crept forward.

"Crap. Crap." Dean jerked us sideways with a push of the oar against roots.

"The children." Ice crawled up my arms under the coverall sleeves. I could do nothing but keep riveted to the scene.

The soldiers on the bank had dropped into boats or grass while their comrades tore into the campers with automatic weapons. Windows shattered and left fragments of curtain waving in the air.

One of the doors opened, and bullets puckered the soft metal. A woman fell out, and a small cat darted into the maelstrom.

Orange flame sprouted from the side of a camper. Fire licked over the roof and glowed underneath. The shots stopped as a second fire sprung up.

"They're killing them all," I said. Dean had turned us around, and I knelt on my seat to see behind us.

"I know. Get down before they see us."

My eyes blurred as flames engulfed half the trailers. A man and child leaped out of a door, dropping to the ground after two steps. The gunshots echoed across the lake.

I spun and dropped to the seat.

Dean's features were sharp and hard. His brown eyes were locked on the scene. I had to hope he wouldn't turn.

We would be moving very far away.

Another gunshot echoed over the lake, then a second. The families were likely trying to escape the burning campers.

"Why?" I asked with a choke that pitched my voice.

Dean couldn't answer for the soldiers. "They're killers. It's obvious. You trust them too much."

"They shouldn't be killing humans, just —" I stopped, barely able to see him through the tears, but I regretted what I'd almost said.

"Cryptids." His eyes finally flicked to mine. "Like me."

A dull thud sounded in a tree behind Dean, and I squinted into the woods.

"Shit," Dean said.

The gunfire echoed, and my eyes widened. Something whistled through the branches to my right.

"Get down," he said. He, however, leaned into the oars and remained a target. Each stroke caught grass or roots.

I spun to see behind us, dropping to my knees on the floor of the boat. My pulse pounded in my ears, deadening the last gunshot. The trees grew thicker between us and the inferno that had been the compound. Black smoke trailed into the air, then drifted south under the wind.

One of the soldiers pushed on the bow of a boat while the man inside rummaged at the back. Roots and grass made it hard to see them.

The rumble of an engine reached us, and Dean's swearing leaped to a new level. "First place we can, you hide. I'll draw them off."

I glanced over my shoulder. "No." On a very selfish level, I knew I'd never survive in the wilds on my own, and without Dean, I might not want to. "Get us to a hidden area, and I'll use my magic."

"Nothing is easy," he whispered as he rowed.

As my comment sunk in, I imagined the men dead at my hands. Part of me wanted revenge for the families at the compound, but I couldn't do it. I wasn't a soldier, a killer. At least, I didn't like to think of myself in that way.

I'd happily send them and their boat into the trees, though, ruin them enough so we could escape and keep running. In one short morning, my life had changed once again.

The sound of their motor pitched as it drew closer.

I flexed out, reaching for the otherness, and found it ever-present, waiting to be used. Pivoting, I focused ahead. We'd need a place to slide the boat out of sight so they wouldn't shoot me before I could ambush them.

My heart pounded harder, but slower. I wanted to hurt these soldiers. I swayed as I thought of Eric, then Roxie. My jaw tightened.

Dean hadn't argued with my plan.

I remembered the storm I'd brought down on Tyrell and Selina. Dean had barely survived, but I'd saved him.

We turned into a broader waterway, and Dean poured his muscles into the oars. Birds circled farther to the north, searching for a new place to roost. We were loud enough that squirrels and raccoons hid.

I almost pointed into a patch of grass, but it would have left no cover. Ahead, roots from a large oak mounded high about the base, offering some concealment.

A flash of pink and blue caught my eye beyond it.

"Moonjir." I whispered his name, and Dean's eyes flashed.

Chapter Two

Moonjir sat on a decaying log with his fox legs crossed at the ankle and an impish smile on his face. His sky-blue fur tinged with pink appeared bright against the shaded browns of the woods behind him. His tail trailed along the rotting log then pointed deeper into the wilderness to my right.

"What is Moonjir doing?" I asked myself more than Dean.

The impossible cryptid leaned back against empty air, and his elbows folded at his sides like they leaned on the arms of a chair.

Once he seemed sure he'd caught my attention, he stood with his tail pluming above his head. With a slight bow, he sauntered to the right and disappeared behind a wide oak.

"We're going to follow him." The strange cryptid had never harmed me, and I'd always believed that he tried to help me in some incomprehensible way. I just wished he would speak something other than riddles.

Dean studied me before he spoke. "Tell me where to go."

The motor behind rumbled too close; I dared not even glance back. As we passed the alcove I'd originally considered, I spotted a log just under the surface that would have blocked us. We'd have been trapped.

"Okay, coming up."

Dean glanced over his shoulder and nodded, "I see it. Hold on."

He pulled the oars one more time, then plunged them in opposite directions. His boat tilted in a sharp pivot, and I clung to the sides.

Moonjir walked across the old lily pads and scum that covered the inlet. He glanced at me, paused, then peered down at his feet. Like a character in an old comic book, he sunk to his chest, then continued walking. Water flowed around him as he brushed a path through the floating debris. He guided us to a circular pool with steep banks rising to a forest.

Dean continued to turn the boat to the right, bringing us to the far side of the large oak that blocked us from sight. The soldiers' engine whined as they followed.

Moonjir climbed the bank four or five yards away. I readied myself to jump out while Dean maneuvered and propped us with his oar. I slipped and landed my left boot in the muck, soaking my coveralls to the knee. I had no grace when it was important. My right leg slid in the mud, and I flopped face first onto the bank with both feet in the frigid water.

I had begun crawling out when Dean sprang from the boat, knelt beside me, and dragged me into the grass. "They might not see us," he whispered.

Moonjir spoke beside us, despite how far away he'd been. "Oh, I bet they will." About two feet from Dean, he lay sideways in the brush with his head resting in the palm of his paw, propped up by his elbow.

I could hear a voice muffled against the engine. Water splashed.

Dean growled, "Get out of here."

Moonjir raised whitish eyebrows. "And miss this?"

I flattened to the ground as Dean did. If the soldiers kept searching down the tributary, they might not catch the dull gray of the rowboat.

The tree and surrounding root mound hid us well. To the right of that, I could see the river through the opening to our little pool. Grass covered much of the far side of the soldiers' path, broken with one lone tree. If I needed to send them flying, it would be there.

When this was over, I would thank Moonjir. His timely help and some luck might have been just what we needed to get out of this situation.

The first soldier crouched at the bow, weapon pointing up the river. I recognized the uniforms and my fist tightened. My last days at Camp Sparta had soured me on the military, though I'd never been overly enthusiastic. Killing an entire compound of innocent people made my teeth clench. Despite an angry urge, I wanted to let them pass without hurting anyone.

The bow of the boat passed the log where Moonjir had been waiting for us.

The man at the back steered with a stick attached to the engine. His head swiveled from one side to the next with an orange beard jutting from his chin. He nearly missed us.

Eyes widening, he saw the boat, then locked eyes with me. Pale eyebrows rose as if he might recognize me. The motor lulled. His free hand lifted a pistol.

I drew the otherness around me in a roar. Air sprang to my call from the woods and the open sky above. Wind bent branches and blew leaves into the air. The water scum beside us rippled. I drove tendrils of targeted gusts at the soldier I could see, at the boat, and into the barely visible man in the front.

The gunshot cracked, loud and sharp.

My magic impacted with enough force that the weapons flew from their hands and hats took flight. The boat toppled as the soldiers scattered into the grass. My power hit, but the angles were wrong. The pursuing soldiers did not fly high, but tumbled across the tops of grass with limbs flailing. The man on the bow who'd been holding the rifle still had a revolver on his holster. For all my fear of killing these men, I only knocked them a dozen yards into the marsh.

"Hmm," said Moonjir. "Didn't really rise to the occasion, did you?"

Dean grunted and grabbed my arm as he stood. "We need to go."

I stumbled to my feet, shivering from cold and the use of my magic. "I'm sorry."

Already the soldiers were moving, stirring the tall grass. I could target them again. Moonjir hadn't shifted from his spot and watched me curiously.

Pushing me in front of him, Dean pointed us north into the woods. "Go." What might be trees and roots one minute might turn into marsh in another, but there weren't many choices. I scrambled forward, waiting for a gunshot from behind.

"Can I come?" asked Moonjir.

"No," Dean's voice grumbled, and I hoped he wouldn't turn. He'd been working hard to control it.

I raced for the thickest trunk and clambered through leaves and brush with it at my back.

A gunshot rang out. A bullet thudded into a tree, and relief flooded my chest. I chanced a glance back to check on Dean. Moonjir loped behind us on two legs with a silly grin.

He passed Dean to run beside me. "That was rather exciting. What have you two been up to?"

"Really not a good time." I tried to mimic Dean's stern tone.

"Very little is as it seems, and a conversation is always in order when there are multiple paths ahead." Studying me, he didn't even glance down as he trotted over the bramble and roots.

I nearly tripped on a vine. "What paths?" There hadn't been any more shots from behind, so perhaps the soldiers were having a difficult time following us.

"Where to go from here?" Moonjir waited for a response, but I didn't have one.

We'd left the little bit we'd owned, including water containers, behind. Dean had his knife on his hip, and I wore his jacket. Anything else we retained rested in our pockets. I could use some water.

The woods ahead dropped to the right, and I veered left to avoid any boggy areas. The scent of pine and brush had overcome the fouler odors of the marsh. The soldiers might give up after a while and we could risk going back for our things. Moonjir was right; we did have some choices to make. I didn't know where to go.

"Don't slow down," said Dean from behind.

I hadn't realized it, but winded and with my legs aching, I'd dropped from nearly a full run. Taking a deep breath, I pushed harder. "How long will they follow?"

"Don't know. Don't want to find out, either."

Despite few evergreens, the forest hid the horizon. "Am I still headed away from them?" I didn't want to run in a circle and end back with the soldiers.

"Sun to our right," Dean said.

"Look at what's real." Moonjir's tone lilted, as if reciting or singing. "I love the bonds you two have made. Connections are important, and especially ones between those who are so different. Remember, you have the power to break them as well as create them."

"What do you want?" Dean's voice snarled with gruffness, on the edge of anger.

"Me? Nothing at all. I have everything. You two are the ones who have left it all behind, once again. I would suggest you be open-minded to new friends."

"Like you?" I asked.

"I'm an *old* friend at this point."

"Friend," Dean muttered.

Moonjir scoffed. "You both could use some new friends. Caitlyn could use a little confidence as well."

I huffed, trying to run in the wet muck. "We're just fine."

"I can see that." Moonjir's tone dripped with sarcasm. He danced ahead of me and pointed into the woods ahead. "Keep on your path, and we'll meet again. You're much stronger than you know, even if you can't save everyone." He slipped to my left side and slowed to a walk.

Trying to peer back at him, I slipped and planted both hands into soggy soil. "Where are you going?" I asked.

Dean stopped and pulled me up by my armpit.

Moonjir shrugged, hands upraised. "Where I am, of course."

I didn't really have any more to say, but hesitated even as Dean pulled me forward. Moonjir made no real sense, but I felt like he wanted me to understand his words.

When I glanced back a moment later, he'd vanished. Sighing, I let Dean lead, and we wound around dreary bogs and rivulets until finally we spotted a break in the trees ahead. Only then did he slow us to a jog. I had no idea where we were, and I doubted he did.

As my heart rate slowed, my chest felt hollow. I didn't want to believe the army would butcher those families as they had, but the images of the man falling with his baby wouldn't fade. We didn't dare go back to our home in the marsh if the soldiers had moved that far up the lake.

"Are we heading deeper into the cryptid zone?" I asked.

"I don't see a lot of choice. Not at the moment." Dean dropped to a walk and put his hand out to hold mine. "We'll figure it out. After all this, I'm not giving up."

"Me either."

"About what he said —" Dean swallowed and paused to stare at me "— about the bonds." He shifted awkwardly with an expression of apprehension I'd never seen on him. "I *do* love you."

Standing in scraggly brush, I nearly started to cry. I'd said the word once when we first set up camp, and he acted as if I hadn't, so it never came up again. "I love you." My hand trembled, reaching for his. "With all my heart."

"Lousy timing." The edge of his mouth twinged, then pulled into a full smile. "I've never said it since — my mother disappeared. I was always afraid I'd lose people."

I couldn't tell if he would say more, so when the pause dragged on, I kissed him. Only a couple tears rolled down my cheeks. I knew he loved me, but it felt so good to hear it.

Dean cleared his throat after a minute and glanced behind before leading us forward.

The stretch of treeless tall grass and occasional brush ahead had probably been a cow field or farm at one time. Copses of trees that bordered it almost hid a road on the other side. We hadn't slogged through wet soil for a while. Walking under a final leafless tree, I stopped.

On the road beyond the field and trees, the soldier standing beside his motorcycle raised his rifle.

Chapter Three

I froze at the sight of the man who reacted like he'd just spotted us as well. He couldn't be from the same group of soldiers.

A bullet whistled in the brush at my knees as the gunshot cracked a fraction of a second later. Birds scattered around us, I leaped to the side, and Dean tackled me as I dropped. Stiff, dead grass dug into my face, and the scent of earthy debris filled my nose. Holding onto me, Dean rolled us back toward the trunk of the tree.

He growled a swear as two more shots whipped through dried brush.

Roots dug into my right elbow before he swung me around the back side of the tree. Dean's jaw tightened and cheek muscles rose in the beginning of his shift into a werewolf. I no longer felt threatened when he shifted. My emotions were frayed, and I imagined his were in no better condition.

His face elongated as he rolled away from me, squirming in his jeans and boots. His black hair had already turned silver.

The soldier kept firing, and the shots were low, aimed to

catch us in the cover of dried brush. One bullet splintered the tree. A quiet, innocent breeze drove in from my left, stirring dead branches and brush.

Dean tumbled three yards from me. I cringed at each bullet, sure they would find him. In the form of a large wolf, he rose on all fours, coated in silver fur. With a flick of his rear leg, he kicked of his last sock. He wore a toothy snarl, and his dark eyes flicked to mine for just a second before he ran away, back the way we came.

I knew he wouldn't leave me. According to what little he would tell me of his past experiences, he retained most of his intelligence, though his emotions ruled him. I couldn't risk him doing something foolish — not without me.

The soldier would move closer, or others would join him and they'd head for this tree. It was wide enough to hide both of us, but the first real limbs were well over my head. To my right, a tree of similar size had a large limb and branches cradled under it.

If I guessed right, Dean would circle through the forest and try to catch the soldier from behind. I wanted to have a view before then. I also didn't want to get shot getting there.

The bullets stopped, and I dove at my chance. Wriggling along the ground, I avoided the taller brush that might sway and made for the second tree.

Burrs caught in my sleeves as I slithered past, or through, some animal's poop. It smelled like a dog, but how would I know? The silence had me believing the soldier crept across the field, getting closer. Perhaps he thought he'd hit us.

The branches of the fallen limb proved impossible to worm through without causing them to stir, so I chanced a quick peek at the field.

The soldier had moved into the copse of trees between me

and the road, but hadn't ventured any farther. He stood beside a trunk, aiming as he scanned the forest. I blessed the wind, hoping it had covered my movement, and ducked to the ground.

Backing up and avoiding the meddlesome branches, I crawled in a circle to my new cover and tried to calm my pulse. Three branches the thickness of my wrist spouted from the limb leaving a thin slit to peer through.

The soldier still waited, and I didn't see Dean anywhere. Pulling a dull groan of otherness to me, I sent a whirlwind in the direction of the tree where I'd first been hiding. He fired twice, then stopped. His eyes were focused there now.

Where are you, Dean? I shoved down a rise of panic threatening to lock my chest and took soothing breaths.

I almost missed Dean. Only as he crawled over a rise on the far side of the road did I catch a glimpse of silver fur. The soldier had no idea. I smiled in relief, then thought about Dean attacking a man. As little as I wanted to kill even the soldiers who had been part of the massacre, I didn't want Dean to murder them either.

The otherness whispered in my ear as I unwittingly began to draw it in. At this distance, I might not do more than topple the man, and that would still leave Dean to attack him. I squirmed. What choice did I have? I cursed Moonjir and his lofty talk of paths. Sometimes there was only one.

I jerked when the distant sound of a motor reached me through the trees then died off again. Of course there would be more than one of them. We were lucky they hadn't been together. Ears listening for the engine, I shifted to get a better view down the road. The trees and dead brush at that end of the field made it difficult.

As a crouching Dean padded openly across the road, I

sent another whirlwind back to the first tree, distracting the soldier.

He fired two shots again.

Dean pounced with the crack of the rifle still in my ears. He caught the upper arm of the soldier and twisted, which sent both man and wolf to the ground. The man screamed in pain, then quieted.

The cold breeze to my left rustled leaves and branches in the silence bereft of gunfire. The birds were gone.

A chill crawled up my back and neck. Only Dean's twisting silver fur showed. I didn't watch but jumped to my feet, dashing for the first tree and Dean's clothes. We might have time to run from here and avoid the second soldier. The first would likely be dead before I made it four strides.

Still aching and weary from our first escape, I fumbled as I grabbed his jeans and green socks.

Dean trotted across the field in wolf form, his silver muzzle darkened. His head whipped from me to the sound of the approaching engine, but he kept moving forward.

I blinked away tears as I found one boot and searched for the next. The engine *was* close. The noise wavered and echoed through the trees, but didn't fade away. "Where the hell did you throw your boot, Dean?"

Wolf tongue hanging out, he panted as he stood next to the tree he'd hidden me behind. I shivered at the blood.

"I can't find your boot."

He grunted and padded past me into the forest. The direction wasn't exactly back the way we came, but toward the right.

I found his second boot as I followed. It had a new bullet hole in the top near the laces. "Found it."

Dean growled, squinting back at the field, road, and dead soldier.

Dropping to one knee, I watched as the second motorcyclist came to a stop, surveying the scene ahead. He likely saw the body and definitely the abandoned vehicle.

We watched as he left the bike running, dismounted, and unstrapped his weapon. He searched in every direction, including ours, as he approached his comrade. A wolf attack would leave a gruesome corpse. He stopped and stared for a long moment.

I couldn't turn toward Dean or his bloody muzzle, so I swallowed the lump down my dry throat and watched the soldier's pain.

He only stayed that minute, then ran for his motorcycle. When he spun in a cloud of dust and left us, I stood, relieved, and continued in the direction Dean had been leading us.

He followed as I cuddled his clothes to my chest. My pulse slowed, but I couldn't feel any emotions. Each step became a chore.

When Dean stopped and grunted, I paused and turned to find him shifting back. Usually, I really enjoyed seeing him naked, like when we bathed in the lake at night; this time I just dropped to the ground as his fur retracted and muscles reformed. The blood disappeared from his face with the muzzle. White returned around his eyes, and he glanced away, as if ashamed.

The birds started to chirp again, now that the wolf was gone.

Silently I handed him his pants with his blade still sheathed at the side.

"Underwear?" he asked.

I almost laughed. "Sorry."

"They were falling apart, anyway."

We weren't going to talk about him killing a man yet. "Commando, Roxie calls it." I didn't even feel the usual gut-wrenching pang of losing her. Numbness draped over my body and spirit.

For the next hour, we walked in silence. There had been too much death for any day. The afternoon warmed until I removed his jacket and tied it about my waist. We passed through a number of abandoned farms, avoiding the buildings and open fields, but their growing frequency made it more difficult.

Thirsty and tired, we came to another field, and I leaned against a tree at the edge. "Across or around?" I asked. A hill rose ahead of us, promising more wooded terrain.

He stepped to the edge, peering around. "Crap."

I straightened. Two people had just turned toward us on the opposite side of the field.

Chapter Four

The pair stood beside a tall pine where the field inclined into sparse woods. Birds called to each other playfully, almost mocking my panic. An herbal, spicy scent rose from the brown bush we'd just stepped through. We were no more than thirty paces from each other.

I squinted in the sunlight, then my eyes widened. They weren't both human.

The cryptid stood tall, a male Duathua wearing only a beige skirt with a colored hem. Around his thin waist he had belted an open-weave satchel that dropped to his thigh. His fingers were overly long, but could have been human. He turned to peer at us; his disturbing dark eyes were a bit too large, his skin too gray, and his chin too pointed. Something flaked on his head, but it wasn't hair. From this angle, I couldn't make out wings.

Beside him stood a short, brown-haired woman, possibly my age, garbed in a long, black coat that rested on the ground. She had a rifle strapped to her back that she moved to her hands while I blinked.

Dean stiffened, obviously sensing a threat. If he shifted into a werewolf, she might shoot him. I couldn't read the

Duathua's expression, but the woman appeared ready to defend him. Why were they together?

"Calm. If you shift, they will attack. Let's just back away." I lifted my hands and followed my own advice, sliding one heel behind the other.

I heard Dean let out a long breath, and he nodded. My own heart pounded in quickening beats. We had to get out fast before he couldn't control his emotions. The morning's terrors flashed through my mind.

"Scouts," the woman said. Her comment accompanied a rise in her weapon, as if she might bring the stock to her shoulder. "They aren't armed."

The Duathua smiled, though not all of his skin moved as it should. His long fingers reached out and rested on her rifle. "Then, we needn't consider them a threat. Simply outsiders." The tone rang higher than I expected, with oddly pitched inflections.

The human woman frowned, still not moving the muzzle aimed at us. "Look at what she's effing wearing." Her short-cropped hair hung just at the bottom of her ears.

Under Dean's jacket, my coveralls would appear military, since they had been. I took another step back and swallowed. "We'll leave. We didn't mean to intrude." We needed to find someplace quiet again. I longed for our leaky lean-to in the marsh.

Deep behind the pair, a small figure, a tween from their size, raced down the hill in leaps. Tiny, silver wings flickered behind bare shoulders at each jump. The Duathua child wore the same skirt about a tiny waist as the adult, but it flew wildly with abandon.

For some reason, this new, younger arrival calmed my racing pulse. Even Dean's tight jaw appeared to loosen.

The adult glanced back, then pushed more insistently on the woman's weapon. He stretched his other hand toward us. "I am called Nur." His head tilted toward his companion. "This woman is called Penny." When he moved or spoke, his skin creased as if too thick, except around his eyes and lips. Turning in time to nod toward the new arrival, I caught sight of his silver wings. "She is named Wati."

The tween smiled brightly and then frowned at the weapon in the woman's hands. "Who are they, grandmother?" Her voice was not that of a child.

I couldn't help but glance at Nur's bare chest, then back to the tween's. At Camp Sparta, we hadn't discussed the anatomy of the Duathua much, except for their wings, thick hide, and that fire proved the best defense against them. Confusion pushed aside my concerns.

"Would you care to introduce yourselves?" Nur asked.

I started out of my surprise and forced a smile onto my face. "Yes, I'm Caitlyn." Tugging at my coveralls, I continued. "I ran away from the military. I'm — we're not scouts."

When Dean didn't speak, I nudged him with my elbow. His lips pursed before he grumbled, "Dean."

Nur finally managed to get Penny to lower her rifle. The Duathua, who I had to consciously convince myself was a grandmother, strode across the space between us. Smiling broadly, the smaller Wati left Penny's side to join Nur.

My tension rose again, but I stepped toward her, not wanting Dean to tense. "Caitlyn?" he asked with obvious concern.

I should have been more cautious, but the friendly demeanor of the Duathua made me think of her more as a person than a cryptid. Penny could have shot us if the pair wanted to cause us harm. I truthfully didn't know what the Duathua as a species could do to us. Neither of them knew I could use magic or that Dean could transform into a deadly werewolf.

Penny and Dean ambled behind each of us with a measure of reluctance until we reached the middle of the field. The Duathua grandmother stood a head taller than Dean, and Wati appeared fully formed, not childlike at all, yet reached my chest in height.

Nur gestured to the surrounding woods and hill. "We have not seen you here. What, Caitlyn and Dean, brings you to these woods?"

I jabbed a thumb behind us. "Actual military. We were hiding on the north end of Lake Marion for a couple weeks, and they found us."

Dean coughed, perhaps thinking I'd said too much. At the moment, the worst threat seemed behind us. Penny held the only weapon. I still guessed her age close to mine, but her sharp, distrustful eyes spoke of a hard life.

"Lake Marion? Is that where the fighters live in the south?" Nur turned. She appeared to have translucent, brownish scales on her head, as did Wati.

Penny's features slackened, then she inhaled and recomposed her frown. "Yes. It's a big lake, though. There are others living there. Were you north of the bridge at Pack's Landing?"

I shrugged and turned to Dean. "I don't know where that is."

He locked eyes with me, and I knew he didn't want to discuss any of this. "Yes. North of Pack's Landing."

My instinct had been to trust Nur, but she *was* a cryptid, and we'd met only minutes ago. I could be too trusting. Old lessons crept in from Camp Sparta, and I forced my smile. "Do you live here?" I asked.

"Our enclave lies north of these woods near the human city of Sumter. A day's walk."

I had asked the question primarily to avoid more questions about our situation, but the name of the city struck a memory. "Sumter?" The soldiers who'd attacked me had been arriving for a trip to Sumter, but that had been weeks ago.

My expression must have changed, because Nur's smile relaxed and Penny cocked her head suspiciously toward me. The soldiers we had just seen could be on their way to Sumter. Tyrell's maps had marked a route in dotted red. I almost searched around us, expecting him to be leading the army across the field.

"What is it, Caitlyn?" Nur asked.

I shook my head for Dean's sake. His reluctance to speak now didn't work for me. "I think the army is heading for Sumter. They had a map. Two circles to the west of the city, maybe targets." Ignoring Dean, I motioned behind us. "They just attacked a human compound, then us. There could be a lot more following."

Wati's smile had never diminished. "Two weeks ago. We turned them back. There are over twenty thousand of us in the Alliance and over 10 percent showed up to fight. We barricaded the roads, and when they fired thunder, our Pahawan attacked and our humans fired their guns." She patted Penny's rifle. "They fled like sunfish."

I didn't ask if the Youth Guard had used their magic or if Roxie had been there. If she lived, they likely wouldn't trust her to go on an attack. My chest hollowed, and I closed my eyes. "Could they be coming back? I'm concerned about the soldiers behind us." Either way, Dean and I would be avoiding Sumter and whatever the Alliance and the enclave were.

"Halimay scouts now," Nur said. "We have many eyes watching for their return. Human and Duathua. It is sad the southern humans have killed our Speakers as we would welcome an alliance with them."

"Speakers?" I asked.

"Our — ambassadors who volunteered to be sent to make peace. Eight souls who have never returned. We hope they were returned to the Void to rest and not held prisoner all these years." Nur's lips flattened, not quite a frown, but I took it as such. "Many humans have anger at our unwilling appearance, but we cannot choose the Displacement, as that voyage is made for us." She glanced at Wati. "No matter how we long for our home."

Wati's smile lapsed. "I will find a path back to Denya and my new eggs. My mate will not be left alone with our family."

I blinked at the small Duathua proclaiming not only that she had a family, but that she believed she could return to them. Both concepts stalled my brain. Dean swallowed loud enough for both of us. He'd lost his mother to the Sorrow. She'd faded before his eyes. Without a thought, I reached for his shoulder to comfort him.

"We thank you for your information about the soldiers. Halimay will take special interest in this." Nur studied us, and her smile returned. "You have said you are leaving. Do you have a destination? All are welcome among the Alliance. We have worked hard to make this new home safe."

They likely meant safe from werewolves, and maybe even someone with magic like myself. "Thank you; we haven't really decided what to do." Dean would kill me if I agreed without a private discussion. I needed some time myself to grasp the Duathua as something other than a cryptid who should be killed. Inside, I cringed at the thought of their diplomats being stuck in labs as soon as they crossed into the Savannah territory. They might not survive the first gunshot.

The Duathua appeared to have a better acceptance and understanding of what happened during the Sorrow. "What will happen to the people, the humans, who disappeared from Earth? I'm assuming they are on your home world."

"Some did appear on Denya and they will be safe, if they are not near the Onikai. Others will have been moved to Yerd, and we cannot believe they will survive. We have no hope for the Duathua who the Displacement sends there." Nur touched Wati's cheek. "I consider us fortunate."

I had not expected her answer. Did Denya mean a world, or a place like America? "Where is Yerd?"

"It is the home planet of Sogoi and those you call were-wolves and vampires. There is no speaking to them with honesty, so we know little, but expect it to be as dangerous as they are."

My heart skipped, and I didn't dare glance at Dean. We could hope his mother had not been taken there. "Three planets?"

Nur nodded. "I forget your people live short lives and have no history of the times before. We Duathua do not live long enough to experience it more than once, but our stories have their own longevity." For the first time, I sensed she held back and changed subjects. "We have some supplies to share, and Penny will likely catch some mammals with her traps, if you'd like to join us for a meal."

Wati appeared excited at the prospect. "Will you tell me of your soldiers? I have considered joining the Pahawan and have Kedi make me armor."

"How old are you?" Dean asked. I seemed as surprised as the others that he'd finally spoken.

"Calculated into Earth years, I would be nineteen." She

gestured to her body, as if that explained something. "How old are you?"

"Seventeen."

"Two days ago. He just had his birthday." It hadn't been memorable, but I'd woven him a pouch and a hat. Both were gone now, thanks to the army.

Wati cocked her head at me and waited.

"Fifteen, last February."

"Humans join their military at a very young age," she said with some awe. "I can't consider the Pahawan until I'm fifty-three and a quarter Earth years. Have you battled the Oni?"

"No." I wet my lips, searching for some way out of her questions. "Do the Duathua battle the Onikai — Oni on Denya?"

"When they attempt to raid. Like your human soldiers. The Oni are much more difficult, like a crabknuckle on a rock."

I smiled as I listened, but I hadn't gotten past her size and age. Nur loomed over us all. Wati had children, or eggs at least. She *was* older than me. The Duathua had been so much more than I'd expected, and so very different. Eric would have loved them. My blood cooled at the thought. I didn't want to remember him — his death, but he deserved to stay alive in my memories.

"Sad memories?" Nur asked.

I forced a smile on my face and blinked aside a tear. "Hard not to."

She nodded slowly. "I imagine my wife Asin still grieving, as I've been here —" She spoke in another language of whistles to Wati.

"Two and three-quarters, roughly, Earth years," Wati replied quickly.

Nur gestured to the shorter Duathua. "That long."

"Two point seven eight at two decimals." Wati appeared embarrassed at her outburst. "I hate approximates."

I glanced at grandmother and granddaughter quizzically. Asking about Nur's marital arrangements would be rude.

Despite all the oddities, the meeting with the Duathua intrigued me. An enclave and their Alliance promised a rest against the threats surrounding us, until Tyrell's soldiers arrived.

Dean stiffened, and Nur glanced to my right over the field. "Halimay arrives." Her voice held a hint of concern, if I read it right.

Chapter Five

Wings blurred on the back of an armored Duathua as Halimay flew just over the tops of dried weeds. Eyes trained on us, they had a glittering helmet that appeared made of glass. With a waist thinner than Nur's, the cryptid appeared almost waspish. The armor on their shoulders appeared shiny and clear as well. In their hand, they held a glass pitchfork with three tines. I wouldn't consider Halimay a male after misjudging Nur.

Nur stepped quickly between us and the new Duathua. She had a concern, and my pulse raced. "Let me introduce you."

Penny studied our reactions, but Wati approached affably with a smile and patted my hand.

The newcomer rose slightly and straightened at Nur's intercession between us. The armor covered them, head to foot. Only an inch-high slit at the mouth let in air. The joints at the elbows and wrists appeared to bend or slide impossibly. Under the thin glass, they wore a similar garment to Wati and Nur, but shorter, more like a loincloth in the Tarzan comics.

Their weapon had three barbed points that they aimed

at me as they buzzed closer. "Who are these?" Their voice was similar to Nur's, though their tone far more threatening.

"Travelers who have had a rough time, from the look of it." Nur spread the fingers of her right hand in front of the weapon, as if protecting me. "Caitlyn has run away from the military camp at Santee, and her friend Dean accompanies her."

Halimay did not seem swayed, but dropped to the ground with a thud, wings disappearing. "The soldiers have moved along the lakeshore and burned out our allies. These are scouts, spies."

Penny glared at us.

Wati's mouth opened in a human expression of surprise.

"It's true," I said, then waved off my comment, "about the burning of a compound, not about us being spies. We've been running from the soldiers all morning."

Halimay glared at me and took a step forward, weapon rising to point up. "That is a soldier's patch. You lie."

"It *was* my unit. The Wolf Squad. I abandoned them."

"Liar."

"They shot Dean's shoe." I flushed at my lame evidence. "If the allies you're referring to are the families in the campers, we saw it." I couldn't help but cringe.

"We don't need to explain ourselves to them," Dean said from behind me. "We can just leave now."

Halimay's eyes flicked over my shoulder, then they stomped to the side, as if to reach Dean. "You will not leave until you have told me their plans. Spies."

"Halimay." Nur moved to position herself between us, but the armored warrior outpaced her.

Dean growled. I couldn't let him get into a fight and expose himself as a werewolf.

The otherness roared as I stepped back with my shoulders flat against Dean's chest. I wove streams of air in front of me, pushing with an insistent force so Halimay couldn't move forward. With Penny's rifle at the ready, I didn't want to appear like I was attacking, merely preventing any harm their Duathua might cause.

Penny still lifted the muzzle of her weapon, her finger aside the trigger. Nur's eyes widened in surprise. I pushed Dean back with a step.

Wati beamed. "A Seyir!"

"Indeed," a new voice spoke from behind us. "Halimay, leave the human to one of her own kind to judge." The woman sounded old.

My skin tingled as I heard her call a grumbling of otherness. "We just want to leave," I said; my eyes returning to Halimay.

The warrior appeared to defer to the older woman and took two steps back. I dropped my wind, and the tingling along my back stopped.

Dean snorted in short breaths, and I knew he fought to control his emotions. I reached for his hand as I turned to face the woman. My eyebrows raised. She stood about five feet tall and wore a neat, yellow-flowered dress. Her white hair had been curled into a bun that added four inches to her height.

"Introductions are in order. Speak with me as we head back to camp." She gestured for me to approach her. "Please. I'm Vanya."

I checked with Dean, but his eyes were flicking from Halimay to Penny. "Okay. But then we leave. We just want to get away from the soldiers," I said nearly breathless.

Vanya laughed. "Don't we all?"

Tugging on Dean's hand to get him to move, I stepped toward Vanya and away from Halimay. "I'm Caitlyn, and this is Dean."

As I neared her, she turned and started walking for the hill. "You've got some experience with the soldiers? I'm guessing from your comments and the uniform." She pointed at my Wolf Squad patch.

"Yes." I nodded, keeping a hold on Dean and in step with the elderly woman. "How do you have magic?"

She chuckled. "I've had it since younger than your age, Caitlyn. On my world, we are rare, but not unknown."

I stumbled, causing her to chuckle again. "Your world?"

"I wondered if the military knew. Humans have been on Denya for almost a hundred generations."

Halimay snarled. "Give no secrets to these spies."

"Bless your heart, Halimay." Vanya glanced at me. "That's the right term, isn't it?"

"Yes." Despite our situation, I had grown to like Vanya, Nur, and especially Wati quickly. However, the idea of humans living on some other planet shocked me into a stupor, and questions swirled in my brain. "How —"

Vanya raised a finger. "I've given you a secret, now your turn."

I swallowed. The biggest secret I had was about Dean, and we didn't know how they'd react. "The people at my camp consider me a traitor. I had to hurt some of them to leave. They might be hunting me, especially if they recognized me this morning."

"Hmm." Vanya kept her eyes forward. "Alright. We'll work on more later."

"She could be lying." Halimay's voice came from behind and to my right. I tried not to imagine their glass pitchfork.

Nur spoke. "Considering what she did to you, she could have disabled Penny and me upon our first meeting. I'm leaning toward trusting her word." The Duathua woman leaned in conspiratorially and gestured toward Halimay. "She's not going to forget soon."

My head twitched as I glanced at Halimay's chest. It would take a while to get used to the Duathua genders, especially without a male to reference. *We won't be around them that long anyway.* The thought made my chest tighten.

Vanya hummed. "She wasn't using but a spit of her power at that. Besides, she's a healer and more that I don't recognize."

I blinked. "How could you know?"

"You felt me touch you. What did you think I was doing?"

The sensation of the otherness had been unusual, but at the time I thought maybe she was preparing to attack, perhaps with electricity like Selina.

"You said the people at the compound were your allies?" Dean asked.

Vanya nodded. "Yes. We have brought them supplies from the ruins of the city. Clothes and other things they cannot find."

"Why didn't you help them?" Dean sounded angry. I hadn't considered his feelings during this morning's horror.

"We offered refuge at the enclave. They chose to live closer to your people." As we began up the incline, she studied him. "Their families worked with us, setting signals for our scouts when the army approached. I do mourn for their losses."

"As do I," said Nur.

Their tones both held empathy for the families. These were Duathua and humans working together. I would not have believed it possible. If it weren't for Dean's condition, I would have hoped for a safe place among them.

I shook my head. There could be no place for us unless they knew how to save Dean.

As I formulated a way to ask about a werewolf cure, hardly an innocent topic, we reached the top of the incline. On the back side were three dark green hammocks that had been strung between trees. A chestnut horse with a splash of white glanced at us while a peach and brown pit bull studied us silently.

Vanya took my arm for support as we descended. "You are welcome to a meal and some water before we break camp. We are returning to the enclave, where you are welcome, if you choose."

Halimay snorted but didn't argue.

I *was* thirsty and always hungry. Besides, I could use a chance to ask about a cure without seeming obvious, even if that meant traveling with them for a bit. At least we didn't seem to be at risk from Halimay's ire anymore.

I responded, purposefully non-committal. "Thank you."

Chapter Six

I smiled at the sight of animals; they'd proved rare even in Santee.

"Odie." Wati blurred past us in flurry of wings to drop down beside the dog.

Vanya continued to hold my arm, even as the decline lessened. "If you do decide to accompany us to the enclave, we can find you some supplies. I'm betting you had to leave everything behind."

A canteen and pack would be welcome and another reason to accompany them. "We didn't have much to begin with."

Penny passed us. "I'll take Wati and Odie with me to retrieve the traps." She gave me a glance, then another behind to Nur or Halimay. Despite Vanya, they didn't trust us.

Leading me to a pack hanging from a tree, Vanya motioned for me to retrieve it. "We've got flatbread and cold beans to start with, unless Penny brings back something." She took the bag, then gestured to a canteen at the base of the tree. "Drink."

I eagerly grabbed the water and turned to offer Dean some.

He knelt in front of the dog, extending a hand so Odie could sniff it. I paused, wetting my lips with my tongue. If the dog sensed Dean's condition, it might not go well.

Odie grunted, stood, and walked closer, letting Dean scratch his ears.

Nur snorted. "He took to you quickly." She joined Vanya kneeling beside the pack. "Still doesn't care for Halimay."

The glass-armored warrior had stopped behind Dean. In response to Nur, she squinted at the other Duathua in a scowl, then raised a shining transparent gauntlet. "This doesn't help."

I shivered, imagining the glass breaking and cutting into fingers. Why would they wear it? Instead of asking, I joined Dean. Odie sniffed my hand and allowed me to pet, but obviously liked Dean better. I smiled when Dean did; he'd been scowling all morning.

This can't last, I thought, and closed my eyes. A craving to belong rose, and I shoved it back down. We couldn't risk them finding out about Dean. He needed a cure. Vanya and Nur were busy, and Penny had retrieved a duffel bag. I wasn't about to strike up a conversation about werewolves with Halimay.

Penny clicked her tongue, and Odie's ears perked. "C'mon. Traps." He whined and rose to follow her.

I thought for a moment Penny might smile at us, but she turned away. Vanya's quick acceptance of us seemed to be having an effect on the others. Wati waved as she left with them.

Dean sat and chugged on the water, but I couldn't get the lingering question out of my head. I approached the two women. "Can I help?"

They had dug out a tin pot with a lid strapped to it and were opening a cloth bag of cracker-like bread. Vanya gestured to the pack. "We've got five metal plates in there and spoons. Pull 'em out. You and Dean can share one."

On the bottom I found the cloth-wrapped utensils and spoke in a calm, conversational tone. "There weren't a lot of dogs in Santee when I first moved to Camp Sparta. The werewolves killed most of them early on."

Vanya pointed to the pack. "Should be a serving spoon in there as well."

My lips twisted, but I dug back into the backpack. I couldn't appear as desperate as I felt. It might be best to wait until we weren't all busy. I produced the spoon, and Nur traded me two pieces of flatbread for it.

I nibbled. It was salty and delicious, and I was suddenly starving. We'd had fish for breakfast. "This is *so* good."

The women both smiled, and Dean grunted around a bite of his. I savored every mouthful when they served us a plate of fat green beans rather than the usual black or red. Dean slid closer and held the plate as I took the first bite. The beans were meatier than what I was used to, and they'd been perfectly seasoned with garlic and onion. I'd thought we'd eat fish for the rest of our lives.

I offered Dean a spoonful, commandeering control of the utensil. He took the bite with a smile, then hummed approval as he chewed. We alternated bites until Penny and her troupe came back.

"Nothing." She offered an apologetic smile. She and Wati shared a plate while Odie tried not to watch.

When they were ready to leave, it took them minutes to break down the camp, and they had everything stowed on the chestnut horse while Dean and I helped clean dishes. Nur stopped beside us on one of her rounds. "Don't spare the water. We've got plenty to last to a safe spring. It's only an hour away."

I had my whole conversation planned for Vanya, until she walked over while I was drying plates. "One of our people made those."

Dean cocked his head. "You're smelting metal?"

Vanya pointed a wrinkled finger at my face. "I said, our people. A Seyir who can work metal, like yourself."

"With —?" Surprise, hope, and a little vanity bloomed inside. She would know so much more about magic than any of us at Camp Sparta. Her people had a history of using their abilities. There had to be a way to cure Dean.

"I got the feeling you can do the same. It's an unusual skill."

I squirmed and turned away, uncomfortable that she could know these things about me. "Only once, in an emergency." I'd bent Dean's cage the night we'd escaped.

As we loaded the last backpack onto the chestnut, I noted in surprise that no one rode the animal. I had assumed they would have the horse for Vanya. There were stirrups and a saddle, but she walked beside Dean and me.

"You should train with metal and develop your skill. There's something else within that I haven't seen, but I am hardly that knowledgeable about the arts." Vanya's voice grew more introspective.

Frowning slightly, I turned back, unsure what she might mean. "Like what?"

Vanya shrugged. "I'm really not sure. I can see a proficiency with air; you would make a fine air sculptor as well." She gestured to Halimay who walked ahead. "We do more with it than just armor."

"I thought that was glass."

She laughed, as did Nur and Wati. "That wouldn't stop a bullet."

"Neither would air," said Dean.

"You would be surprised, young man. That is Kudara, fashioned by a Seyir."

It took until late afternoon for an opportunity to broach my question of a cure for werewolves. We'd refilled our canteens quickly using Vanya's ability with water. The terrain included the strange pine forests grown in rows that were broken by trails, the occasional dilapidated building, or copses of oak and maple.

The area appeared uninhabited, and Wati explained that incursions from the werewolves and Oni had driven many of the last humans to the enclave. "Whole families had been turned, adding to the population of werewolves," she said.

My pulse sped as I turned to Vanya. "Is there no cure? A powerful healer perhaps?"

Vanya studied me. "Got to be careful with trying to heal that. Early on, a Seyir from my world tried to save a woman who got bit, but she turned ill and died."

I cringed, remembering how sick Dean had become when I attempted it. A cure could be a risk, but without it, we'd never be able to join a community. "There has to be something that can be done for them." After these past few hours of talking, I'd been considering joining the Alliance, if they would accept us.

Nur spoke from behind. "We have never asked Iandil. She has been here the longest of our people, that we know of."

Heart pounding, I swallowed. "She's at the enclave?"

Vanya shook her head. "No, she remains with a group of Pahawan west of us at one of our original camps. They still hunt for those Duathua who are stranded here from the Displacement. Iandil worked — works tirelessly to gather our people and foster relations with yours."

I didn't show my excitement, but when Dean held my hand, I squeezed it. His response didn't indicate a resounding yes, but we had someone who might know of a cure. Despite all that had gone on this morning, I was the most hopeful I'd been since we left Camp Sparta.

Ahead of us, Halimay clacked her weapon against her armor and fluttered into the evergreens. She pointed the spear tips to a cloud of sparkling reflections. "The Onikai have been sighted near here," she shouted.

Chapter Seven

I glanced along the rows of sweet-scented pines. The birds continued chirping without care. On one hand, I could see far down the tracks; on the other, rows of thick trunks created huge areas where anything could be waiting. We had a single weapon and our magic.

Halimay rose above the trees.

Vanya continued walking without missing a beat, and I had to double step to keep up with her. A chill hung on my shoulders. "Will they attack?" I asked her.

"If they find us. The Pahawan will be combing the area to repel the attack. They send raiding squads hoping to find stragglers."

Like us, I thought. "How close are we to the enclave?"

"It will be dark when we arrive."

Penny, who had been leading the chestnut horse with her rifle strapped on her back, jumped into the saddle mid-stride and dug into one of the packs. Wati buzzed into the air beside her.

The clear blade Penny pulled out had a curved Kudara edge that jointed oddly to what looked like a wooden grip. Wati took it and buzzed over to hand it to Nur. The second knife she slipped into her own belt, and a third went into Penny's. There were none offered to Vanya, me, or Dean.

Penny dropped down and unslung her rifle as she resumed her walk. Her eyes were sharp and face tight. Odie trotted beside her, sniffing the air. Conversation had disappeared, but our pace continued, slow and steady.

I rubbed at my sleeves, searching the woods around us. Dean touched my hand and I flinched, then grabbed his tightly.

The rows ended ahead at a more natural forest. I wanted to sprint for it. The others might as well, but Vanya was too old. We kept to her pace.

Even though our initial contact with Halimay hadn't been very warm, I was grateful for her armored presence and warrior-like demeanor. I didn't doubt she'd be the first one to dive into a melee with cryptids. If bullets couldn't get through her strange armor, then what chance did teeth or claws have? I dismissed the image of the Onikai painted on Camp Sparta's classroom walls.

We made it to the mixed forest of pine, live oak, and leafless trees where I could watch Halimay more easily and search the dried brush for some sign of lumbering cryptids. We crossed a road, and our cover disappeared; we began to trek across an abandoned field where I felt exposed.

Vanya clicked her tongue. "Here they come. On the right." The others repositioned with Penny and Nur facing that direction.

Odie growled and stalked toward our right with the hairs on his back bristling.

There the grass rustled and swayed. A bush ten yards away jerked. The chestnut whinnied and sidled away.

I had never experienced knowing we were going to be attacked by such a large, unseen force. Fear rooted me.

Less than ten paces away, animal-faced Onikai burst

from dried brush, suddenly looming. They had spread their ambush, so some were farther away and others terrifyingly close. Their dark fur had been dusted with sand and dried vegetation that spilled off as they ran. Their eyes were dark, nearly blending with their brown fur. Two sharp bottom teeth jutted over their upper lip like yellowed tusks.

Dean and I both jumped backward. My breath came in short tugs at the air. My heel caught in weeds, but Dean righted me with one hand and then brandished his blade. It looked too small for this fight.

Penny fired, her gunshot cracking the silence as her bullet took one in the shoulder at five paces away. The beast exposed sharp carnivorous teeth as it roared. For a moment, the Onikai swayed, momentarily left behind by the others, then stormed forward.

Odie snarled and darted ahead of me for the closest, ripping at a furry leg, then darting away from a sweeping paw and claws.

The shortest of the Onikai raced for the horse and Penny. The chestnut snorted and galloped away as Wati rose to the air, her blade ready.

Halimay bellowed foreign words as she dove at the group, causing two to turn to face her. Wings flattening against her back, she drove her spear and body into a howling beast.

Nur stood before Vanya, her wicked blade ready as one of the attackers raced toward her.

One of the Onikai barreled at Dean and me. I summoned a shriek of otherness and slammed a spiked gust into their chest. As they toppled backward, they yelled words in a guttural growl.

Odie harried the back leg of one who ignored the dog and bore down on Dean and me. I managed a quick blast of air, spinning the creature off course.

My next step backward caught vines and dropped me on my ass.

The Onikai I'd spun stumbled to the side, then too quickly righted themselves with strange, grumbled words. Their expression had changed to a semblance of anger or rage, though I couldn't say what gave me that impression. Their eyes locked on mine.

Dean's knife dropped to the ground, and I heard him grunt. A new panic rose in my chest.

A step to my left, Penny fired a second and third shot into the attackers. I flinched at each one as they deafened my ears. My eyes never left the Onikai I'd attacked. Fear had left, leaving only a cold calculation that I might not survive. I worried more about Dean turning in front of our new allies.

My adversary leaned in as they ran for me, still ignoring Odie even though their legs were matted with wet fur from the wounds. They left stains on the dried brush.

Sitting on cold ground, I pulled in howling otherness and slammed the cryptid solidly in the chest with a gale of air. A claw flashed an arm's length from my face before they were thrown off their feet. Snarling and yelling, they landed six yards from us.

Silver fur darted past me and joined Odie in pursuit of the Onikai. Dean had shifted.

I would have frozen again at that moment, had Wati not let out a pained scream to my left. It pierced my ringing ears. Penny fired a fourth shot, and I turned to see Wati sailing away from us.

The Onikai loomed above us. I could smell a dank, musty odor. Black nails sprouted from the fur of their massive feet. If I leaned forward, I could stretch and touch it. A shiver raced across my back.

With a blur of dark fur, they knocked Penny's rifle

away. The creature's body shifted, knees telegraphing the next swing that would tear through her.

My breathing stopped, and my eyes focused on the swaying hairs of the Onikai's feet. I could see them clearly, even a glimpse of pale gray skin beneath. As the Onikai dipped forward for its deadly strike, I drew in the otherness. I felt lighter as it filled me.

I screamed as I rolled to slam my palm onto their foot. Otherness squealed in my mind as I connected with their body, squirming through muscle and instinctively seeking a familiar organ.

Sobbing, I burst the Onikai's heart. *His* heart.

He said something as he died, but I couldn't hear it through the clamor and ringing in my ears. The cryptid's knees buckled, then the full body crumpled to the ground and fell away from me.

His foot slid away, and I lay dragging in breaths.

Dean. I had to find Dean.

Chapter Eight

I lifted my head and wearily pushed up from the ground. The Onikai I'd killed stunk of musk and something sour. Halimay flew an inch above the grass, stabbing down at one of the attackers. Her mouth opened as if she were shouting, but I heard nothing over the ringing in my ears.

Penny jerked her focus to my right, so I turned to find one of the cryptids running away. Blood-streaked silver fur leaped behind it, along with Odie.

I flinched when a furry foot nearly trampled the grass two feet from my hand. Another of the beasts fled, loping in the general direction of Dean and Odie.

The Duathua, Vanya, and Penny all knew about Dean. Shakily I rose, turning farther to my right where Nur stood behind us with a bloodied blade. She watched Dean, or maybe the retreating Onikai.

Vanya studied me.

I flushed in shame. They'd trusted us. We hadn't directly lied about Dean's condition, but certainly hadn't mentioned something that might change their reaction to us. It was a betrayal on my part.

Vanya reached out her hand and placed it on Nur's back. The otherness whooshed in my mind, like water pouring from one bucket to the next. The Duathua woman took in a deep breath. She had a gash on her far shoulder and blood dripping down her arm.

Unable to handle Vanya's unreadable gaze, I turned the direction Dean had run. Penny left my side to dash toward Wati, who lay struggling in the brush.

With Dean and Odie hidden by the grass, I spotted only three running Onikai over the tops of dead brush.

Halimay fluttered ahead and to my left, glaring after the remnants of the ambushers. Her armor had clouded in patches about the helmet and shoulders. Two tines remained on her spear. When she flicked a glower back at me, I could read her rage. She had the right to be angry with me. We'd deceived them all, and she had been right not trust us.

Too tired to think and too ashamed to face any of them, I stumbled on wobbling legs and moved away from the Onikai I'd killed. My foot stepped on one of Dean's boots. With all of my usual grace, I fell to my knees and palms. Tears blurred my vision.

Dean wouldn't follow the Onikai too far. He wouldn't risk himself. I'd seen how careful he'd been, attacking them and leaping away, like Odie. However, Halimay or Penny might try to kill Dean if he returned. Maybe they'd just let me leave their group. Dean would find me.

Crawling on hands and knees, I gathered his jeans, socks, knife, and boots. More so, I avoided facing the others. One by one, they had moved to Wati, who appeared to be trying to wave off their concerns.

Vanya smoothed a bent wing, and I heard the otherness crackle.

It made sense that we could heal the Duathua, at least with some experience. I could certainly kill cryptids with it. The werewolf I'd killed didn't feel the same as the Onikai who had been speaking. *A murderer and a liar.*

Pushing myself to stand, I focused on tucking socks into boots instead of chancing their condemning glares. I could make out a louder note or two of their words above the diminishing ringing.

The Onikai I'd killed stretched out maybe seven feet, bigger than any man I'd seen. His dead eyes stared at nothing.

The cryptid would have killed Penny. Though she was close to my age, I couldn't guess about her training. She'd frozen without her weapon.

I wouldn't have let her die. I couldn't. Knowing I'd kill the Onikai again in the same circumstance held little solace. That made me a willing murderer.

Focus. Finding Dean mattered, as did securing a safe place to stay. I doubted the latter existed between the army, the Onikai, and now the Alliance. Halimay hadn't stormed over and tried to poke me, so there was that.

I slid Dean's knife into the sheath, balled his clothes, and straightened to face Vanya. None of them might speak to me, but she had vouched for us. I owed her a goodbye.

She studied me. With a motion to the others, she left Wati and ambled toward me. Her expression held no hints.

I smiled apologetically when she stopped a pace away. "I'm sorry. I didn't dare say anything."

"This is why you asked about the cure. His color is wrong, silver instead of mottled white. Did you attempt a healing?" she asked.

"Yes. I was there when they bit him. I tried again later, but it makes him sick." I almost spoke of Eric's healing of my own infection, and stopped myself. "He can control it, mostly."

"When does he turn?" Her eyes held none of the warmth they had before, just cold, analytical curiosity.

I blushed. "Whenever he gets strong emotions."

Her lips twitched, but remained flat. "Obviously, he doesn't attack you. Others?"

"Soldiers and other werewolves when threatened." I hadn't mentioned the *killing* of the soldier, and wasn't about to.

"Penny is worried about Odie." Finally, her unreadable mask cracked and her eyebrows furrowed.

I had to hope Dean and the dog would continue to work together. "They appeared to be okay."

"They did." She focused on my hands. "You saved Penny. She knows that and is rather disturbed — divided. Halimay, of course, votes to kill Dean, and possibly you. Nur and I are opposed. Wati has no interest beyond protecting you, especially since you protected Penny. They are close."

I flicked a glance at Halimay, who glared. Nodding, I pointed northeast, hopefully. "I understand. I'll leave. Dean will follow me."

Vanya's lips pursed. "When you killed the Onikai, another force pulled, not just death."

I shrugged. "I wasn't thinking clearly, just reacting."

"Nur felt it physically as well. You affected gravity." She tilted her head with a light twist. "It's spoken of, though I've never witnessed it. There are stories that we will not get into. Have you done it before?"

I blinked. "Maybe. When I freed Dean from Camp Sparta." Even the raindrops had seemed to pause and float when I'd called the storm. If I could affect gravity, it was a useless power, yet Vanya seemed focused on it.

She nodded and touched her lips in thought. "You cannot join the Alliance with Dean as he is. Does he, too, want a cure?"

He'd dismissed my comments, but I knew he did. "Yes." A small spark of hope rose in my chest.

"I believe I can convince the others to allow you to stay nearby, while you search for this cure. We could provide for some of your needs, and there is some level of protection in the area I'm thinking of. Dean would have to restrain himself for his sake and ours."

I smiled, nearly crying. "He can. He will. Do you believe there is a cure?"

Vanya shrugged. "I know but a spoonful of what our magics can do. However, we will train your abilities. I am curious about your use of gravity. I won't be the only one. I will speak for your inclusion in the Alliance."

"Thank you."

"Don't. It won't be easy. Many will oppose working with you two." She nodded behind me. "Go get Penny's horse, Bella, while I talk Halimay through this."

I wanted to hug her, but just jerked wearily and searched behind me. Bella stood a good hundred yards away at the edge of the field with her head down munching on something.

Dragging physically, I marched off at my best speed for the moment. Not only would we have a place to rest, but I'd have a chance to find a cure. No matter what else had happened, I couldn't have asked for a better situation. There would be people, too. I loved Dean, but new conversation beyond fish, survival, or the books we'd read would be welcome. The only thing I missed about Camp Sparta, outside of not eating fish, was the people. I dared to hope the Alliance might have preserved fruit or peanut butter.

As I got halfway across the field to the horse, I hoped

Dean might pop up. He'd find me. I had the usual general sense of his direction somewhere to my right. Once, he'd commented how easily he could track me by my scent. That conversation hadn't gone well.

Chapter Nine

By the time I returned with Bella, Penny's chestnut mare, Odie had come back. Wati stood shakily with two pink scars on her left side. They appeared bright and highlighted the gray tones of her pale Duathua skin. Her expression saddened around the eyes when she saw me.

Penny took her horse with a stiff nod. Nur offered an unsure smile, the first to show any warmth since they'd learned of Dean's werewolf infection. I kept scanning the area around us for him.

Vanya pulled free a canteen and handed it to me. "It might be best if you kept a few paces behind, so Dean feels safe approaching you."

I understood the logic, but it layered onto my own shame and their distrustful glances. "I'll do that."

From the packs, Penny pulled simple tunics laced at the sides for the Duathua to wear. The Alliance group forced Wati onto Bella and stepped into an easy pace without a glance back.

My earlier excitement withered as I waited until they were ten paces ahead. After our ambush, I would have rather been closer.

A couple hours later, at sunset, Dean approached us from my left side, strolling nude through the bramble of a thin copse of trees. More houses had cropped up here and there, and our path had included some roads, especially where they led over rivers. Wild fires had raged in some areas, leaving us to walk through younger growth in wooded sections amid blackened older trees.

Halimay circled over the canopy but made no sign of attacking. I would defend Dean if it became necessary. As Dean angled toward me the last few yards, the others stopped. Wati watched us while the others pointedly busied themselves without turning toward me. Odie, surprisingly, trotted over to check on Dean with a companionable wag of his tail and a grateful whine for the scratches around the ears.

"Are you okay?" I offered Dean his pants and didn't stare — too much.

"Nauseous." His eyes flicked at the others with distrust. "Can we leave them now?" He jabbed a thumb behind him in the direction he'd come.

As he climbed into his jeans, I fidgeted with the laces of his boots. "I want to continue with them. They have a place outside of their enclave where we'll be able to stay while we search for a cure. They know so much more than I do."

"Caitlyn, no." He settled his jeans on his hips, then reached for my shoulder. "We can make it on our own. I don't trust them any more than I do the military."

Boots cradled in one hand, I hugged him with the other. He smelled like wood and leather – and not from his jacket that I wore. "We need to find a cure. I love you. I want — you." I blushed at the comment, holding him tighter so he couldn't see.

"No." He coughed. "To the staying with cryptids thing. I love you."

"There are humans with them."

"Penny would likely have put a bullet in me if she weren't fighting something bigger."

He might have been right about Penny. I released him and handed him his shoes. "Please. At least take a look at where they are offering us. You won't know until you check it out."

Dean plopped to the ground, wiping down his foot. "Nothing is easy. Especially not you."

I smiled, and then hid it. "Thank you."

The sun painted the clouds above with orange and purple, and shadows obscured the group ahead. Halimay's faded armor glinted with colors as she moved away, ahead of Vanya and the others. Two other flying shapes in armor reflected light, forcing my spirits to sink to the pit of my stomach.

Odie noticed and trotted back toward them.

"What is it?" His voice low and fast, Dean must have caught my expression.

I swallowed. "More Pahawan. Two of them are talking with Halimay."

"We really should leave." Dean shoved on his socks and fought with a boot.

The three Pahawan fluttered toward us, circling within easy sight before they dropped down to the group. Dean stood and watched them with me.

"Vanya will explain," I said.

"What will she explain?"

"I have a power she wants to study."

Vanya did most of the talking, though the warriors in Kudara armor peered at us more than her. My pulse rose with each second it took her to convince them. If they didn't agree, I might not be able to fight off three of them and Penny's rifle.

After a minute, the conversation spread to the others and some decision led them to removing packs from Bella. The other two Pahawan took to the air and flitted away.

"Well, there's that," said Dean with a hint of positivity.

Nur, Vanya, and Halimay began to follow, while Penny and Wati led the chestnut mare toward us. We moved to meet them, and Dean touched his stomach with a grimace.

"Nauseous?" I asked.

"Odie is likely as sick. That Onikai blood burned."

"You were very — brave."

"Foolish. I know. I couldn't help myself." He tapped the canteen; I'd saved some water for him.

I slid it off my shoulder, smiling hopefully at Penny and Wati. Penny's deadpan expression gave me no clue to the situation, but Wati's hesitant smile gave me some hope. She held two large pieces of bread, and my mouth watered.

Penny stopped. "We'll be taking you to an area west of the enclave. Most of it will be roads from here. It'll take three hours. By morning, Vanya will know if you can stay there or have to leave." Her voice had been as indecipherable as her face, until the end when her tone grew more forceful, as if warning us to behave. "We are to accompany you throughout the night." She frowned when Odie rubbed against Dean, begging for a hand.

"Thank you. I'm sorry for deceiving you. It's why I wanted to leave in the first place." I didn't want to make excuses for my behavior. "I have been craving someone to chat with and —"

Dean raised his eyebrows. "What? I chat."

"Two words at a time."

Wati laughed and handed me the bread. All of it. I offered one to Dean.

Penny studied us, then forced her frown into a flat expression. "Let's go. The area's clear of the Onikai."

I stuffed bread in my mouth as I nodded.

We followed her to a road ahead and to the right. Wati took the chatting seriously, and we exchanged stories about Camp Sparta and her home life and family she'd left behind. At twilight, the road led to a burned area centered on a church and its buildings. A sluggish river traveled under the road through a pipe.

As night fell and the cold sunk through my coveralls, Dean refused to take his jacket. Our pace had increased without Vanya, but even the exertion didn't warm us. We passed through an empty town, most of it gutted from fires.

Under stars and clouds, we took an intersection to the right, and Wati's chatter with me got her in trouble.

"If I were Pahawan, I'd be preparing for the attack."

Penny spun. "Wati. They told us . . ." She let the warning trail off.

The night air had me freezing, but the shiver came from deeper. "The army?"

Wati swallowed, appearing abashed.

Penny replied, "We aren't to discuss this."

"How long do we have?" I asked. It was selfish, but I had the right to worry. Our life had a glimpse of being normal or at least safe, and now the army would attack again.

She turned away, leading Bella faster.

"I've got more reason to worry about them than you do." After this morning's attack on the families' compound, that likely wasn't true. "Okay, the same."

Penny's cold voice snapped with harshness. "Then leave in the morning. We don't need your help. Can't trust it."

Her comments were like a slap. The Alliance had built a community I should hope existed. Duathua, even though they were cryptids, and humans had bonded together peacefully against the violent cryptids and the people who had raised me. Shame twisted my lips, but I didn't offer any excuses or apologies. We walked in silence past abandoned communities and farmlands.

I *did* want to be part of the Alliance and *would* be willing to help defend it. *Would I be willing to kill, again?* They might not want us, though. If I could cure Dean, then this wouldn't be an issue.

Dean spotted an armored Pahawan flying ahead and motioned to it silently.

Penny turned off the pavement onto a dirt road that crossed a small creek that ran through a pipe underneath. We immediately left what turned into barely a trail for a forest of pine trees growing in a row. The scent helped enliven me, but exhaustion ached in my muscles. Dean held my hand after my first stumble and managed to keep me upright. The smooth surface had kept my steps steadier.

Through a small copse of scattered trees, we came to a low house in the middle of a yard growing wild. Crocuses had sprouted around the back entry, and Penny tied Bella under a tree there. She pulled out a pair of blankets and the lantern, handing the first to me and the latter to Wati. "Get them set up," she told Wati.

"Thank you," I said.

Penny eyes were sharp. "Don't. I voted to send you packing."

Too emotional after the day, I just sagged to follow Wati. Tomorrow we would know our status, and I might just want to move on anyway. If they couldn't tell us details about the army attacking, then I didn't need to wait around and find out the hard way. I'd gotten a lead. Iandil and her Pahawan might reject us outright, but I intended to try anyway.

Chapter Ten

I woke alone in the musty room they'd left us in.

Outside the sky hung gray, perhaps predawn. Birds called, but the house remained eerily quiet except for the floor creaking as I stood. Wati had given us a rough woven blanket that I'd snuggled around myself; Dean created his own furnace. I shivered in the cool morning air, grabbed his jacket, and shoved myself into it.

I found a canteen and leaned down to retrieve it, and my legs ached as I bent. We hadn't been walking much the past few weeks, and yesterday had been a chore.

The house wasn't in bad shape despite being coated in dust. I could see where someone had patched a window in the larger main room. The night's rain hadn't made it through the roof at least. The kitchen appeared more used than anywhere else and had saddlebags on the counter.

Through the window, I found Dean talking to Wati while Penny leaned against a tree watching them. Rain had wet the grass out back, and tinges of green were showing. The clouds were thick and threatening. Odie sniffed through the brush but stayed close to Dean.

I stepped onto the porch, catching a glance from Bella,

Odie, and Penny at the first creak of boards. "Good morning," I said to Penny, despite her lack of expression. At least she didn't glare at me.

She mumbled something that I took for a cheerful response. Dean watched me step down to the backyard, though he didn't leave Wati. As always, the little Duathua nearly fluttered and bounced as she spoke, appearing animated, excited, and unaffected by yesterday's injuries.

Wati spotted me. "Caitlyn! Did you see the blueberry bushes back here?" She pointed at dead shrubs.

Smiling, I strode past Penny and went to check. "I hadn't. We had a small blueberry patch in Santee." The families at the hotels did, but I'd tried them once. They were delicious.

She began pointing at the scattered trees in the back. "Peach trees. Pecans. I think that's an apple. I found blackberry bushes near the woods." Wati grabbed Dean's hand and led him to an area with slightly different weeds. "I bet this was their garden."

I held the smile, but a tinge of jealousy rose as Dean allowed her to tug him along. He must have noticed my expression as he pulled away and met me.

"It's going to rain," he said. "I didn't wake you."

I hugged him. "How long have you been awake?"

"An hour maybe. They were making noise."

Wati bounced to land beside us. "We waited for breakfast until you were up. We've got jam." She smiled broadly, and this close, I noticed she didn't have canines. Her teeth were thicker and flat.

"I love jam." Mostly — but I'd like anything that didn't include fish. Fish for breakfast had been the worst.

Wati led the way, and Penny straightened but let us pass, then she followed us inside. Dean's searching glances told me he wanted to speak privately. My dreams had been tense, and the mood rekindled with each moment in the crowded kitchen. I worried about the people of the Alliance with the army attacking, but my real focus lay with Iandil and the hope of a cure for Dean.

"How far away is Iandil?" I asked.

Penny's expression hardened, and she spoke before Wati could. "Deal with Vanya and Nur about that. I'm sure they'll be here soon."

I nodded, my lips tightening, and accepted some of the bread with jam. Beyond my expectations, my knees buckled slightly at the taste. "Amazing," I mumbled through the first bite.

Wati beamed and waited for Dean's monosyllabic grunt of appreciation. Penny never took any, as if we weren't clean enough to eat with. I had begun to dislike her.

After we finished eating, I took a lap with Dean around the house. Stagnant green water surrounded a wooded section of the front yard in a weird setup.

Dean glanced back when we had some distance. "We should leave. Forget this Iandil."

"I want a cure." I wanted all of him. It hurt every time we got close and he had to pull away because of his emotions.

He frowned. "I don't trust them. They don't trust us."

"Who else can we find who might know about any of this?" We paced along the drive with the scent of rain threatening its return. "Vanya literally grew up using magic. Nur knows of other Duathua who have dealt with all this. Iandil has been here for years. What if she has a cure and we walk away? I won't."

Dean kicked at the dirt, too wet to blossom into dust. "I love you. Can't say no. Never give up. Right?"

I smiled. "Exactly." Bumping into his shoulder play-fully, I wrapped an arm around him and pulled him closer for a kiss. "I love you too." We were safest with his bits fully dressed and outside in the chill air. It was cuddling at night when he'd been unable to control his emotions, or me mine.

Through the woods to our right, another house had its roof patched at the corner closest to us. Maybe someone else lived beyond the Alliance enclave. I released him and pointed it out silently. After a few more steps, another house to the left by a road at the front came into view. I didn't want to meet anyone and explain ourselves.

"Let's go back," I said.

As we returned, Halimay, with her broken weapon and clouded armor, rose into view over the house. She watched us for a moment, then fluttered back down out of sight. Nur or Vanya had probably arrived as well, if not both. I sagged, unsure of how the morning might go.

I worked my mind into imagining they'd be sending us away from the enclave, too busy with the upcoming attack to deal with Dean and me. My argument would be to allow us at least to visit Iandil before we left. If a cure existed, it would be helpful to everyone, not just us. By the time Odie jogged around the side of the house, I had grown stiff-backed and strode with sharp steps.

I detected muffled conversation inside the house as I passed the corner. One of the voices sounded like an angry Penny; that gave me hope. Vanya was sitting on the steps of the back porch, examining her hands.

"What did they say?" I asked.

She turned her face to us with a quiet smile. "Good morning, Caitlyn. Dean."

I flushed. "Sorry. Good morning." Stopping a couple paces from her, I fidgeted on one foot, tapping the other toe into the grass. It really smelled like rain.

"You'll be staying here, conditionally," she said.

My heart fluttered, and I couldn't help but smile broadly.

"What conditions?" Dean asked. His voice was abrupt.

"That you do not transform, for one, Dean." She studied him until he nodded. "That you actively search for a cure during your time here, with one exception."

"That is?" I asked. I didn't want to do anything but search for a cure.

Vanya stood and approached me with steady eyes. "Are you willing to fight your comrades in defense of the Alliance?"

Comrades. "Youth Guard?" I asked.

"If you mean those your age with powers, then yes, along with the regular military they are building. The force is larger this time."

For a brief flicker, I imagined Roxie among them, but they wouldn't trust her, not after she tried to help me. My face hardened as I imagined Selina whipping electricity into the Alliance ranks. I only knew a few of them, but I'd rather live in their world than the one Tyrell and the military were trying to build. "Yes."

She took my hands in her cold fingers. "My people now know of your potential and would consider you an important ally. They wanted to come en masse to speak with you, but allowed me to have time alone to adjust, as well as train, before you head off to visit Iandil."

I questioned her concept of my potential, but didn't argue. My mind locked onto visiting Iandil. "I can go to Iandil today?"

Vanya rolled her eyes slightly. "Later. For now, some training. We will only have a day's warning when they begin to march, and they've cleared the way effectively, so perhaps less. We've got scouts, but so do they. It could take them a week, or two days, to gather their forces. We will use some of that time training." She kept my hands in hers and addressed Dean. "This will be yours, at least for now. Go inspect it and determine what you might need."

"I can wait," Dean said. He had his obstinate expression.

She let go of my hands and gestured to the back door. "Go now, young man. Give us some time to talk."

I tugged at his hand. "I love you. I'll be fine."

Dean searched the sky, then the woods behind before grunting and stepping away from us.

Vanya led me deeper into the backyard toward Wati's blueberry bushes. "Have you trained with your magic?" she asked.

I nodded. "Every day blowing wind at targets."

She snorted. "This will be different." Vanya sat on the wet grass in her light dress, and I followed suit. "Can you hear the life force?"

"The otherness? Yes."

"Good. Save us some time." She motioned for me to come closer, and I slid across the wet grass, wiggling until our knees nearly touched. Resting her palms on her legs, she reached her fingers forward, one hand up, the other down. "Touch my fingers."

I mimicked her position and touched her wrinkled fingertips. A breeze drew the scent of pine trees from the nearby forest. My butt was wet and about to get wetter as the air brought a mist of moisture.

"Close your eyes and listen for the life force."

I did, then spoke. "I can hear it when it's being used, not like this."

"You hear it during motion and action. We listen now for it as it rests."

The winds played through the trees, Bella snorted on occasion, and snippets of conversation rose loud enough in the house for me to hear as a muffled echo. The otherness had no sound.

"It's going to rain."

"Even better," Vanya said. "Eyes closed."

I shut them and fidgeted. Ringing had started in my ears, but I knew she had me searching for something else. The high-pitched peals happened on occasion, especially when in silence.

We sat for what seemed like an hour, and the rain came. A light sprinkle slowly soaked us. Vanya never moved; I peeked.

"I—"

"Shh. Listen."

Anger grumbled inside me. I wanted the safety of this house and the potential support and camaraderie of the Alliance, but I didn't hear anything. Asking Vanya now about going to Iandil might just make this futile training take longer.

A door creaked at the front of the house, and Odie scrambled from somewhere on the porch to run through the grass. Bella snorted. Vanya sat there, eyes closed.

I sighed loudly, trying again to hear anything.

"Shh," she said.

I shifted through rebellion, frustration, and finally leveled into determination as the rain stopped. Imagining what the otherness sounded like when I called it, I worked back to the sense of it being there. As I did, I swore I heard a hum.

Holding my breath, I worked my way back again from that moment when I would reach for power, but before I had.

"There's a hum," I said.

"Good." Vanya said. "Now listen to it."

I blinked. "For how long?"

"Longer than you have. Shut your eyes." Hers were closed.

Letting out another dramatic sigh, I began the process again, finding the hum, then held that mindset. It wasn't monotone. There were rhythms in it, though not repeating. In a way, it reminded me of having Selina and Roxie talking in our barracks while I drifted off to sleep. Noise, but not defined.

Distracted, I dropped it, but I picked it back up again easily.

"The life force, what you call the otherness, pervades everything around life."

"I—"

"Shh. Listen." She remained quiet for a minute. "Reach out your 'hearing' to the house. Does the humming change?"

I did, and it did. "Yes."

"Dean and the others are there. Each of them is alive and adding to the sound. Explore."

I did, and the humming changed, but not in a way that allowed me to identify Dean — that would have been cool. We already had our werewolf connection from when I healed him. I could reliably point in his general direction. We were so close all the time, I had to focus to notice it.

"This is easier for us than someone like Dean. He will never hear it."

"That's why I can use it." The hum dropped, but I pulled it up again.

"Exactly. For my people, it is a known effect of life, and we are trained to search for it early. The life force has been subdued here on Earth for a very long time."

"How?" I asked, holding the hum of the otherness.

"Magic. Long ago. A failed attempt by your people to protect yourselves; one that doomed the other planets."

I snapped open my eyes. "Wait. What?"

Her lips twitched. "Shh. Listen."

"No, what do you mean we did this? We did this? How long ago? Why?" I shook beads of water from my eyebrows. "Are you saying we caused the Sorrow?"

Vanya pulled back her hands and opened her eyes. She was soaked. "Yes, our ancestors. I don't know how far back, but it is considered to be over five thousand years ago. The why, we'll leave for another day."

My jaw tightened with her words. I wanted the blame for the Sorrows, my isolation from my family, and Dean's curse to be someone else's fault. "No, tell me now."

Vanya smiled. "Bless your heart, Caitlyn. You'll have to wait. There will be more training. First, we have to go to Iandil. Your mission. Let's gather the others." She stood more easily than I expected, leaving me frustrated on the wet ground.

"Who's going?" I asked.

"All of us. It's dangerous that far west."

Leaning over to rise, I pressed my palm on the wet ground, mud oozing between my fingers. Squinting after Vanya, I was pleased to see her own bottom muddy.

I'd learned something about the otherness, but I couldn't be sure it would be useful. The frustration of her last comments and my present sogginess soured any sense of accomplishment.

At least we were heading to Iandil, even if it meant Halimay coming along.

Chapter Eleven

I hadn't known that Nur and Vanya had brought us supplies until we packed some onto Bella for the trip to Iandil. A collection of cooking equipment, dried food, and even books were stored in the kitchen cabinets. I eyed some of the titles hungrily, as I hadn't seen them before.

They made Wati ride on the chestnut mare and Halimay took to the air. Penny stayed beside her horse, while Nur and Vanya took the lead. We walked down the driveway that Dean and I had traveled earlier in the morning, when it wasn't muddy and dotted with puddles. My soaked coveralls chafed.

Odie had taken to walking at the back with Dean and me. "So, that didn't look like your usual training." Dean and the other locals had often hidden in the bushes and watched us at Camp Sparta.

"Not at all." My lips twisted to the side. "She said some strange things about the Sorrows."

He glanced sharply at me. "Like?" His mother had vanished in front of him, and it might be our ancestors' fault.

I spoke quietly, almost not wanting to tell him. "Vanya

said that someone with magic in the past somehow caused all this. She didn't explain it."

Dean's face hardened, then he stared at his boots. "Then, can someone with magic now bring them back?"

Wati turned, a good five yards from us. "Yes, if they push them just right. Not pull." She would have to have pretty good hearing to catch our conversation. I needed to remember that.

In fact, Nur turned. "Wati." Her tone held a warning.

"It's true. You know what she told us."

Nur glanced at me with a slightly curious expression. "It has been tried."

We'd closed the distance to Wati, and Dean spoke. "How can you bring someone back?"

Wati beamed. "You can't do it that way, that I know of. Alia, a Duathua Seyir, said that one of her people returned, pushed from Earth by one of you. She got caught in the Displacement a few minutes later and thought there was some connection. Not very happy about it."

Dean sagged slightly, but my curiosity spiked. "What do you mean, pushed?"

"I don't know. You're the Seyir." Wati's eyes fixed tightly on mine. "Want to try? I really want to go home."

My head jerked back and my skin tingled. "No. With you? I don't know how to do that. What if something went wrong?" I hadn't ever thought about how the Duathua felt getting stuck on Earth. The army had always made it sound as if it were some nefarious conspiracy to attack humans.

Wati pouted. "I don't mind if you practice on me. I have two new eggs on Denya."

I noticed Penny glaring at me, and from her position twisted toward me as she walked, she likely had been the entire conversation. Wati really wanted to go home, and I had stirred up a fantasy of hers that they probably would rather be left asleep. My ears warmed.

I flashed an apologetic smile to Penny and toward Nur, who turned away from us. "I don't think I can do that."

Wati nodded silently, then turned forward. Bella's heavy scent clung to the breeze.

The sides of the road remained similar to our trip to the house where we'd spent the night. Fields with shrubs had been farms at one time. Some sections were burned, especially blackened forests around houses that indicated the fires had spread. We crossed rivers and over one longer bridge through what appeared to be a swamp. It reminded me of fishing, the massacre of the families, then Moonjir.

I joined Nur and Vanya as were passing a field on the left with a tall metal tower. "Do either of you know Moonjir?"

They shared glances, then shook their heads. "Duathua or human?" Vanya asked.

"Neither. He's a fox with blue fur, tinged pink at the tips, and a really big tail."

Nur nearly stopped, her tall form pitching as she twisted toward me mid-step. "A Sogoi? He can change his appearance?" I couldn't tell from her tone if it meant excitement or concern.

I shrugged. "I haven't seen that happen." It wouldn't surprise me. "When we first met, I used my magic to try and make him get out of my way. It didn't work at all."

"Where did you see him?" Nur asked.

"The last time was when we were running away from the soldiers right after they killed those families."

Nur stopped, and Bella snorted as we all followed suit. "You saw this Sogoi more than once. You called him Moonjir. You spoke with him?"

She seemed to be in disbelief, so I jabbed at thumb over

my shoulder at Dean. "We both have seen him, a few times."

"What did this Moonjir tell you?"

I shrugged. "Weird stuff about paths and bonds. Making decisions."

"About things not being what they seem," added Dean.

"What do you know about them?" I had tried to remember the exact words Moonjir had said, but they jumbled as I thought of his mocking personality.

"Sogoi. Tricksters. We have never seen one, but we have stories aplenty on Denya." Nur studied me. "He has obviously taken an interest in you. After we were here a while, we thought the tales an exaggeration when we didn't come upon one."

A sprinkle of water drifted onto us from the laden clouds above, and Nur continued walking, prompting us along. Vanya remained close by my side while Dean shadowed us on the other, half a step behind.

"Has he tricked you?" Vanya asked. "Suggested you go somewhere or lead you somewhere where there was danger?"

"Nope. In fact, the last time he showed us a safe place to hide so I could ambush the soldiers."

"Then he speaks of your powers?"

"Not really, but he talks about my potential, making bonds."

"Breaking them too," said Dean. "Sounds like he's trying to be a Zen master."

Nur glanced back at the others. "What kinds of bonds?"

Dean sighed. "I think he said, 'I like the bonds you two have. Connections are important, like between different people. You have the power to break them.' I thought he meant Caitlyn should dump me."

I raised an eyebrow. "Not." We were passing through a

graveyard covering both sides of the road. A breeze had risen, driving into us.

"He said he was a friend and would see us again."

Vanya peered past me to Dean. "Do you remember everything he's said?"

"Naw, that part's still fresh. He's a bit of a dick. I try to forget about him as soon as I can."

Nur threw an arm out to warn us to stop. Halimay dove down into a burned forest along the road just past the graveyard. Dean snarled. Penny's gun cocked behind us.

Then I saw the werewolves. Breaking out of dried brush and blackened trunks, mottled white and gray blurs raced toward us along the left side of the road. The rusty fence at the edge of the graveyard on each side corralled us on the pavement. The sprinkling rain began as three of them bounded toward us, only thirty yards away.

I couldn't let Dean turn in front of the Alliance. The otherness roared in my ears, and I leaned forward with intent. The rising storm, even thin, left plenty of thick air for me to work with.

Wati gasped as it swirled toward me and I concentrated on the swath ahead.

Penny fired, but I was too focused to register the gunshot. I built a winding gale that slammed into the lead werewolf. A section of it I split off to carry the cryptid into a flailing arc over its pack. The stream of air continued to the next, hitting it from the side to toss it out of our sight. Whipping back, I caught the third at its legs and flicked upward. All three werewolves were out of Dean's sight in seconds.

I reached back for his hand, not willing to take my eyes off the road ahead. Halimay darted in the direction of one, glaring at me as she did so. Shaking, Dean took my hand, and I heard him taking careful breaths, relaxing his emotions.

"I didn't sense them," he whispered. He'd always felt the pack who'd turned him, as I felt him.

I didn't like Penny behind us with a rifle, but didn't turn around. Halimay had disappeared, and I assumed she now chased the werewolves away. Odie had paced a few steps ahead of us, but stopped, tense and alert.

My chest lightened as I peered at the woods and brush ahead. The werewolves did not appear to be returning. I wanted to laugh, but everyone had become so quiet and serious. Then again, I couldn't hear very well after Penny's gun had blasted behind us.

Vanya touched my arm, and I flinched. "That was impressive. They taught you this at Camp Sparta?"

I breathed deeply and nodded. "Yeah."

"Your comrades will be with the military. Are they as skilled?"

Memories of Selina killing Eric flashed in my mind, and my smile dropped. "Yes. Not all with wind. Fire. Electricity."

"How do we effing stop them?" Penny asked harshly from behind.

I turned to face her glare and replied hesitantly. "I —"

She held her gun facing the ground with white knuckles. "Are you going to help us or side with them?"

"I'll help you, the Alliance." Thoughts of harming others of the Youth Guard did not come easily. I cringed inside.

"How do we stop them?" she repeated.

Standing in the chill rain, it felt like my blood drained from my face. My training had never been anything other than planning to attack cryptids, as I'd just done. Beyond that, I had no idea how to stop an army or people like me. "I don't know."

Vanya still rested her hand on my arm. "That's alright.

The Pahawan have been working through some strategies to counter the military. We're better armed being warned of the magical abilities of your kind."

Penny snorted, tearing her eyes off me and focusing ahead.

"We are prepared to retreat as well," said Nur. "It has been discussed at length with all of the Alliance."

I hated that Tyrell and the army posed such a threat for these people. "I'll do everything I can to stop them." The words felt empty, knowing what I might be up against.

"The scouts will have an idea of what we are facing, once they begin to advance." Nur seemed to be trying to soothe us all, but it wasn't working with me, nor Penny.

Stiff and gripping her rifle, she left Bella with Wati and joined Odie at the front. Together they inched forward, scanning the woods.

Dean squeezed my hand, attempting to reassure me, but I couldn't even offer him a weak smile. The threat of the impending attack clung to me like vines wrapped around my heart.

Halimay returned, and we all began walking again. Dean and I hung back with Wati and Bella.

"Her sister was killed by werewolves," Wati said quietly. "She was alone before we found her. I wasn't here yet."

Dean swayed his head. "No wonder she hates me."

"That's not all." Wati carefully did not return Nur's glance. "Until two weeks ago, we've had a spy at the enclave. One of your people. A young man who had come to us for refuge and became a friend to many of us. He arrived the day after the last attack by the army. Penny was among those he befriended. One of the Pahawan caught him meeting with an army scout."

It made sense why we were mistrusted, when the

Duathua had been open to humans before. "So our arrival is suspicious."

Wati nodded. "To them. *I* believe you."

Dean scoffed. "I would think my — condition would exempt me from being a spy. Everyone would like to see me dead, or in a cage at least."

He made sense, as usual. However, I doubted the Alliance could see beyond their present plight and experience. Penny surely wouldn't. It explained why they were accompanying us to Iandil.

If we found a cure for Dean, they might accept us better. I didn't know if we had time for that before the attack.

Chapter Twelve

We walked through a section that could have been Santee from the buildings. Many had been burned, and the rain dislodged the reek of wet ashes. It didn't rain hard, but the sprinkle had a chilling effect to dampen the mood. Our footsteps were wet slaps as water coated the road.

"Humans like to live very close to each other, but alone, don't they?" Wati asked.

The burned-out husks of houses were only a few yards from each other in this section. "I guess. I lived in a kind of barracks and always had a roommate."

"Barracks?" Wati asked, pointing to a short, blackened husk of house.

I gestured ahead to a two-story house still intact, though charred. "Taller than that and four times the length. Each floor has small apartments."

She peered at Dean. "Did you live there too?"

He snorted. "No. We wanted nothing to do with the hotels or such. It was a small house. Big enough for us . . . big enough for my sister Bettina, Angelo, and Donna."

Wati appeared surprised. "Do they miss you?"

Dean stared ahead. "I don't know. Not likely after they found out." He gestured to his body.

"Oh. They don't like werewolves."

Dean took a long minute to respond. "Neither do I. They killed my father."

We passed a brick church that appeared to have survived the fires, but the windows and doors were busted open. There had been a few brick buildings, but most were scorched and missing their roofs. As businesses cropped up along our path, those that weren't wood and had metal roofs appeared to have survived. The drizzle subsided, but the threat remained in the cloud-covered sky.

Halimay landed on a flat roof ahead where the road inclined, perhaps to a bridge. She appeared to be talking to someone, but I didn't see anybody.

When we reached her, and she didn't come down, Nur and Vanya came to a stop.

"We will eat here. I think those werewolves are tracking us." Vanya nodded behind and to my right.

I spun, but other than a blackened business, I didn't find anything. "How do you know?"

She pointed to her ear, then dug into the saddle bags on Bella. Listening to the otherness obviously had its benefits.

We ate the delicious flatbread with a hearty bean paste that filled me quickly. The whole time, Halimay remained on the roof, and we all studied the surroundings carefully.

"They'll wait until dusk to attack again," said Nur.

Vanya nodded, then cocked her head. "They're injured, but driven."

Reaching gently toward the otherness, I searched for the point where the humming started. I smiled gently when I found it. Even as I ate, I stretched out in the direction Vanya had indicated. The humming did change, but I couldn't tell where the werewolves were.

We left the bridge over the railroad tracks instead of crossing it. We wound along some streets, crossed the tracks, and continued to head west, where we seemed to leave the denser, burned-out city.

The rain held off, but the sky had darkened by the time we reached a larger road and turned right. Fewer of the houses had burned, and whole sections of woods were untouched by fire. I was worn from half a day's travels, yet Halimay continued to spiral over us protectively. She appeared tireless in her vigilance, whereas my footsteps had grown wooden in their pace.

When she swooped toward the side of a building at an upcoming intersection, I woke from my dullness.

Penny's gun barked out two shots, and I saw a gray form drop from where it skulked across the pavement. Bella snorted and shuffled behind me. Dean stood close at my right shoulder.

Halimay disappeared behind the building, and I drew in the otherness just enough to cause it to murmur. When the next white and gray werewolf darted around the corner, Penny caught it with one shot.

Breathing steadily, I waited futilely. Halimay bounced into view much deeper in the neighborhood, then disappeared.

"The last one is retreating," Vanya said. Her declaration caused Penny to relax.

Penny studied Dean. "It doesn't bother you?" she asked him.

He scoffed. "If I had a rifle, I'd be the first to shoot."

His response appeared to surprise her, though she let it drop.

I took a deep breath, in then out, glancing around at the slick pavement and muddied sides. The sky was darkening across the east, leaving the lighter gray to my left. Scanning there, I caught a glint of armor.

"Vanya," I pointed to the pair of Duathua flying toward us, Pahawan from their armor.

"Iandil's scouts. They would have heard the gunfire." She and Nur turned to face the new arrivals.

I would have mistaken either of them for Halimay until I saw their broad smiles.

They flew swiftly, just above the height of the metal fences surrounding a field of a nearby business. As they approached, their legs dropped, and they landed in a jog. They held the same odd three-pronged spears made of Kudara, hardened air. I longed to touch the improbable material.

"Nur!" said the Pahawan on the left with a deeper tone that might have been masculine. "You have not traveled this far since last summer. What brings you?" They glanced over our heads. "Halimay?" Neither of them gave me or Dean a second glance.

"We've come to speak with Iandil," Nur said, but both of the Pahawan appeared more interested in Halimay fluttering across the street to land before them.

The Pahawan on the left spoke loudly in a boisterous laugh. "You seem to have lost a tooth off your Rizulat, old woman!"

"Left it in an Oni, old man." Halimay almost sounded cheerful. The three tapped their weapon points together, as if in greeting. Her voice grew serious, and she glanced at me. "We have much news to discuss with Iandil, Quim." Then she began speaking in their odd language.

My chest tightened. These Pahawan would likely view Dean and me with the same animosity we felt from Halimay. I reached back for Dean's hand, and he took it. I could feel his pulse in my palm.

The two new Pahawan studied us, asking questions in their language to Halimay. Nur gave them a moment, then joined them. A moment of paranoia stirred through me, but Selina had been a longtime friend before she'd betrayed us to Tyrell. They wouldn't have brought Wati if they intended a fight.

They said nothing to us before they flew off into the dwindling light.

Nur waved us onward, taking the road that led toward their flight. Halimay took to the air again.

Wati spoke as Bella clopped beside us. "They will let Iandil know what you're looking for."

"Iandil, of all of us, will be the most understanding of your quest," Nur said without turning.

"Why is that?" Dean asked.

"She has worked for a long time to find peace between all species, even attempting to treat with the Oni. Some consider her too tolerant, but many of the Pahawan look to her wisdom." Nur twitched her head. "She has the scars to prove her benevolence."

"Bless her," said Vanya.

In less than half an hour, the two Pahawan returned with a third as we plodded down a nearly dark road. The chilled evening wind blew at our backs. Halimay dropped quickly beside Dean and me with her Kudara boots clacking onto the asphalt.

The three new Pahawan landed in the same easy jog beside Nur and Vanya, leaving Penny to circle back. Wati jumped off Bella, excitedly bouncing forward to join them. My palms grew sweaty. We stayed with the chestnut mare. Odie loped back to us, and Dean knelt to pet him. Either they had come to refuse us access to Iandil, or this was she.

"Nur," the newest Pahawan said with a gentle and

affable tone, "the troubles sound dire. Before we discuss, would you introduce me?"

"Indeed, Iandil." She motioned us forward.

I rolled my muscles, trying to relax, and reached back for Dean's hand.

Wati bounced on her toes. "I'm Wati, grandmother. I want to become a Pahawan. First, I need to get home to my eggs."

Iandil tapped her forehead, then leaned over to touch Wati's. "I am pleased to meet you, granddaughter."

I doubted Wati had three grandmothers, so perhaps the name referred to a generational gap.

The other Pahawan, including Halimay, crowded us as I approached, but Iandil waved them away. She wore the armor but carried no weapon. Her tone was amiable. "Welcome. I understand you come to us under unique circumstances. I am Iandil."

I nodded, a bit too enthusiastically. "I'm Caitlyn, and this is Dean."

"Caitlyn, Dean, would you walk with me and answer my questions?" she motioned to the road ahead.

"Thank you." Hopefully, I could squeeze my questions between hers. It had gotten dark enough that I could only make out the horizon where shaded trees met a lighter gray sky.

The three of us led with the dull clank of boots and hoofs following. "Let us speak first of the infection. How is it that Dean is able to control himself?"

"I was there when they bit him, and I tried to heal him right away."

Her head tilted sideways to view me. "With the life force?"

"Yes. I can heal. It didn't work all the way, just a little."

Iandil hummed. "I'm not sure that's been tried before." She nudged her chin toward Dean. "What did you feel?"

He spoke reluctantly. "Fire. Like my blood burned."

I pivoted toward him. "You never told me that."

"I'm not complaining." He continued responding to Iandil. "I got sick afterward. Fever."

"That is common, yes. After the sickness, you didn't have the urges to shift and join your pack?"

"Some. Caitlyn tried to heal me again, and I got sicker. I could sense them and the desire, but I wanted nothing to do with them."

"Heal him again?" She peered at me.

"I could tell I hadn't fixed him, so I tried some more." I'd ended up sick myself, but Eric had been able to help. "Is there a cure?"

Iandil didn't answer. "When do you react?" she asked Dean.

I flushed and stared at the ground. The night chill soaked through my wet clothes, but my cheeks were warm.

Dean's eyes flicked to mine. "Strong emotions. Like when the Onikai attacked. I thought they were going after Caitlyn, and I became furious." Gratefully, he'd chosen that example. He didn't mention our failed attempts at closeness, nor his mutilation of the soldier.

"Is there a cure?" I asked again.

Iandil shook her head. "I have never heard of anyone not fully turning. What you two have done is amazing."

I didn't want her amazement. "There has to be someone. A Seyir? Maybe someone stronger?"

She studied me, obviously not believing there was a cure beyond what we'd done. I'd been cured, but the infection might have already been weak, coming from Dean. "It is a magical infection, so one might believe that it could be countered with magic. The manifestation is so quick that I don't believe many have been able to act as you did."

I fidgeted, wanting an answer or direction.

She pointed toward a steeple off to our right. "This is where we will stay the night. Some might have concerns, but I have a room where you will be isolated. Please do not judge their reactions too harshly. I have much to discuss with the others tonight."

The tightness in my chest dropped, and my shoulders sagged. Iandil did not appear to have a solution for Dean. The Alliance churned in crisis because of the army. Focused only on having Dean as a lover and being accepted into the Alliance without their hateful reactions, I found it hard to put their situation ahead of my own.

The past two days had worn on me, but I hadn't come to her for a room. My tone petulant, almost whiny, I felt selfish. "So, no one you would recommend who might know something?"

Iandil smiled easily, stiff gray skin folding with the effort. "Yes, child. Two suggestions."

Chapter Thirteen

At Iandil's response that she did have not just one lead, but two, I stumbled and would have face-planted in the wet grass if it weren't for Dean's quick reactions. He caught my elbow.

"Who?" I asked.

"We'll discuss in the morning. I have questions as well." She stepped gracefully over to Nur and Vanya to suggest a larger meeting with them.

My exhilaration, kindled by her earlier promise, I doused in frustration. Lips twisting, I didn't argue or whine. At least we wouldn't be walking in the dark with were-wolves and Onikai about.

A massive church in pristine condition comprised Iandil's base. We wound through spiked barricades while the dark form of it slowly took shape. The taller, main section had a massive steeple, and the front doors were open, revealing a hint of flickering light inside.

After a word between Iandil and one of the other Pahawan, Dean and I were escorted away from her and the main group to a connected low building that angled out from the church. I could use a chance to dry off and get warm. My stomach growled, and I glanced back at Bella and the saddle bags with food. We hadn't even taken a canteen.

The Pahawan opened the door to a small, beige room obviously meant for sleeping, since it contained a blanket and mattress in the corner. Reaching overhead, the Duathua fiddled with a lantern, and it clicked with a sudden bright light.

"Stay here." The voice sounded like the one named Quim, but the joviality in his voice had left.

"Toilet? Water?"

"We'll bring you something." He motioned us through the door and closed it behind us.

I should have mentioned food. In the windowless room, a door behind the bed led somewhere. I stood, unsure if I should strip and wrap the blanket around me.

"Comfy," Dean said. He pushed the mattress aside and opened the door to expose a defunct bathroom like those we had at Camp Sparta.

I tugged at the two blankets, then went to the door to pull off my boots. "Iandil seemed nice enough."

Dean flourished his hands toward our accommodations. "Love the digs."

I frowned, not having heard the term before, but I assumed he was griping about the room. "It's dry, but I'm hungry."

"Hopefully they feed their prisoners."

"We're not prisoners." I peeled off his leather jacket.

Dean raised his eyebrows, crossed the room, and opened the door. "Hey, if there's anything to eat, we'd appreciate it."

I heard a muffled response from our guard, but didn't give Dean the satisfaction of acknowledging it. Unbuttoning my soggy coveralls, I faced away from the door.

He had a smug expression when he closed the door.

"Our valet will consider it." Dean kicked out of his boots and peeled off wet socks.

"Are you okay that I'm pushing for this?" I squirmed out of the wet coveralls, and he averted his eyes. I hated that.

"Yeah. I love you. Not giving up is good. Right?"

I wrapped a warm, dry blanket around myself and faced him as he stripped out of his jeans. "I love you too, and that's why I don't think I can — give up on curing you."

"Saving me."

"What?"

"You tried to cure or save me when we met. That was cool. Now it's become your mission to save me." He grabbed the blanket I offered him. "I get it — considering we can't do anything without me wolfing out."

I wilted slightly, unsure what I'd done wrong or what he objected to. A cure meant the same as saving him, in my mind. Too tired to try to unravel it, I sighed. "You do want to be cured, right?"

"Yeah." His tone held an assurance.

Wati and one of the Pahawan were the ones to deliver two canteens of water, food, and an ominous plastic pail that I assumed would serve as a toilet from its faint, lingering odor.

She remained as we sat to eat and drink. "I heard Iandil say she had people for you to visit, to continue your quest."

The flatbread, while delicious and hearty, had become commonplace, while the raspberry-honey jam we were dipping it into held my rapt attention. "Yes. Do you know who she meant?"

"No, but I'm excited."

I assumed that meant we'd have the whole group as an escort again. "Me too."

"Have you given any thought to helping me?" she asked.

My eyebrows dropped, studying her. "Oh. You mean

pushing you back to Denya? I wouldn't know where to begin."

"You could try anyway." Wati's expression was hopeful. "Not tonight. You must be tired."

I held off taking another bite of delicious bread and jam. "What if I did something wrong?"

"I'd take the risk."

"I'd feel awful."

"Not if I asked for you to do it."

I shook my head. "Even if you asked."

She drooped slightly. "I understand. I just really want to get home. I've been here thirteen months, according to your calendar. Our eggs will be hatching soon."

It wasn't long after that she left and we turned out the light. I wanted to sleep and have my conversation with Iandil, but lay there stressing as Dean drifted into a light snore.

By the time I woke in the morning, I had to use the stupid pail, but he'd tucked it in the bathroom. Without a window, I couldn't tell whether the sun had risen or if we'd woken ridiculously early.

"Is it morning?" I asked.

Dean remained in the bed, though I knew he'd rather be outside. "I think so, love. When do you think we'll get going?"

"No idea." I didn't want to be in a blanket when they arrived, but my coveralls were nastily damp, and I had no interest in crawling into them in that condition. I thought of Roxie and called the otherness to extract the water into a puddle on the floor.

Dean pointed to his jeans, flat on the floor. "If you're in the mood."

I stared at him flatly, but in a few minutes, we had passably damp clothes and a decent puddle of water.

Dean chanced opening the door to a gray predawn sky. "Morning, bud."

Someone grunted in reply to his snark.

Chilly air blew into the room, setting me to shiver. "Let's wait until it warms up, Dean."

"Later." Dean closed the door, and we only had to wait a few minutes before Penny came to retrieve us.

Her expression was unreadable, but it didn't hold open hostility. "Vanya asked me to come get you." She turned and started toward the end of the building.

I grabbed the canteens.

Dean raised his eyebrows but walked with me. Our guard followed behind.

The building we had slept in was larger than I realized as she led us around the far side instead of toward the main church. I could see the bristling barricades clearly in the gray light. Made of small trunks and some large branches, they would not be easy for Onikai to pass through, but a werewolf could crawl under the spikes.

In the broad field behind the building, Vanya waited alone under a dented metal pavilion. Without any of her usual grudge, Penny nudged her chin toward the woman, then left us. Our guard remained standing beside the building.

"Sleep okay?" she asked as we approached.

"Yes. I was tired." I wanted to hear what Iandil had to offer, but didn't need to be rude with Vanya. She'd stood up for us since the beginning.

"Good." She peered at Dean. "This might be a little boring for you, young man. We'll be training for a couple hours."

My eyebrows shot higher, but Dean just shrugged and pointed at the Duathua guard. "Should I go play cards with my new buddy?"

Vanya chuckled. "The Duathua have a dice game favored by the Pahawan. Tell him I want him to keep you occupied so you don't interfere."

Dean reacted with surprise. "Totally joking."

"Go on." She waved him back toward the guard. She motioned for me to sit on a bench.

Gratefully, we wouldn't have to sit on the still wet grass. "Listening?" I asked.

"You catch on quick."

We spent until well after sunrise there, while Dean did in fact kneel on the sidewalk playing some game with the Pahawan. Vanya coached me into sensing them there, then reaching out to the comparatively empty hum of the fields around us. My stomach churned with hunger and growled when we finished, but I felt a little proud of my newfound ability.

Vanya led me back toward Dean. "Try to keep it alive when we're walking today to test it."

"Where are we going?"

"Iandil will explain. She wants to see your ability with gravity, as do I."

"I don't know how to use it."

"Have you tried?"

"Not intentionally."

She studied me with one eyebrow raised. "Then you don't know if you don't know how to do it."

I sighed; the magic didn't have much use anyway. "I'll try."

Vanya led the way into a door where Iandil, Nur, and a slew of Duathua, mostly armored, were talking in a large room that reminded me of an oversized classroom. Windows near the door added light, but otherwise they sat in the dark. The room smelled like some sort of spice.

My pulse rose, barely able to see their expressions. Most

of the Duathua sat at a long table, and they were ranged in height from Wati to Nur. I would have guessed them all male, by their flat chests, but knew better.

Iandil rose. "Caitlyn, I trust you slept well?"

"Yes, thank you."

If I'd been with my Wolf Squad unit, or alone with Dean, I might have been more forward. Surrounded by imposing Duathua felt somewhat intimidating, and I did want Iandil's help. I waited as she approached to stand before me, looming in her glass-like armor.

"Would you attempt to give us an example?" When I nodded, she led me to a pair of chairs away from the group. "There is some curiosity among us about the ability, as it might be tied to older magic that Seyir of present do not appear to possess. It might be an aspect connected only to Earth, though that seems unlikely."

I sat where she gestured. "What older magic?"

"Those that deal with bonds."

Her comment caused a shiver down my back. I tried to remember Moonjir's exact words about bonds and connections. "What kinds of bonds?"

"There are so many, but gravity is one of them. Kudara making is one that has been retained by our people." Iandil sat in the other chair. "Could you try to release the bond of gravity around us?"

There were some concerned murmurs from the Pahawan. Dean leaned on the wall by the door. Wati watched me with too much expectation and excitement.

My stomach felt empty, and I eyed Dean and the exit. I really didn't want to fail at something I'd never tried in front of a large group. Early embarrassment at Camp Sparta flickered through my mind.

"Release the bond of gravity? I don't really know how."

Iandil loomed over me from the other chair. She shrugged. "No one knows until they try, correct?"

"Sure," I mumbled.

With air, I had a real sense of what I moved. Water, too. Healing had an innate sense when I gathered otherness and pressed it into the body, then reacted to the response.

I tried approaching gravity like healing by gathering it in a dull roar of otherness. When I pressed it down into the area around us, I sensed the air, even the metal and plastic of the chairs, and the concrete of the floor, but not gravity. I pushed the otherness into it anyway.

The leg of my chair buckled and bent, scattering me to the floor. I folded onto my side, picking out a chuckling Dean. Face pressed against cold concrete, I confirmed there was still plenty of gravity.

"Yeah, not sure that worked," I said.

Iandil leaned over to offer a hand. "Let's try it again."

"That sounds like a blast. Perhaps without chairs?" I stood, then joined her sitting cross-legged on the floor. I pushed my softened chair a good distance away.

Again, I gathered in the otherness and focused on the concrete below us. I could sense the finite particles bound together, without the usual clarity that I felt from air or water. My own body I could feel clearly in my otherness sense, and Iandil's only vaguely. Hoping I wouldn't cause her some physical damage that would bring the Duathua warriors down on us, I tried to push into stone and flesh, then upward. The action immediately drained me, like I'd called down a hurricane.

A sharp snap jerked me out of the attempt. A yard-long crack had grown along the floor. Taking deep breaths, I laid back and stared at the dark ceiling. "Not working."

"Not, it seems, as intended." Iandil stood, offering me a hand.

I waved it off. "Let me take a minute."

A worried Dean appeared at her shoulder, along with concerned Pahawan. They escorted Iandil away from us.

"Wait," I managed. "You said you had two names for us."

Iandil continued to walk away. "Yes, I talked with Vanya about them last night. She agreed and will be taking you there today."

I closed my eyes and smiled, laughing at myself. Vanya had known all morning and never said a thing. If I'd had the energy to move, I would have bounced with excitement. I had a fear that the impending crisis with the army would crush any hopes of us pursuing Dean's cure.

Dean knelt beside me and took my left hand. "You okay?"

"Ready for a nap."

"That's not going to happen." An impish grin formed on his lips. "Wati says they have food for us."

I opened my eyes. "Okay." The Duathua were clustered together, talking. "Where?"

"I thought that might get a response. She set us a table in the front corner."

Sighing, I shifted onto my elbows, then offered him a hand. "Drag my sorry ass up. I'm hungry."

Chapter Fourteen

An hour later, I wasn't surprised to learn that our same crew would be traveling together again. The morning sky held only a few clouds, and the air carried a clean springtime scent. Halimay joked with a few of the other Pahawan, which made me uncomfortable. I had thought her incapable of pleasantries, but she simply had not changed her hostile disposition toward us.

Penny, as she and Wati stored supplies on Bella, actually didn't glare when I offered to help fill the canteens. "Sure. I'll pour."

I jumped to grab the first, a cylindrical water bottle that had a plastic cap screwed into the metal. "Do you think we'll run into trouble today? I mean, the Onikai, then the werewolves yesterday. I hadn't realized how dangerous it was here."

She positioned the pail of fresh water to pour into my container. "Never know. Oni are rare this close to the enclave."

I blinked at her casual response, not because of the content, but her easy tone. I'd gotten so used to her bite that I hadn't thought of her as just someone my age stuck with the aftermath of the Sorrows, like me. "I'd really rather not deal with either of them again, but the Onikai were terrifying."

Chilly water sloshed onto my hand before she corrected the flow. "That's only my third time. Usually the Pahawan hunt them down." She backed off the water as the container filled. "Thanks, by the way."

"For what?" I fumbled the cap with my wet fingers.

She motioned with spread out fingers ahead of her. "Killing with a touch. Effing scary, but damn, it worked. I would have been dead."

I winced and focused on the lid. "I don't like using that magic. Killing at all, really."

Penny scoffed. "Pretty hard to survive out here without defending yourself, or are you thinking of your Seyir comrades at that camp?" Her head lifted to study me.

I tightened the cap, not wanting to think of that at all. "I've had to fight them before, rescuing Dean." It wouldn't be the same. "They wanted to take him off to the labs and study him."

"Should have just . . ." She stopped, letting her words drift off, then replaced the full canteen with an empty container.

I assumed she would suggest they should have killed Dean, but we never finished the conversation. Wati joined us, and I finally learned about the Denya witch named Kisharn who we would be traveling to see.

"He lives with about a dozen human kids, south of the enclave. Kisharn never would join us, but he's good friends with Iandil."

"How far south?" I asked.

Wati shrugged. "Three hours, I think."

It took longer than she expected, and late in the after- noon we crossed a bridge. Once we'd walked past the marshes and waterways, the air smelled solidly of spring with more scents of fresh leaves and blossoms, than decay. The wind had picked up from the south, but there wasn't any sign of rain from the light clouds.

Halimay hesitated over a dirt drive to our right, waiting for us to follow. As Bella turned the corner with Wati, Odie circled around Dean and me. Halimay flew along the tops of the trees to our right, but we all watched the woods on both sides. The sun had started to feel warm, my coveralls had dried, and I wore Dean's jacket tied around my waist.

Vanya motioned me to join her and Nur. Dean stayed back with Odie and the others. "Try to listen as we walk. It is difficult to split my focus consistently. The practice is good, though."

I slipped into the mode and located Halimay and the others. "Am I looking for anything specific?" I asked.

"No. Shh. Talking splits focus."

Nur chuckled lightly, but remained silent.

I sensed nothing unusual, though I might have caught some animals in the woods like rabbits or foxes. A waterway cut in to border the right side with a stagnant canal. It reminded me of the short inlet by Camp Sparta. My thoughts drifted, and I had to focus to listen for the otherness again.

Scanning far ahead, I found three distinct hums. Tight and higher pitched, much like Vanya herself. I gestured excitedly, and she nodded. They moved away from us and beyond my hearing quickly. Nur watched us with a bemused expression.

The tighter hums ahead returned. A solid mass, rather than distinct. Halimay paused in the air, and we all came to a stop. Far down the road, where I sensed something, there was motion.

"Kisharn?" I asked.

"Fairly sure," Vanya replied.

I sensed a stiffness about Vanya and Nur. What relationship did they have with Kisharn? Halimay circled back toward us and landed beside Nur as we waited.

There were four teens my age walking behind a bald man with a roundish figure. As they drew closer, I could make out the dark vest he wore over a bare chest. His expression held no malice, but he didn't smile at the sight of us.

I jumped when Dean took my hand. "Doesn't look impressive," he said quietly.

Vanya stepped forward, greeting Kisharn, and he coolly returned with informal politeness. They obviously knew each other, but I saw no warmth. The three males and one female teen had tight expressions. Their mix of skin tones and shapes told me they couldn't all be his family.

"We have an unusual request and news of the military to the southeast."

"Mobilizing again? I doubt they'll find anything of interest out here by the water; few do." Kisharn's eyes were dark and sharp. He had a pinkish quality to his face as if from exertion or a light burn.

"Agreed. The request is for healing of an unusual kind." She turned and gestured Dean and me forward. "This Seyir, Caitlyn, attempted to heal this young man of the werewolf infection, and nearly succeeded. Your concerted method might be applicable, if you were willing to attempt to cure him. Caitlyn believes it possible."

He studied Dean, then cocked his head and addressed me, "Why do you believe this?"

I wasn't about to mention my own circumstance. "Because it partially worked. I might not be strong enough." Neither Vanya nor Iandil had given me any idea what to expect; from her comment, I suspected we would try a group healing.

"In what way did the healing work?"

"He didn't join his pack, he only shifts if his emotions get out of control, and — I could just tell during the healing."

Kisharn addressed Dean. "What emotions? Anger, fear, lust?"

"Yes." Dean's tone sounded as dry as the man's.

"How do you control them?"

Dean sighed reluctantly. "I take deep breaths. Focus on logic and action rather than reaction."

Kisharn's bottom lip lifted, as if impressed. "Where did you learn that?"

"Reading books." Dean showed no sign of warming to the man.

With a shrug, Kisharn pointed down the dirt road from where his group had come. "Very well. We'll give it a try. Might cause more harm than good. There's a barn at the end of the drive; you two wait for us there. I want to find out more about this military threat. Strip down and wash up, Dean."

I didn't move. "Wait, what do you mean more harm?"

"Healing isn't something you force, and we'll be forcing it, so there might be consequences. Head to the barn, or leave." Kisharn's eyes were black steel.

Dean nudged me forward.

Kisharn turned to Vanya. "How do you know they are massing for an attack?"

The group of teens warily parted to let us pass. The scent of sharp herbs clung to them. They wouldn't acknowledge my nod as we stepped forward.

"They are staging at a place they used to call Summerton. It is the same location they used a few weeks ago before the attack. This time, they've sent smaller patrols ahead and cleared out any humans along the path to the town called Pinewood. We've had to risk Pahawan scouts. Once they begin, we're only a day away." Vanya's voice trailed farther behind us as we walked.

"I guess we witnessed what she means by 'cleared out any humans along the path.' Those soldiers make me sick." Dean's angry tone ended in clenched teeth. He really needed to remain calm.

"Are you sure you want to do this? Take the risk? Maybe the other person Iandil thought of has a safer option."

Dean shrugged. "Might as well try. Fish are biting."

A silver pole barn waited at the end of the dirt drive with the left side built into sheds, creating a shadow. I practiced my listening with the otherness and thought there might be someone deep in the woods to our left, but no one inside the barn. The canal to our right had plenty of buzzing, maybe fish. A small dock rotted at the end of the road.

In the shade of the pole barn were two large barrels connected to spouts from the roof. A picnic bench in decent shape sat in the center. Junk and automobile parts were piled by the sheds.

"Want to take a bath with me?" he asked with an impish grin.

"Might not go over well if you wolf out before they get here."

He eyed me up and down. "Pretty likely, too."

As we reached the shade and he started to strip, I listened again. If anyone was peeping, it wouldn't matter. It sounded like plenty of people would be ogling Dean soon. I sat on the sturdy bench of the picnic table and enjoyed the sights.

"Missed a spot," Moonjir said from the shadows.

I slipped off the bench and landed on the concrete pad with my elbow. His bright fur reposed across a padded car bench by the sheds. "Moonjir, what are you doing?"

"Watching," he said. Head on his hand, elbow shoved into the dark cushion, stretched down the full length with legs crossed at the knees, his pose reminded me of the last time we met.

Grappling the top of the table, I pulled myself upright. "Here? Why now?"

Dean snorted, and continued washing with water out of the barrel. There was no sign of Kisharn or anyone else.

Moonjir studied Dean. "I think he's fine, just as he is. Don't you, Caitlyn?" Before I could reply, he gestured down the road. "I see you've made new friends."

His initial surprising appearance had my heartbeat racing. He hadn't shown up when I'd been listening, and his blue and pink fur would have been hard to miss. The Alliance had called him Sogoi, trickster. I should probably be more careful with him.

I straightened. "They explained a little bit about your people."

In a languid, graceful move, he shifted into a sitting position and smoothed the fur on his cheek. "I do hope it wasn't *all* bad."

"Cautionary."

Moonjir shrugged, ear flopping. "For good cause."

He didn't argue the point, and for some reason that assured me. "What do you want with me, Moonjir?"

"What anyone would, Caitlyn. To be your friend."

I doubted that. "Why?"

"Who wouldn't? You're good-natured, perceptive, curious, and downright enthusiastic, most of the time."

My lips pursed. I would pay attention to his words this

time. He'd talked about meeting new friends, paths, and bonds before. They'd become relevant in time. "That's very nice of you to say."

"Well, I wouldn't mention your dreadful fashion sense, or the fact that you're overly optimistic, especially in others, and not confident of your own abilities." He stood, pacing in front of his seat. Scratching at his cheek highlighted the pink tips at the end of blue fur. "Dean is a good balance for you. He's as perceptive as you, but more direct and bold. I'd say, if you're having trouble picking sides, check with him."

I was about to dig into his previous comments about bonding as it might help with what Iandil wanted me to try, but he stopped pacing and leaned forward to peer past Dean down the dirt drive.

Kisharn was leading his teens and the rest of the entourage toward us. Still a good distance away, I could make out their shapes.

"Oh, too many questions, I think. I'll see you soon." Wiggling fingers goodbye, Moonjir began to fade where he stood.

His body didn't turn to vapor or anything like that, I could just see through him to the junk beside the sheds. The motion of his fingers continued, catching my focus.

"What —?" My mouth dropped open.

Moonjir smiled. His teeth were fully visible and white against the shadows, then they winked away.

Dean laughed, louder than I'd heard from him in a while. "Cheshire Cat. *Alice in Wonderland.*"

I snapped back and forth between staring at Dean and searching for Moonjir. "What?" My question was about the character he'd mentioned.

Rumbling with chuckles, Dean waved at the space where Moonjir had been. "A book. Maybe we'll find a copy someday. You'd like it."

My chest remained tight. "What did all that mean? It had to mean something."

Dean shrugged. "Maybe." He turned and faced the coming crowd, turning his butt cheeks squarely in my direction.

It took me a moment to refocus over his shoulders to Kisharn, the Alliance people, and a growing group of teenagers. Everyone had an emotionless expression, except for Wati with her usual beaming smile.

"You don't have to flaunt it." I took three steps to rest my hand on his shoulder.

"Yeah, touching me right now might be a bad idea. I love you, but I'd like not to announce it to everyone." Dean's tone obviously teased me, but I removed my hand.

"Love you, too," I whispered.

Kisharn spoke to his teens as they approached, too quietly for me to hear.

I tried to loosen the tightness in my chest with a deep breath, but I just twitched. One of the younger female teens broke off to the sheds, followed by a young male. The rest marched resolutely toward the picnic table in the center of the floor. Their steps echoed against the metal ceiling.

I suddenly regretted the entire attempt, but I couldn't make that decision for Dean. "Are you sure?" I whispered.

"No regrets."

I had them, since I had no real reason to trust Kisharn or his group. He said this could go badly. We could pass for the moment and check on the second lead Iandil had, though I didn't know if it would be any better.

The girl returned with a stiff, folded tarp that had a mildewy scent and began covering the table. There were a dozen teens circling the far end of the table, and a couple helped her.

The boy's eyes were blinking rapidly as he brought a coil of yellow rope.

"What's that for?" I asked.

Kisharn raised his eyebrows. "To tie him down, of course. He might shift during the procedure, and I won't risk everyone over your sentiments. Face down, arms at the side of your head."

Pulse racing and mouth open, I shook my head at Dean. We needed to stop them.

He just chuckled, heading for the table. "Let's do this."

Chapter Fifteen

In the crowd of teens, the scent of sharp herbs grew stronger. They tied the yellow rope over his arms and head, then across his back, and finally against his thighs. If he shifted, it would take a minute before he could get out, but he would; I'd seen him wriggle out of tighter clothes. I hated this.

"Sit on the bench at his left shoulder." Kisharn motioned with a brusque gesture. He took the side opposite me and placed one hand on Dean's neck and the other on his shoulder.

Vanya, thankfully, stood near me and took Dean's head. "We'll go slow, right Kisharn?"

"We'll go as the body wills."

Six of the teens began taking places on the bench, hands touching his skin. The others formed a ring around us, perhaps to attack Dean if he shifted.

He watched me with a smirk, and I was glad he lay facing me. "I hope this works. Either way, we are never talking about this afterward."

Penny chuckled somewhere behind me. Even Halimay

had come in to observe, or maybe to stab Dean if he turned into a werewolf.

Kisharn's tone changed as he spoke from the stiff coldness to a warmer, teacher's tone. "The infection is known to be a magical bond inherent in the species on their world. It allows them to be connected as one mind when they are hunting in a pack. The connection, when they infect humans, wants to align them to their form and to their bonded group. Any possible healing comes from disconnecting that link. How that presents itself to the human perception, we do not know. Do you, Caitlyn?"

Surprised he had asked me in the middle of his lecture, I faltered before speaking. "It was like a blackness in his blood. I burned some of it away. Later, there was much less."

He watched me over Dean's dark locks. "Very good. Burning it away is likely your comprehension of severing the connections. We start in the blood and see what we find." His tone reverted to teacher. "As we work together in a body, we become a body. There will be a sense of oneness if we let it happen. Each success will feed to the others, guiding them in providing what the subject needs." From his glances to us, the latter comments were for Vanya and me.

"We stop together as well, I take it?" Vanya asked.

"Some have been known to drop out early, but this case is different. Dean, do you believe you can control yourself, if you shift? We will step away in any case, if you do."

"Yeah, sure." Dean's voice was tight. He had to be nervous.

Kisharn glanced to a couple of the teens outside, then nodded. "We begin."

I winced as the otherness roared around me from the group; my own call sounded faint in comparison. As I moved into Dean's body with my healing, I could feel every-one, as Kisharn had stated. A pulsating rush swelled inside me from the experience. Excitement and a rising sense of power came from being joined in a purpose.

Even as I investigated his blood, finding the darker elements that didn't belong, I knew the others experienced similar revelations. We prodded as one, in all areas of Dean's body.

He stiffened, and the exultation felt selfish and cheap.

I focused on cells dark with the infection and pushed, trying to sever the connection. They resisted and tore, some breaking their bonds.

Dean shook and grunted as we pressed harder.

In our larger pool, I could sense Vanya's concern as she worked carefully at the blood in his head and brains. It eased my concern to know she worked there.

As before, Dean's blood seemed to steam and roil with the healing. His knees knocked on the tarp-covered table. His grunts had turned nearly to a continuous hum, almost a whine.

The infection did not yield easily, and blood cells felt like they ripped before we could dispatch the darkness.

Dean screamed. I jerked my hands off him, as did Vanya.

"Stop," she said. "We are causing damage."

Kisharn and his followers continued. I stood and pulled at Kisharn's hands. "Stop."

I was a bit surprised when Penny stepped to the table and helped me pry one of the man's hands free. He blinked, then let us pull the other hand off with ease.

"It is not done," he said in a distant, dreamlike voice.

Wati had begun swatting at the teens, forcing them become aware. In seconds, we had Dean free of them.

He gagged, coughing and limbs trembling.

"Dean?" I pressed my face near his, but his eyes were unfocused. What had I done? I could feel the damage at the end. His body would need to clean away broken blood cells and replace them. What little progress we had made would not cure him. It had been worse than nothing, and we'd been warned.

Kisharn showed no remorse, simply gliding out of his seat, shaking his head. "Not possible. Perhaps when the infection is still new. It would be an interesting procedure to try on someone who'd just been bitten. We have learned from this, though."

My throat croaked with raw scratches. "Untie him."

Kisharn noted Dean's trembling limbs. "He could still turn. We'll leave him to your ministrations. Leave the grounds by nightfall. We've done what we could do." His group followed him toward the front of the pole barn.

While Penny and Wati began to untie Dean's legs, Vanya touched my shoulder. "We need to try and heal what we damaged."

She was right. I scrambled back onto the bench and put my hands on Dean's back. Vanya took Kisharn's seat.

"Easy. The body will know what it needs." Her words were calm and reassuring.

As we healed, Vanya and I bonded as a team. I could sense her care as we explored. The ministrations were intuitive, aiding strength were the body needed us. Dean stopped shaking and coughing, then fell asleep. Penny and Wati worked around us, loosening the yellow rope that had left red lines on his skin. Nur released Odie, who whined as he licked Dean's fingers at the edge of the table.

I couldn't help the tears that dropped into my lap and soaked into my coveralls. My throat thick and closed, I rested my head on the table and cried.

We had pushed when we shouldn't have. I had hoped

for a simple cure, but that appeared less possible now than ever. Worse, we had no idea how much damage we'd caused Dean.

Moonjir had called me overly optimistic. He'd been right.

Sitting there, I didn't want to even consider Iandil's other suggestion, but we couldn't stay. Kisharn had made that clear.

Chapter Sixteen

When we packed a groggy Dean atop Bella and left the barn, the sun had already dipped low in the sky. Wati took to the sky with Halimay, though her flight wasn't as sure and smooth.

"I can walk." Dean's voice croaked, and his face paled.

"You'll slow us down. Leave your ass in the saddle." Throughout the whole ordeal, Penny had been supportive. I felt relieved that she had begun tolerating us.

Odie trotted alongside Penny but kept an eye on Dean.

I jogged a step and caught up to Nur and Vanya. "I really think we should just take Dean back to the house."

Vanya sighed. "I might agree, but it will be dark for half the walk if we try. Vinnie will let us camp at his compound. We can leave in the morning. He's not a healer, so don't worry."

"Then why are we going?" I had yet to get a clear answer from her.

"I'll let him decide if he wants to explain. I do understand why Iandil suggested him."

"Human?"

"Yes."

I rolled my eyes. "From Denya?"

"No."

There didn't seem to be any harm in going to him if he couldn't try any magic on Dean. I hated that my hopes for a cure were crumbling. My own energy sagged after using so much magic. There were only about two or three hours of daylight left. "How far is it?"

"A couple hours. The rivers branch around us here, good for keeping the Oni and werewolves at bay, but we'll have to keep to bridges." Vanya glanced at Nur. "There's still a few stragglers out here who haven't moved up to the enclave. We help them out when we can."

Nur cocked her head. "Vinnie has been one of the few outsiders who helps us. He's developed a refinery for lamp oil using beeswax, among other things. We trade with him."

I really didn't see why Iandil had sent us to him. "That's nice. Why won't he move up to the enclave?"

"He hasn't been ready to leave his home." Nur's tone sounded odd, and I guessed I would find out soon enough, if Vinnie wanted to explain.

"He'll have a place for Dean to rest?" I asked.

Nur nodded. "I'm sure. He's eccentric, but very nice. We have always valued our relationship." Her words held more meaning than what I could glean.

My steps were nearly a shuffle, scuffing against the occasional crack in the asphalt. Our quiet life in the marsh seemed like a lifetime ago. The soldiers had broken everything Dean and I had been building together, and then I had dragged him on my fool's quest to cure him. The Alliance couldn't offer us true safety with their rightful concerns over Dean's condition and the army preparing to attack. I doubted Vinnie would be our answer.

I jumped when Nur placed her hand on my shoulder.

"Dean is okay. You'll have a place with us, even if some will make it uncomfortable."

"What about the army?"

"We survived their attack before. If need be, we'll retreat. I believe they are only here for the military base and what little it holds."

"What base?"

"It was called Shaw Air Force Base and once held strange flying machines. Scavenging has taken most of what the fires left. When we first met members of your army, they attacked my people and rebuked even humans sent to engage in talks. We would have happily let them investigate the base." She patted my shoulder. "I want you to know that we will advocate for you among the Alliance, Vanya and I. Be assured."

Her words did make me feel more welcome among them. I was surprised how quickly I'd accepted the Duathua as people, even friends, after having been trained for years to be ready to kill them. Exposure to Moonjir had already tainted my assumption that all cryptids intended me harm.

The afternoon's warmth faded with cool breezes from the north that accompanied the descending sun. Dean drooped forward as if ready to sleep on Bella's neck. Shadows grew long, burying the road and all of us but Halimay flying above. As we approached an intersection with low fields ahead, the Pahawan darted there, circling to search the exposed area. Halimay paused mid-turn as we watched, the sun bathed her armor in golden light.

Penny jogged to the front, rifle ready. Her pace slowed, but she pulled away from our group, closing on Halimay's position at the intersection.

"Keep an eye out." Nur searched the woods around us

for a threat, and I followed suit, dropping to the end of our line.

The woods were bare limbs and dried brush except for the pines dotting them. The height of the trees and the density filtered the golden sun, barring a glimpse as we walked. I listened as Vanya had taught me and sensed only the lightest humming from local wildlife.

"It is but more scouts." Nur spoke more assured than she had previously.

Ahead, two more flying, sun-sparkled Pahawan had joined Halimay in the air. They gestured with their weapons away from us and toward the south. The Duathua landed when Penny arrived, as we were only a couple dozen paces away. The warriors' expressions were hard as they focused on us. They likely knew of Dean and me. If we did stay with the Alliance, I knew not all would welcome us.

I hung beside Bella, taking the reins from Wati so she could run ahead to join the group. Nur and Vanya had reached Halimay, their voices audible but not clear. The sun burned close to the horizon, a golden ball touching the treetops.

"Are you sure?" asked Nur, her voice tight. Her wings flicked, as if preparing to fly.

The Pahawan were focused on me or Dean, but one replied, "They have brought supplies, and their scouts have moved north in large numbers, as before. There are fifteen of the children in uniform." The warrior pointed at me, even as I brought Bella to a stop five yards from the group.

The army had brought three units of the Youth Guard. I cringed, wondering who they had brought. Selina was a top candidate, and dangerous. I feared for the others who might be tossed into this attack. Surely, they would leave Roxie behind at Camp Sparta.

Even Wati's smile had disappeared. Her wings flashed in the sun as she flitted toward me. "The army will be marching in the morning. We'll have to go back."

I nodded. "Now?" After the damage I'd already caused Dean, I could forgo our visit to Vinnie. "How far away from the Alliance are we?"

She shrugged, jerking her gaze toward Dean as he stirred.

"What?" he asked groggily. His eyes tried to focus on the Pahawan ahead of us.

"Rest, Dean." I reached back and patted his knee.

"The army will be marching in the morning," Wati said to him. "They'll be at the enclave by tomorrow evening."

He straightened, nearly toppling over. I grabbed his leg. "It's alright. Rest."

Vanya spoke from behind me. "He needs rest. We will stay the night and leave at dawn." She spoke to me and Dean, as well as to the others. "Nur. Halimay. You head out now. I can deal with Vinnie tonight and get us on the road tomorrow."

Nur studied me and Wati. "The army cleared the roads to the east of any eyes. I imagine that is the route they are planning to take, but their scouts will make it difficult to confirm. Perhaps we should chance the night and leave together."

Vanya shook her head. "You cannot be sure of their path. Eyes are needed. We will be four hours ahead of them and safely back before the attack. You are needed to set the defense."

"We are prepared," one of the Pahawan boasted, tapping the base of his Rizulat on the street for emphasis.

"Not for an evacuation." Nur's voice was firm but pained. Slowly, she nodded to Vanya, then peered at me. "Then, we will all be needed to defend."

After a moment, I understood her meaning. "I'll be there," I said. "I'll help fight off the army." I guessed I might be the only one trained to use my magic for battle.

Halimay and the Pahawan retained their steely, cold gazes, but Nur nodded her head toward me. "Thank you."

They rose into the sun and flew off to our right. Vanya wasted no time setting us on the road to the left. "We are nearly there."

Penny took the reins from me, and I rested my hand on Dean's leg. My pulse rang steady, if not slightly faster. The army and some of my friends would be attacking the Alliance. I had betrayed my unit at Camp Sparta for Dean; now I would fight them in earnest. The thought made my stomach churn.

First, I needed to get Dean somewhere he could rest. That meant meeting Vinnie and hoping we fared better under his hospitality than Kisharn's.

I would also learn why Iandil had considered the man a possible aid in searching for a cure.

Chapter Seventeen

The sun at our backs, we left long, disfigured shadows creeping along the road ahead. Ungainly and alien, they bobbed and merged as our boots scuffed along the asphalt. The scents of spring clung to the chill air as the breeze whistled through the woods to our left.

Bright white light flickered through the shaded forest where the road turned slightly. "What's that?" I asked.

Vanya peered ahead, then nodded. "Vinnie uses electricity for his spotlights."

Once, the entire world had run on electricity; there was proof of it everywhere. I'd only witnessed it at the labs, and that brought terrifying memories. "Why? Doesn't he make lamp oil?" My pulse sped, and I forced myself not to assume the worst about Vinnie or the people who led me and Dean here.

"His choice."

Wati bounced to rise the height of our heads, wings fluttering. "I've never seen electricity. We have two trucks at the enclave, though; I guess they have electric lights like glowing bug eyes." She dropped back down, beaming.

My grip on Dean's leg tightened. "Does Vinnie have a lab?" If they were bringing us to one, would they tell me?

Vanya opened her canteen. "Not really. He's got a huge machine shop out back, and the refinery has a couple enclosed buildings. The only laboratory I've seen was in the city, Sumter."

A bee buzzed past us with a deep hum. Dean started to shift, and I tugged his leg, waking him slightly. Wati noticed, and her smile dropped.

"I'm glad Dean is better." Her tone sounded as sure as my confidence in his health.

"I should have never gone to Kisharn's or trusted him."

"You want eggs — babies. I can understand that."

My face flushed. Dean and I had never discussed children. A passionate kiss without him turning would be nice. "Still. It didn't work, and he might be worse now."

Wati glanced toward Vanya, walking ahead of us. The woman said nothing.

Penny turned with a smirk. "I think Caitlyn's looking for the fun stuff before babies."

Heat raced to my ear lobes, but I smiled. It was the first time Penny addressed me by my name.

The woods remained thick to our left, but fields opened around a house on the other side of the road. The roof had been damaged, but parts had been rebuilt, and a tight chain-link fence surrounded it. The dried brush of the fields had been flattened as if trampled. Past a small copse of leafless trees, a similar field encircled a second house. Vinnie's lights ahead and to the left broke through more often, and a white glow leaked to the road.

Again, panic bubbled into my chest. I never realized electric lights would remind me so forcefully of the labs, but flashes of uncontrollable terror gripped my thoughts. A very real part of me wanted to take Dean and flee. Only my trust of the others kept me walking.

The lights took shape atop tall poles. The sun behind had nearly set, and the colored clouds would have stood out if not for the searing brightness. Chain-link fencing lined the front, much like Camp Sparta. Multiple layers cordoned off angled black shapes that I did not believe were houses. More akin to pole barns, they had steeply slanted roofs that reflected light like glass despite their pitch-black coloring.

"What are those?" I asked.

Wati fluttered higher to see better.

"He calls them solar power panels, and somehow makes electricity with them." Vanya sounded as impressed as me with the structures.

Small beige boxes at the base were shaded from the electric lights. The closer we approached, the larger Vinnie's compound grew. Three layers of fence surrounded the front and closest corner; probably circling the massive property. Along the road at the center was an obvious gate with smaller lights and other equipment. With the panels standing taller than us, I could not see his house or machine shop.

The buzzing of bees grew louder as we neared the corner. Motion blurred near the little boxes. "Bee hives?" I asked.

"Yes. He uses the wax and some of the oil from his crops to make fuel. I know little of his process." Vanya's tone drifted, as if preoccupied.

My anxiety simmered just under the surface while Vanya led us toward the gate. An occasional bee threaded between us with a hum, but little else moved under the bright lights. Dean roused to blink at the sight but said nothing. I took one last glance back down the road to the setting sun, then continued beside Bella, my fingers gripping Dean's leg.

When we came within a few yards of the gate, Vanya motioned us to stay in the road while she approached it. Well-worn tracks led inside over crumbled asphalt. The lights were too bright for me to see far down the drive.

A man spoke, his voice sounding as if his head were stuck inside a washing tub. "Closed for the night. Come back at the dawn. Peace."

"It's Vanya."

A moment of scratching noises came before he answered. "Out for a stroll?" A loud click sounded from the gate. "Whose kids?"

"We should talk about that." She stepped forward with a motion for us to follow.

"Inner bailey. Give me two minutes."

As Vanya swung open a loose gate, it squeaked.

I had no idea what an "inner bailey" was, but I did think it might be nicer to be inside the fence. A wolf howled somewhere behind the property, causing me to inhale sharply. Dean straightened, his hands tightening on the horn of the saddle. It appeared we'd gotten to Vinnie's just in time. As tired as I was, I didn't want to fight werewolves, or even regular wolves, in the dark.

A corridor enclosed by the second layer of fence held a wide drive lit by regular lights that kept me squinting. The third layer of fence sat only three yards behind that.

Vanya held the gate. "Don't touch the metal. Electricity." She shut the fence behind us, and an ominous click echoed.

"Do you think that's a pack out there?" I asked.

"Nope." Vanya stepped quickly past us to take the lead.

The howl rose again, and shivers crawled up my back. Odie huffed, standing stiff. I held Dean's jacket closed against me with the other hand on his leg. He sagged in the saddle.

Impossible to tell at first with the intense lights, the drive led deep into the compound past the black panels and bees. It appeared to be only fields behind that, but the light pointed outward at the fences, or here inside the fenced-in drive, leaving the rest a dim mystery.

"Does he live alone out here?" I asked.

Vanya sighed. "Not exactly."

"What does that mean?"

She didn't answer, and my previous concerns over a lab leaped into a ball in my throat. Wati wouldn't betray us. I let paranoia race inside my brain until I was convinced Penny had only been nice because they'd decided to lock us up. I barely realized our corridor ended at another gate and more lights square in our eyes.

"What's shaking?" Standing on the opposite side of the gate, Vinnie, an older man, broad of build, wore a flannel shirt with rolled sleeves and stained overalls. His white beard curled all the way down his chest, while the rest of his face hid under the shade of a cap. He had a holster under his left arm with the grip easily within reach.

Vanya jabbed a thumb over her shoulder at Bella. "Boy's been bit well over a month now, and able to control himself."

I nearly reached out for the otherness, expecting a squad of men to come out for us. My trust in Vanya wavered, but I didn't react.

As he peered at Dean, Vinnie's head lifted, giving me a glimpse of a wrinkled face and sharp eyes. "Ain't possible." Disbelief and hope hung in his voice.

Turning to gesture at me, Vanya said, "She did it part ways when he was first bit, before it infected him completely. We just were at Kisharn's, trying to push it all the way."

Vinnie took a step forward, studying me, then turning back to Vanya. "Is it possible?"

"Dean got sick, but it's another piece to the puzzle. Iandil thought we should check with you and see if you've come upon anything new. We haven't discussed it for a few years. Boy could use with a good night's sleep. The day's been hard on him." She waited for a response, then continued. "We've been traveling with him for two days. He shifted once when we were attacked by Onis, but he controlled himself."

Penny nodded. "We killed two effing werewolves. He didn't blink."

Vanya pointed to each of us. "Penny. Caitlyn. Wati. Odie."

He dug in his pocket, pulled out a small black box the size of his thumb, and pointed it above the gate. "Guest house ain't being used." A dull click sounded, then a green light flashed at the side.

"Just the night." Vanya stepped forward. "Army's on the move toward the enclave. We'll chat while the boy rests. Caitlyn's about exhausted from trying to heal him today. It went rough."

Vinnie opened the gate, watching Dean. "Army hasn't been out this way since the winter before last. I got trouble coming?"

I shivered, remembering the families the military had killed.

Vinnie misinterpreted my shaking and motioned me forward. "Let's get them warm, then we'll chat, Vanya. Weather's been wonky since the Sorrow started. Temps run about ten degrees cooler now compared to two decades ago. Axial tilt hasn't changed. I've yet to figure it out."

Once I passed the blinding lamps, the glow around us easily marked a low house to the left with its own fence and gates. A row of tanks stretched to the right, and multiple large buildings rose farther back. The border of lights around the entire compound encompassed a huge area.

The wolf howled again, and I froze. It sounded too close to be outside the fence. Penny reacted as well, reaching for her gun. She stopped at Vanya's abrupt gesture.

Vinnie studied us, especially Dean, then began walking toward the fence around his house. "That's my son. He got infected after we had most of this built. A stupid accident. We got him tucked away before he turned. So, you can see I'm searching for that same cure you are. I'll want to hear more about this healing with that nasty Kisharn."

I stumbled in the dark, and then blinked. Iandil had likely hoped that Vinnie had made some progress, but he hadn't. "I'm sorry."

"Yeah, me too. I keep hoping that if I do find a cure, my boy will still be in there. As it is now, he'd kill me if he could." We followed the fence to the back where it branched to surround a tiny house and yard with a gazebo.

We reached the gate at the side of the small house, and he pointed his device at a box there. The click was audible, and again a green light flashed. He lifted the little black box and smiled. "All the radio frequencies of the world gone to shit, but this still works if you get close enough."

Wati peered at the device. "What's radio frequencies?"

I hoped she wasn't asking me. Radio had been mentioned in some older books.

"Electromagnetic waves of a certain bandwidth — shape." Vinnie's explanation made less sense than his first comment. "They're distorted now, at least at any reasonable distance. Useless. We might have had a chance if communications hadn't tanked. That, the disappearances, and man's propensity for violence let the Sorrow dwindle us to 10 percent of our previous population. If I've calculated correctly."

"Twenty percent," I corrected. Our civics classes had been quite clear about the causes, but I'd never heard anything about communications; just the riots, the cryptids, and those who faded from the Sorrow. He had to be wrong about some of this. Telephone poles and their wires were for communications. "Most died before the army held back the cryptids."

The gate squeaked as he opened it and motioned Penny and Bella through first. The wolf howled again, but closer I heard a pig grunt and a few chickens cluck. I peered into the darkness but didn't see a pen or roost. I swallowed, suddenly hungry and craving eggs.

"The cryptids were the problem? Is that what they teach you?" He pointed to my Wolf Squad patch.

I nodded. "We have civics classes."

Vinnie shrugged. "Victors write the history." He started counting on his fingers. "Ranking of the death toll and their sequence in the timeline: starvation when the infrastructure broke down and cities were on their own, riots over resources and whatever else we could fight about, the disappearances from the Sorrow, and long after that the werewolves and Oni populated the zone enough to be a problem. I lived this nightmare."

Vanya tugged on my arm and led me through the gate. The white lattice gazebo in the back appeared in the best shape I'd ever seen one. Unpainted concrete blocks with thin horizontal windows and a slanted roof made up the house, newer than any I'd ever seen.

We gathered in the back by the gazebo while Vinnie closed the gate behind us. He never turned his back on us. "Fence is electrified; don't test it. I'll open in the morning.

Tie the horse so it don't get a shock." He gestured to the gazebo and then glanced at Odie. "Best keep him inside with you."

My mind still fumbled with his interpretation of the Sorrow's history. "Why don't you think the cryptids were a problem?"

He studied me, stroked his long beard, then glanced at Wati. "The werewolves and Oni were very low populations in the beginning. I'm guessing there's a density ratio between the people who disappeared and their appearance. There's certainly a correlation to the frequency of human disappearances, or cryptid arrival toward the centers of the zones. Those humans closer to the center were already gone, or they did have more to deal with in the beginning. Now, populations of werewolves have grown, and the Oni are moving out from the center."

Wati cocked her head. "Do you think if I went toward the center, it would be easier to go back to Denya? Where is the center?"

"Don't know that you can go back, and I'd say the center is near Whiteville, North Carolina. I've got coordinates based on the perimeter I've come up with." He pointed to the back door. "Get him inside. There's six bunks. Plenty of room."

I jumped to help Penny, and together we eased Dean off Bella. The horse nickered but stood firm.

Dean stunk of toxins and the sweat that carried them out of him. "Shit. I got nothing." His leg tried to fold when we got him to the ground. Together, we held him between us and ambled toward the building.

Vinnie opened the door, reached inside, and a light filled the room. Two sets of bunk beds lined one wall. The bottom of each had white pillows and green blankets. I hadn't had a pillow since Camp Sparta. Now I was hungry *and* exhausted.

We eased Dean up the two steps and into the closest bottom bunk. Oddly, pine scented the air. I began tugging off his boots. Penny and Wati were outside. The inside of the house stretched as big as my living room with Roxie. Unlike our apartment, though, the light mounted on the ceiling worked. A single set of bunks was set against the opposite wall next to a door at the back, likely a closet.

Vanya rested her hand on Dean's forehead. "We need to get him to drink some liquid. Juice would be best."

"Broth?" Vinnie asked.

"Sounds good." Vanya pointed to the closet door. "Bathroom still work?"

He scoffed. "It's not like anyone broke it since you were here last."

Vanya's face spread into a grin and she winked at me. "You're in for a treat. Indoor plumbing. Shower. Hot."

Vinnie tapped my shoulder. "With me. We'll get him some broth and more bedding."

I followed the gruff but friendly man out and around the house. As they unstrapped saddlebags, Penny and Wati watched me with curious if not envious expressions. The hens were still clucking lightly. As Vinnie unlocked a gate between us and the house, I peered into the darkness. More fenced corridors connected the house to what I believed the roost. There were more, but I had a difficult time unraveling the overlaying link fences into any semblance of order in my mind.

His house smelled weird, like a cross between the camp clinic and an old basement in an abandoned house. There were hints of cooked meat as well. My stomach growled as I followed him into a dimly lit kitchen. He flicked a switch and I squinted at the bright light.

"Don't mind the mess. It's just me and Gizmo." He strode into a living room where a pale blue light glowed across a clutter of shelves, stacks of books, and more stacks on tables.

"Who's —?" I stopped when I saw the source of the lighting. An entire alcove had glowing panels. Some had images from outside, one with Bella stomping silently beside the gazebo. I'd seen them before, at the lab. Cold ached in my bones, and I shivered.

Vinnie didn't appear to notice my panic and clucked out the side of his mouth.

Transfixed, I barely registered the fluffy cat lifting its head from a second chair in front of the panels. "I —" My mind flipped through images of electrodes and sickening shots, dead roommates, and a sweaty technician.

"You okay?" He strode over and stroked the cat, then waved at the panels. "My pet obsession, especially in the winter." After a moment of not getting a response from me, he gestured for me to follow him toward another door. "Linens are in here."

I stumbled behind, happy to leave the sight. He had the light on when I arrived. Metal shelving, jammed with supplies, lined the room. A single easy chair sat beside a strange guitar and a black box with wires attached to it. Frowning, I studied the flat guitar. It didn't even have a hole in the center.

Vinnie started pulling out blankets and pillows, then noticed my interest. "I ain't Billy Gibbons, but I keep myself amused." He shoved a pile at me and I took it absently.

"What is that?" I asked.

"Guitar."

"It's flat and there's no hole."

"Electric."

That made no sense, but I didn't argue. As we walked

back to the living room, I focused on the books rather than the glowing panels and strange images. Tired, rattled, and hungry, I couldn't process another thought. Maybe in the morning.

Vinnie stopped, grabbed a book off a pile, and added it to mine. "*Clean Sweep* by Ilona Andrews. In case you can't sleep. You can keep it. I think there's two others in here."

"Thank you." Something to read sounded wonderful, but not tonight, not while the army marched and Dean couldn't walk.

I balanced the book on the pile and followed him to the kitchen. The load wasn't heavy, but I could barely see. He opened a fridge, and a light went on inside it. Food lined the shelves in a variety of containers. The ones I'd seen usually had mold everywhere. Peeking over pillows, I watched as Vinnie put a bowl into a machine, pressed beeping buttons, and it began whirring. Under a dim light, the bowl turned in a continuous circle.

He grabbed cooked meat out of the fridge and caught me gawking at the bowl of broth. "Microwave. Heats things."

"With electricity?" I asked.

"Yep. When the power plants failed early on, most people had no idea how to survive without. Only a few nuts like myself were preppers."

The machine beeped and I jumped. "Preppers?"

"Preparing for the collapse, just in case." He pulled out the bowl and juggled all the food under one arm along with a pail to water Bella and Odie.

"You wanted this?"

Vinnie laughed as he headed for the back door. "Hell no. Just expected something like it. Those first few years were hell."

I followed, trying to imagine what the world had been

like with electricity, and fit some of his comments into what I'd learned at Camp Sparta. Some of it fit. The rest boggled my mind. He kept talking as we headed back to the others, but I had trouble focusing. Dazed, I let Wati help unload, though she seemed most excited about the towels I hadn't seen Vinnie put on the stack.

After spooning some broth into Dean while they talked, I ate the cooked honey-drenched meat, unsure what it was. Odie got some of the meat while Wati and Vanya each had a jar of mixed vegetable preserves. Dean slept like the dead, but felt better when I probed into him with healing. We still had a long march ahead of us tomorrow, then the army. I hadn't fully registered the concept of fighting yet, but I could probably deal with it after some sleep.

Vinnie left us to get some feed for Bella with promises of eggs, bread, and cheese for breakfast. Vanya got Wati comfortable with the shower controls and gestured for me to follow her outside to the gazebo benches.

"We've listened to the life force without, now listen within. Each living thing carries its own note. With practice, you'll read them as an orchestra of sounds. Begin inside."

I could barely keep my eyes open. "What? Now?"

Chapter Eighteen

The night air had dropped to an unwelcome chill, Wati and Penny were inside trying out a hot shower that I'd never had, and I was bone tired.

"I don't want to practice tonight." My butt hovered an inch above the bench, ready to stand and go inside. I'd thought Vanya had wanted to talk to me about Vinnie, Dean, the army, or anything other than listening to my inner otherness.

She gave me a light shove, causing me to sit. "It'll only take a few minutes."

Outside of the little yard, something clicked and whirred quietly, like an engine but muffled. The hens clucked, and I peered into the darkness, searching for the source of the noise. I gave up and sagged on the hard bench.

"Sit straight. Listen. Find the life force around you, then turn it inward."

I had no idea how to do that, but I did settle into listening. The hum came easily, and I quickly sensed Bella, Vanya, then the others inside the house. Dean's hum was low and dull. My posture fought to curl, thinking about what we'd done to him with Kisharn's group. Dean and I deserved someplace safe.

"There is no cure, is there?"

"Shh. Listen."

"Vanya, did Iandil think Vinnie might have learned something?"

She sighed. "He's been searching for a while. Testing blood. For a brief period, he worked with someone who understood science, but that person left."

"What do I do?"

"You've already done more than anyone expected. Somehow you altered the infection enough for Dean to maintain control."

I thought of our midnight cuddles suddenly interrupted when he couldn't hold back from shifting. "Not well enough." It was selfish.

"Give yourself a little credit. Shh. Listen."

I frowned, straightened, and listened to the otherness. Curious, I stretched across the compound to find the heightened buzz of Vinnie in his house and the chickens with bundles of low pitches. My neck chilled despite the jacket when I found Vinnie's son. A sharp high pitch vibrated; restless, angry, and predatory at the same time.

"Now hear your own life force. Focus inside." Vanya's calm voice gave contrast to the werewolf.

I inhaled and readily withdrew my listening from the cryptid. The hum from my own body had some rhythm to it, as if tied to my heartbeat or flow of blood. In a way, it felt like the first stage of healing when I sensed the body. There vibrated a deeper harmony with the complex activities of organs and flesh. Lungs expanded and contracted, intestines shifted food and liquid, my stomach churned with the recent meal, and all added to the sound. My arms shivered against the cold creeping into my bones, and I heard the change.

As interesting as it was, the cold and fatigue pushed at my nerves. "Okay, now what?"

"Shh. Keep listening. Focus."

I rolled my eyes, but hers were closed, and it went unappreciated. *What did a hot shower feel like?* Vinnie's house, his whole compound, had been a staggering wonder. I'd known about electricity and that it had been used before the Sorrow, but didn't truly comprehend it. Machines that kept food cold and could make them hot. Pictures that could see outside. His theories seemed more reasonable for mastering so much. Powering a guitar with electricity made me question, though.

"What do you hear?" Vanya asked.

"Rhythms. Blood flow. Breathing." It wasn't difficult.

"Good. Inside that are finer elements. Your very thoughts will have an effect. Try to see the sound."

I scowled. "You can't see sounds."

Her eyes remained closed. "Are you truly hearing the life force, or is that the way your mind interprets it?"

First she told me to listen, then she questioned whether I heard sound or not. I scoffed and closed my eyes, trying to see the otherness. In an attempt to focus, I pulled on the power lightly, a tug. The sound grew louder, but it didn't drown out the rhythm. The elements still remained, even highlighted.

"What do you see?" Vanya asked.

"The inside of my eyelids. Black with spots."

Her voice sharpened. "Be serious. You're doing well, but we'll not stop there."

I sighed, making sure she could hear, and focused. Just to attempt something, I turned my head down, as if staring at my body — with my eyes closed. The view did appear to change. Frowning, I swung my head back and forth. It could have been my imagination, but gray static flowed and ebbed beneath my eyelids.

The rhythm harmonized with it, and I stopped moving. My body, my whole body, head and all, took a glowing shape. The world seemed to pause with me floating in it. Minuscule dots of light made up the gray. They all vibrated or flowed.

"Wait. A grayness. Moving." I could see where some were more than dots. Filaments of pale light emanated from me and extended into the relative darkness. "Shit." My eyes popped open. Part of the vision remained.

I flexed for the otherness with a gentle reach, and light poured toward me. Some of the lines grew brighter. My heart raced, and the rhythm sped, flashing faster. "I can see it — the otherness — the life force." I relaxed my grip on the otherness and watched it dim.

"Good, we'll work on it more tomorrow during the trip."

I turned, or rather focused on Vanya. Much as I'd seen myself, her rhythm was seated before me. One of the lines from me stretched to her. "Why are we — connected?" A myriad of networking extended from her, some pointing toward the house where Dean slept. I searched and found some of my own lines flowing there.

"That is very good. Some never see the bonds we create."

Her words caused me to shiver. Hadn't Moonjir said something similar? "Do the Sogoi see this?"

Vanya stood, her connections shifting. Many rooted into the ground like tethers. "I'd guess so, but maybe you will ask your trickster next time you speak. The answer might be a riddle, but even riddles have answers. C'mon. You're next in the shower."

As I stood, my vision partially reverted to show the

more static elements of the gazebo and surrounding fence. I hadn't let go of the awareness yet. It didn't interfere with me navigating the steps. Vanya's downward connections trailed on the ground like a dress.

"This is so strange." My pulse still raced, mostly from excitement. Vanya had praised my accomplishment, and Roxie had always said I craved approval, but it still felt good. I had learned something. *A lot.* Each stride toward the house felt like floating.

Vanya faltered slightly on the step. As old as she was, I imagined this day had been wearing on her body.

"Thank you," I said.

She paused, studying me and forcing me to stop. "Our ancestors, here on Earth, somehow manipulated the connections, disrupting some and creating others. They did so because there are entities on this planet that have been here for a very long time. They are legend. Their name comes from Earth, Amarati or Sempiternal. The unchanged and everlasting. Somehow, they are connected to the Sogoi and manipulate humans. I do not understand their nature, nor what they want. Your friend might."

My chest tightened. She meant Moonjir. "Manipulate humans?"

She stared at the ground at her feet, not at me. "The Epics are obscure, but they do carry that warning along with those who can control bonds. We transcribed the Epics here on Earth from our memories. There is a copy at the enclave. If all goes well, I will translate it for you." Vanya turned and grasped the doorknob. "Please, do not speak of this, except to ask your friend."

The door opened, and steam flowed around us.

Chapter Nineteen

Long after I stepped out of the luxurious water and dried myself with fluffy towels, I dreamed of the hot shower. Painful but wonderful water had pierced through my hair to scrub my scalp. Blossom-scented soap had lathered my entire body and pooled at my toes. The air itself had turned moister than a summer day. Decadent heat had soaked into every inch of my body. Cold was a distant memory.

An icy hand grabbed my shoulder. As I turned, black-pooled eyes gazed malevolently into mine.

I screamed and sat stiff in my bunk in a pitch-black room.

"Shit! What?" Penny's voice barked the loudest, but I'd woken everyone from the stirrings. Even Dean grunted.

"Nightmare." My breathing whistled in and out of my nose. An ache rose around my ears and neck from my pounding pulse. "Nothing."

"Effing middle of the night." Penny's grumbling muffled with the rustle of blankets.

"Caitlyn?" Dean's voice was weak.

Odie stuck a cold nose against my elbow. I crawled out of bed, freezing as the blanket dropped off me. "I'm sorry,

Dean. Go back to sleep." My pulse pounded, from the nightmare as well as the excitement of him waking. "I love you."

"Thirsty." His voice grated.

Someone else moved from their blankets as I felt my way to him. We should have left a candle lit. "Let me get the canteen."

A dim light went on, framing Wati in the bathroom door. She flashed a smile at me, partially closed the door to minimize the brightness, and crawled back into her bed. She and Penny had fresh clothes to change into, and they had gifted me a pair of clean underwear.

We'd left a canteen under Dean's bunk last night, and I retrieved it. He lay pale on his pillow, the blankets pushed aside. His eyes followed my movements, then blinked slowly. "Gods, I ache." He took the canteen and raised onto one elbow to drink.

Vanya watched me, unmoving.

"How do you feel?" I whispered.

Dean grunted and handed back a near empty canteen. "Like I should piss."

I pointed to the bathroom and stood back, offering a hand. He rose awkwardly, faltering and swaying, but grasped my hand and stood on shaky legs. We walked to the bathroom as he blinked and studied the bunks and bathroom door. When I led him in, his eyebrows rose at the sight of the working light, even as he squinted. He tugged me in with him when I started to leave.

The door closed quietly enough with a turn of the handle. The room smelled of blossoms. My coveralls stunk. Dean tentatively pulled up the toilet lid and swayed.

"Sit," I said.

He frowned, grumbled, then dropped his jeans. I blushed, and he sat. "Where are we?" Dean asked.

"Vinnie's."

"Should have known. That's so helpful."

"A compound owned by a guy named Vinnie. His son is a werewolf."

Dean glanced sharply, then blinked at the light. "That is why they thought he might have an answer. But, you said 'is,' so I guess Vinnie doesn't have a cure."

"I'm sorry." I was more so to see him shirtless, pants at his feet, with nothing we could do.

"Yeah, me too."

He finished and started to stand, nearly buckling at the knees. I grabbed his arm trying not to ogle. We'd been nude plenty of times, but I still flushed. He stabilized, then glared at his jeans around his ankles.

"I'll get them."

Dean pivoted toward the shower. Water still coated the bottom, and droplets hung on the tiled walls. "Does that work?"

I beamed. "Hot water."

"Do not tell me that." He grinned, then nearly fell.

"Let's get you to bed."

"The hell with that. The patient needs a bath."

He did. "I love you, and you need a good scrub, but you can't stand in there."

An impish grin spread across his face, and I knew he'd suggest I strip and help him. My own disappointment must have shown. Shifting here inside Vinnie's compound would be disastrous. His expression died. "Yeah. Love you, too. Nothing is easy. Get the water going, and I'll crawl in."

I smiled, holding back tears. There was no cure, and we would never have the moments other lovers could. My throat thick, I lowered Dean to the floor. The knobs of the shower blurred in my vision, but I remembered where to turn them. As I held my hand in the flow, waiting for it to heat, I clenched my teeth and fought the crushing pain in my heart and the sob that threatened to burst through.

Lathering his hair dampened my sleeves, but we were able to laugh about it awkwardly. Toweling him dry proved difficult, on all accounts.

Before we got his pants on him, a knock came on the outer door, and I could hear Penny cursing. Hurrying, we found Vinnie entering as we opened the bathroom door. He smiled and raised his eyebrows. His expression sobered as he focused on Dean. "Feeling better?"

I held Dean who leaned against the door frame. "You're Vinnie?"

Vinnie wore gloves and a thin jacket. He placed a thermos and mugs beside the entry way. "That's me." Beard bobbing, he nodded, then frowned at Vanya, still wrapped in her blankets. "Why didn't you turn on the heat?" His chin lifted. "Damn. I'm sorry. I should have reminded you, Vanya."

He reached to a box near the outer door and tapped at it. Something whirred under the floor. "Breakfast? Sun's almost up."

None of us declined, and Penny was recruited to help him in the main house. Wati's expression dropped to a pout until Vinnie waved for her to come along. I settled Dean back into his bunk, and he stretched out with a grunt. Warm air blew from thin vents where the floor met the wall. A faint burning scent drifted in the building.

Vanya studied me. "Bad dreams?"

"They weren't, then they turned."

"We've got a long walk, then a fight when we get there."

Dean hummed. "I'm going to slow you down."

"You'll be on Bella," Vanya said.

He offered a light grunt, as if ready to fall asleep again. I was tired, but breakfast sounded too good, and there might be eggs. I watched his eyes close. His black, damp hair had gone from wavy to ringlets against his olive skin.

Vanya disappeared into the bathroom, leaving me in darkness as Dean drifted back to sleep with slow breaths. My emotions were raw from the past twenty-four hours. In pitch black, I glazed in his direction, even as Odie tucked his nose under my fingers so I would scratch his ears. It had been dark when the others had gone outside, and the slits of windows gave no hint of a coming dawn. Perhaps Vinnie would prefer if we were on our way.

I blinked when the bathroom door opened and light spilled out. Time had slipped away, but I felt like she'd been in there a while.

Her feet scuffed as she put on shoes and wrestled with her belongings and a saddlebag. "Will you have a problem fighting your own people?" Vanya asked.

I shook my head absently. "No, I only had two real friends when I was there. They killed one when I freed Dean, and the other helped, so they won't trust her." Mentioning Selina would dredge up bitterness best left ignored. She would likely be with the soldiers. I didn't want her dead. I didn't want anyone dead.

"Is it revenge that drives you to help us?"

I sighed and turned toward her. "No. I just want a safe place for me and Dean." We had gone from running from the army, to hope for a cure, to settling for a quiet house in the woods. I would have to accept that.

I started when the door opened and frigid air blew in an amazing aroma of food. Penny led the way holding two plates covered with metal lids. Eggs were certainly involved, and meat. She passed me and held one to Vanya. "Eggs, peppers, onion, and cheese, grits and butter. Effing biscuits." The last word came out emphasized, and I wondered what it was. I'd had grits once.

Wati followed and handed me a plate that I tried to take without snatching it. My stomach rumbled. Vinnie came last with a handful of rolled napkins and three plates stacked on top of lids. He noted Dean sleeping and cocked his head before tucking a plate and cover under the bunk, then dropped down onto the one on the opposite wall.

I pulled off the lid and found eggs blended with vegetables and white cheese, yellow grits with melted butter, two strips of thin bacon, and two fluffy pieces of bread with butter and perhaps honey dripping out of the middle. Maybe Dean and I could just stay here.

Vinnie handed out the napkins with silverware tucked inside. One of the plates was for a grateful Odie.

Dean stirred, sniffing audibly. "Is that bacon?"

Vinnie pointed to the thermos he'd left earlier. "And coffee if you like it black with honey."

Chapter Twenty

As we ate, Vinnie finally broached the subject of Kisharn's healing group. Vanya and I took turns answering his questions and describing the process. Dean mumbled through a biscuit some comments about his experience. I would have felt guilty if I weren't blissfully stuffing my face.

I'd never had biscuits before. They were drier than cornbread, but delicious with butter and honey. The salty bacon I'd had on a few rare occasions. Vinnie had a captive, if not terse, audience for his questions.

Wati's meal consisted of grits, biscuits, and jam. I didn't ask why she didn't try at least some of the eggs and cheese. She broached the question about Vinnie's son. "Are you going to take your son to Kisharn?"

"If Kisharn will try, I'll bring Michael to him. Assuming the blasted army doesn't come out this way. I really hoped they'd amuse themselves on their side of Lake Marion."

She glanced at Dean. "Kisharn was really scary."

Vinnie poked at his meal. "Sounds like it. I've run out of choices. Even if the world hadn't crashed and burned, I don't think science would have given us a cure." His fork stopped moving and he stared at his plate before turning to study me. "Perhaps, depending on how this mess with the army turns out, you'd consider coming back here and seeing where we stand with Michael." He lifted his plate and smiled. "I know you enjoy the food."

I did want to help. The man hurt over his son, obviously. "I'll try."

He forced a smile. "Most a man can ask for."

In a short while, Vinnie forced a dozen jars of honey into our saddle bags before he escorted us back out the gates. The sky had turned predawn gray, and wind whipped at us in gusts. Much of the compound in the front consisted of tilled fields until we got to the row of black panels. They circled the inside of the three fences. Some of the bees crawled on their boxes hidden underneath, but they didn't bother us.

Dean appeared ready to sleep in his saddle, but his color was better.

"You taking route 15?" Vinnie asked.

Vanya nodded slowly. "Quicker. Should be safe. The army cleared out any of our people along the route to Pinewood, so we think they'll take the same path as last time. The Pahawan are keeping their distance, but watching. Besides, we're a few hours north of their staging area."

Vinnie had donned a hat when he'd retrieved our gift of honey, and he tapped it as he turned to me. "Miss Caitlyn, I do hope you both come back and visit."

I forced the smile. "I hope so." My future, at the moment, rested uncertainly between the army and the Alliance.

We left him standing at the gate, watching. The crisp chill hung in the air, and I had Dean's jacket tight around me. Vanya and Penny led Bella ahead, leaving me and Wati walking behind.

She tugged at my sleeve and spoke quietly. "You were

practicing last night with Vanya. Will you try and push me back to Denya?" Her expression ranged from hesitant hope to pleading while I stumbled a step at her question.

"I can't. I don't know how."

"How do you know? Vanya says you're learning quickly." Wati gave a quick glance toward the others. "She can't know we're trying."

"I'm not," I said. "What if something goes wrong?"

Wati shrugged. "I'm willing to risk it." Her chin rose. "If you were trapped on my world, separated from Dean, wouldn't you try anything?"

I couldn't argue with that. Without responding, I slid into the listening mode and examined Wati with my new sight. She appeared much like Vanya had last night, with speckled gray rhythms dancing throughout her body, and connections that threaded out to me, the others, the ground, and beyond. What could I possibly do to send her back to Denya? I shrugged. "I don't know where to start."

"The Epics say that bonds are the cause of the Displacement. Vanya said that you changed bonds when the gravity shifted last night."

I scuffed my boot toe, drawing glances from the others. "What?"

Wati laughed nervously, avoiding eye contact with Vanya. When she did speak, her voice lowered to a whisper. "Right before the two of you came back inside, everything became lighter. Even Odie noticed."

I frowned, trying to remember. I'd been so tired. "I didn't realize."

She nodded vigorously. "Vanya said it was because you were working with Seyir bonds and the life force. She is very impressed with your abilities. We all are." Wati added the last comment hastily, as if I might be insulted.

Stunned, I barely registered that we passed the intersection where Halimay and Nur had left us. We followed their path north. "I wasn't —" I hadn't meant to alter gravity. Doing so didn't seem useful, especially if I only did it by accident.

"Send me home," Wati pleaded.

"How?" I asked.

Her expression drooped and she shrugged. "Break my bonds here? Push me home?"

Vanya shifted ahead of us, gesturing Penny to continue forward while she waited for us. "Some training, Caitlyn?" I guessed by her study of Wati that she knew what we were discussing.

I smiled feebly. Listening already altered my vision with the rhythms and connections webbing between us, the earth, and far beyond. "Okay."

Dean leaned forward, and I dashed, thinking he might fall. He'd been dozing since we started. I reached his side as he jerked up, readjusting his grip on the saddle horn. "I'm okay. Awake. Awake." His tone sounded better than during the ride from Kisharn's.

"Be careful." We didn't have a choice to stop and let him sleep. The army moved behind us somewhere, to the west by the lake.

Vanya gave me a moment, then gestured for me to fall back with her. "Let's focus inside again as we walk."

I almost didn't speak, then blurted out, "I affected gravity last night."

It took Vanya a moment to respond. "You did. I suspect Wati told you, as somehow, you didn't notice it. The effect was minimal."

"I was tired."

"You should be careful about manipulating the bonds. We do not know what the consequences might be. I question allowing Iandil to request such a test." She studied me.

"We will focus on mapping out ourselves, not others, not the world around us."

Massive fields surrounded us, not tended as Vinnie's had been, but wild as most were with dense shrubs and even young trees bending under a strong southern wind. The sun had yet to crest behind us, though the sky had paled to blue. The walk warmed me comfortably as I did as Vanya suggested and explored the rhythms of my body. As before, I couldn't help but notice the connections between myself and others, the ground, and those that stretched into the distance.

Sunlight peeked from behind our backs, casting long shadows. Houses and barns dotted the fields. One cluster occupied a scorched section where a fire had blackened the trees but left them alive. When the fields gave way to heavier woods, it did not take long before we came to a more heavily burned area with dead, scorched trunks and roofs mere black timbers. We'd been walking an hour, and I'd been practicing the rather boring inspection Vanya guided me on when our pavement ended at an intersection and continued forward as a dirt road.

Penny glanced back. "Straight?"

"Yes," Vanya replied.

Far from us, to the left, a single gunshot sounded. I couldn't see down that road, but I was glad we hadn't been planning to go that direction. Penny moved her rifle off her shoulder. I jogged behind Vanya, who had sprung toward the others.

I arrived as they were peering down the road. "The army?" I asked.

"Scouts, at best. We still have our own in this area, and no warnings have gone up."

I remembered the glitter in the sky when the Onikai

were nearby. Dean had roused and searched the road with us, though his eyes were lidded and squinting.

A second shot urged us into motion. Vanya gestured right. "C'mon. Change of plans."

Away from the gunfire seemed a good idea. I rested a hand on Dean's leg as Bella was turned. The sun had crested the horizon to our right and caught in my eye.

Penny still had her rifle out and walked backward for a few steps until Bella and Dean were aimed away from the gunfire. The wind whipped at my yellow braid.

Glancing behind us, I caught something glittering at the treetops. "What's that?"

The sun lit the Kudara armor of a Pahawan as they crashed into the top of a pine tree. Tangled, they lost flight and plummeted through branches to the field below.

"Pahawan!" Wati yelled. She took flight before any of us could react.

"Wati!" Vanya and Penny snapped in unison.

The young Duathua paid them no attention, flying low along the road. If that had been the scouts, perhaps firing at the Pahawan, then Wati could be in danger. I stepped forward, reluctant to leave Dean.

Penny cursed. "Odie, stay." She burst past at a full run, and I followed.

Wati flew faster than we could run and darted into the rough field on the left side of the road where the Pahawan had fallen. Woods loomed on each side of the road ahead, but I could make out no soldiers. Belatedly I reached out, trying to listen to the otherness there. My senses were faint at that distance. By the time Penny and I broke from the road and crashed through winter-dry brush, Wati had dropped out of sight close to where the Pahawan had fallen.

Scents of spicy herb from crushed plants were blown

across my face by the persistent gusts of wind. The sun shone brightly at the edge of my vision where the field stretched far to the south before more trees were visible. In my usual grace, my right ankle wrapped under a stiff stem, and I flew into the air behind Penny. As I slammed into the vegetation and rolled, she glanced once and swore, but didn't stop.

I scrambled to my feet, a dozen paces behind her, and broke into a full run. Penny's rifle bobbed in her right hand as she leaped effortlessly over obstacles and outpaced me. In my perception of the otherness, I could sense where Wati had stopped near the dull rhythms of the Pahawan. He hadn't survived the fall. As Penny arrived, Wati's crying reached me.

Breathless, I reached them as Penny tugged gently on Wati's shoulders. "We have to go," she whispered to the Duathua.

The Pahawan had been shot. The armor had two clouded sections, reminiscent of Halimay's Kudara after the Onikai attack, with one dot of red that leaked blood. Under the armor, in the clearer sections, blood covered their chest. I grimaced at the sight, then peered around us.

Stretching my senses of the otherness, I found two approaching humans. Surprisingly, they were to the north of us, stalking through separate copses of trees. "Soldiers," I hissed. My steady heartbeat rose, pounding in my neck.

Penny snapped from Wati, crouching with rifle ready. "Where?"

From where we were, she wouldn't be able to see them. If we returned to the road, or even headed east into the field where we'd come from, they would soon see us. I pointed to their respective positions to the north. "We're going to have to go south."

The woods where the Pahawan had fallen offered a bit of cover before the long stretch of field to the south. It was a long run to the distant woods on the far side. Our only hope was they would not be searching for us when they reached the Pahawan's body. The blinding sun to the southeast would help as well.

Wati had recovered herself at my warning and nodded. Penny took a moment more, lips tightening and eyes narrowing, before she too agreed and led the escape. Even facing away from them as I ran, I tracked the two stalking soldiers through the otherness.

Each harrowing stride, I expected a gunshot. I knew they weren't at the body, but I couldn't be sure they hadn't seen us. The field ahead seemed impossibly huge. We wouldn't be safe until we were hidden in the woods.

Chapter Twenty-One

Running through dried brush with wind whipping our faces, I began to worry about Dean and Vanya. Surely, she'd keep him from running after us and tuck him somewhere safe. Then again, she might have no idea about the soldiers coming from an unexpected direction. We'd nearly headed toward them.

Penny outran both Wati and me. The little Duathua would have moved faster flying, but would have also been more obvious. From my senses, the soldiers hadn't even approached the road yet. In a sharp moment of panic, I spread my search of the otherness for anyone waiting ahead of us.

We angled to the left, east toward the sun, where the woods bordered the field even as it continued to the south. Someone, a human, soldier or local, hid stationary deep among the trees.

"Penny," I rasped, half yelling and half fearful of making any noise. When she glanced back, I frantically waved my hand against going where she headed and pointed to the right.

As a group we shifted, Penny and I both glancing at the

woods where I'd sensed the person. Slightly to our right, one of the tall metal frame towers rose into the sky, reflecting some of the morning sun.

With no one giving pursuit, I hoped our hasty escape went unnoticed. The crashing, crunching race seemed impossibly noisy for anyone to miss.

The soldiers behind were just at the edge of my senses. The unmoving figure in the woods grew closer, and I doubted I could sense anyone we were barreling toward. Our entire fiasco was getting worse. I didn't blame Wati, though; she'd gone to help one of her own.

Penny dove into the brush, and it took me far too long to see the two soldiers ahead, just breaching the edge of the woods where we were heading. Wati rolled into a ball to my right, and I fell face first into a bush with tiny black seeds that stuck in my hair.

"Did they see us?" whispered Wati.

Penny crawled toward us, barely moving the tops of the dried brush. "I think so."

"I can't sense them yet." If it came to it, I had plenty of already moving air to work with. Roxie had always teased me about my weak air magic, but it had been a joke. Wati and Penny didn't question my comment, nor my earlier warnings, so they might have been used to Vanya's abilities. She had better be keeping Dean safe.

We huddled a few feet from each other. Penny crouched on her haunches, rifle ready. Wati, on hands and knees, watched me pick a black seedling out of my ear.

The two approaching soldiers rang with tension. They moved swiftly in a direct line for our position. "They saw us."

"Can you?" Penny raised her eyebrows and blew as if putting out a flame.

I nodded with a questionable tilt to my head. "Yeah. What then?"

Penny pointed almost directly at the person who hid in the woods. "We need to go that way and catch up with Vanya."

Pointing at an angle bisecting our two problems, I spoke. "We'll need to go around them. Once we hit the woods, we'll take a wide path around."

"You do your thing, then lead, and we'll follow."

I didn't love her idea, but waiting for the soldiers to come chat sounded worse. If they had this many scouts out here, Tyrell's approaching army must be huge. "Let them get a little closer."

The two soldiers were both male, and their rhythms were frenzied and alert. They might think they were hunting Duathua. If bullets could shoot through Kudara, how had the Alliance stalled the last attack? After seeing the Pahawan shot from the sky, I had a lot less hope for the upcoming battle.

Pulse pounding, I waited a tense couple of minutes until our stalkers were about sixty yards away. Then, I called the otherness. The air I reached for was behind the soldiers. I wrapped heavy, thick gusts of wind already moving in force with my magic. The angle and direction I sculpted the air brought dual gusts in human-sized blocks into their sides, pushing upward at the last second.

The two made no noise when I hit them. The impact blasted them in an arc that we could see from where we hid. Weapons wrenched from their grips, they flailed a good twenty feet high and twice as far. I didn't wait for them to land.

Penny and Wati were close behind when I burst out of the brush toward the woods. My hiding person didn't budge or even shift, but I dared not get too close.

We ran toward the sun. It destroyed any chance of me being able to see even the brush ahead of me. I fell once, tumbling on my knees and recovering before Penny tugged at my elbow. The tops of the trees started to block some of the sun as we closed the yards between.

A few more strides and I could see at least the brush. The trunks of the trees were blackened from a long-dead fire, but they'd survived, and bushes filled spaces between.

My legs were wobbling as we dashed past a live oak with languid limbs and gray-green leaves. Giddy, I wanted to laugh or cry. Wati beamed mischievously as we slowed to a jog.

Even as we reveled in our sanctuary, I sensed a new group of soldiers directly ahead. A tall, burned-out building stood between us.

"Gods, more." I stopped, bringing Penny and Wati to a wary halt. "How do they know where we are?" I asked.

"They're heading for the effing gunshots," Penny said. She panted, rifle pointed forward. "How close? Can we hide?"

"They're in a line, heading this way." With a sigh, I gestured where I didn't want to go, farther from Vanya and Dean and toward the area the army likely controlled. With soldiers behind us and a mystery man in the woods to our left, we had no choice. I winced as branches and twigs snapped underfoot when we began to run.

I hadn't thought they could hear us, but I was wrong. Either that, or they caught some unlucky glimpse of us through the trees.

First one of the guns rattled off a chain of gunfire, with accompanying bullets whizzing through the trees around us, then the entire trio fired at us. Splinters rained down on us, then leaves.

We reacted with barely any thought. Our path changed,

and we ran wildly for the field where we'd just escaped. It lay in the most direct line away; the worst choice, but our only real option. The maelstrom of metal against wood roared like a storm with the thunder of gunfire. We'd be trapped, pinned by the soldiers who had shot the Pahawan and the other two, if they survived.

Growling, I gathered the otherness, locking in on our three pursuers even though my back faced them, and I ran at a crouch. I formed three separate tornadoes to drop down from the heavy winds above them. Unseen by their victims, the tips of the whirlwinds grew and stretched toward them. They would be silent under the gunfire. I gritted my teeth as I plunged each of them down to their separate targets. I had no idea what the effect would be, but the men were whisked into the air along with dirt, leaves, and soil.

The gunfire stopped as we ran into the field and the massive tower loomed in the sky. My breath ragged from exertion and the use of my magic, I gulped in air even as I crouched. We'd left soldiers here, and we didn't need them attacking.

"Wati!" Penny dashed back past me.

It took three steps to stop my momentum, and another to spin around. My face chilled and my chest tightened. Wati lay crumpled by the live oak.

Penny dove onto her knees beside the small Duathua form. Wati's skirt darkened with spreading blood. She wasn't moving.

Chapter Twenty-Two

I ignored any of the other threats around us as I dashed to them. From the blood-soaked clothes, I feared Wati might already be dead. Penny trembled as she hesitantly touched Wati. I couldn't see either of their eyes. Wind gusted through the forest, scattering leaves around them.

My senses retracted from the more distant dangers and focused on my friends. In my perception of the otherness, I understood the injury before I reached Wati. Chaotic rhythms spasmed around the wound in sparks of gray light. A bullet had lodged in her hip, nearly into the joint of her left leg. She might live, if we could stop the bleeding.

My ignorance of Duathua physiology might have stopped me, were the bleeding not so heavy. Nearly bowling Penny over in a clumsy landing, I yanked up Wati's skirt and slapped both hands on pink-gray skin.

"Help her," Penny croaked in a near sob.

Wati barely held consciousness from a blow to her head, not the shock of the gunshot wound. A vein or artery started closing immediately along the bullet's path, but I had to get rid of the metal. The moment I understood that, I felt the metal soften, oozing out through the hole it had created. My healing of the Duathua felt no different than it did on a human. The rhythms of the otherness played a large part in showing my magic what to do. Of all the skills, healing flesh came the most natural.

I manipulated the bullet much as I had done with the bars on the cage that had held Dean underwater. It came more naturally to me this time. As the metal coagulated on her bloody hip in a blob, I wiped it off with momentary disdain and then anger against the soldiers who'd fired at us.

"What —?" Penny drew shallow breaths, cupping Wati's cheek with one hand so that it did not rest against the leaves.

As I worked her body as a whole, the bark embedded in the scrape on her forehead pushed away while I eased the swelling inside. Wati's eyes flickered open, and pain tightened her features. It would ease in a moment. Forcing flesh to heal quickly always hurt. I could not be sure she'd feel the cracked bone knitting, but that would take the longest to complete. Even at best, it would be partial. Time would do the rest.

"We don't have time," I growled to myself.

Penny stiffened and straightened, still on her knees but searching around us. "Are they coming?"

Flesh joined deep in Wati's hip, and she spoke around the pain. "Send me home."

"I don't know how." Fatigue from using my magic hunched my shoulders. The soldiers would find us. We couldn't move her. They'd kill Wati, or send her to a lab. Even if it took the last of my strength to fight them off, I wouldn't let that happen.

"No," whispered Penny, and I heard the love in her voice. She didn't want to lose Wati.

Wati reached out a weak hand to touch Penny's wrist. "Please, let me go home. My eggs, my mate."

Penny let out a sob, then turned to me, tears streaking her cheeks. "Are they coming?"

Releasing my focus on healing Wati, I stretched out my senses. The two I'd attacked earlier were alive, but injured and crawling to the west away from us. I found a man dying or dead behind us, his rhythms faint. Beyond that were the other two, moving, though toward each other rather than in our direction.

I stiffened. The hiding figure moved slowly toward us with a heightened rhythm and a predator's stealth. "Yes." I nudged my chin toward the wood past her. If the attacker reached the edge of the trees, he might have a shot.

"Send me home." Wati's eyes teared. She had to know the fate of her people at the hands of the army.

"I —" My excuse died on my lips. What choice did I have? I hadn't even tried.

Penny's eyes glazed, and she focused on my hands and Wati's bloody hip. "Do it." She sucked in a sob. Her voice cracked, and the words that followed were the softest I'd heard from her. "I love you, Wati."

Wati choked on unspoken words. Her moist eyes closed.

Straightening, Penny growled. "I won't let them take you. I'd rather lose you, knowing what they might do."

"I love you, Penny." Wati took in a breath and focused on me. "Please."

I nodded. Perhaps it would be as easy as healing. I drew in my focus, watching Wati's rhythms. Her connections stretched tight in so many directions. Should I try to disconnect them?

Instead, I closed my eyes and firmly imagined pushing against her with the otherness. Nothing happened. I took a breath, dismissing the thoughts of the man creeping toward us or the soldiers still hunting us.

There were so many connections. I pressed against them with the otherness, but they didn't sway or bend at my touch.

"It's not working."

"Please. I want to go home." As she spoke, a bundle of lines changed their vibration by the subtlest amount.

I wet my lips. "Think about home. About your eggs. Your mate. Your family. All you've lost."

Again, the bundle of lines vibrated. Unsure, I pushed the otherness into them, not to disconnect, but to strengthen, to heal. I swore they thickened and brightened. Still, Wati remained.

I cocooned her in otherness, smothering her with as much as I could call. Where its noise had been the steady pour of a shower, it rose to a roar. I set my focus to weaken all connections that did not lead home and reroute them to the bonds of her world, family, and love.

Gravity loosened. My own connections were being eased, and I could see it. The otherness around me drifted, untethered. It took no real energy to do it, more like healing than moving wind.

When Wati popped away from Earth, I was nearly sucked in with her. I felt the tugs of my own bonds.

Penny gasped, and her reaction jerked her across the grass by an inch. Like the otherness, she floated. A second twitch of her leg made it worse. I released the otherness and felt weight push me down like a firm hand.

"I did it." I hoped Wati had made it back to Denya. The impossibility of it, and the fear that I'd done something horrible instead, gripped my chest.

Penny cried, then sobbed, one hand touching where

Wati had been, the other limply holding her rifle. She didn't turn to me, and I feared what I might see in her eyes.

I blinked, and my pulse rose as I searched toward our creeping mystery man. I might have saved Wati, or maybe not, but we were in an impossible situation ourselves. Blood coated my hands, and I wiped them on my coveralls.

"I'm sorry, Penny. We've got to leave."

Chapter Twenty-Three

The metallic scent of Wati's blood clung to me, despite the tugging gusts of wind from the south. Branches rustling and leaves fluttering prickled caution up my spine, but we couldn't stay at the edge of an open field.

I tugged at Penny's elbow. "C'mon." My expanding sense of the otherness told me we had the creeper to worry about the most, and I gestured in the opposite direction from him. It would lead us farther from Vanya and Dean, but I saw no other choice unless I was willing to fight him. I didn't have the energy left.

When Penny wobbled to her feet, I started into the woods in a crouch. My own legs were too weak to run, but I wanted to keep a solid scan of the otherness so we didn't run into another group. The sun had risen higher during our failed escape. The wind whipping through the branches made noise, but not enough to cover our footsteps.

"This way." I gestured to the south, hoping to curve around the two survivors of my tornadoes.

"Okay." Penny's face drooped. Tears had left trails, and her eyes were red. Her earlier hardiness was gone. It hurt to see.

The mystery stalker had stalled close to where Wati had been shot. The two survivors from the tornadoes I'd created had regrouped and were heading toward him. "I think we're going to lose them." They would expect one of us to be wounded.

Penny didn't respond. The wind dug through the trees, bringing the scent of rain. I couldn't decide if that would help or hinder us. Whatever fire had gone through the area, it appeared to whither out where we passed the end of the blackened trunks and the sparse canopy of pine and live oak grew denser.

The two survivors aiming toward a point behind us strengthened my hope. "Will Vanya wait for us or continue on to the enclave?" I glanced back at Penny, so she might respond.

She gave me an uncaring shrug. "I don't know."

A cluster of rhythms ahead brought me to a dead stop, and she stopped so close to my back, I could hear her breathing. The rustle of her clothes told me she readied her weapon.

There were three people approaching at a running pace, directly for us. In the time it took for me to stop, I could hear them. We couldn't go east, where I wanted to go; that path might expose us to the survivors of the tornadoes. I snarled and turned west, deeper into army territory. "We're going to have to find a place to hide, quick."

"Are you sure?" Penny asked, though she followed.

"Absolutely not. However, I've got three ahead, three in the opposite direction, and four somewhere out on that field where the Pahawan died."

We scampered through the forest, making more noise than I wanted. A storm would be welcome at this point. I slowed us when the trio who'd been running straight for us dropped down to a jog. We hadn't gotten that far off their path. Every time I glanced back in their direction, I prayed I wouldn't face-plant in the brush.

A fallen tree ahead seemed a perfect place to hide, so I gestured Penny toward it. In another minute, the trio would pass and we could try heading east again.

The trunk of the snapped pine angled down from where shattered wood still partly attached to a waist-high stump. The bark had worn off in some spots, and insect holes dotted it all. We both rolled over the top near the middle, then crouched low to walk closer to the higher end. Penny knelt to peer under it into the woods with her rifle muzzle notably extended, though she wasn't aiming yet. A gunshot would be our last resort unless we wanted everyone to know where we were.

"Thank you," she said.

I blinked and jerked my head to her. "For what?"

"Wati. I effing hate you for pushing her back, but you had to, and she wanted to go. Always had."

I didn't reply. Wati might be safe, safer than we were, I hoped. It was surprising that Penny admitted to hating me for doing it. Her tone didn't carry any type of anger, more sadness than anything. I crawled down beside her, whipping my blond hair out of the way. Over the wind, I didn't hear anyone in the woods.

All of the soldiers around us had slowed, perhaps searching for us. To the east, the two survivors were close to the mystery man, but they hadn't closed the gap and were walking slightly spread out. The trio continued on their path, but slow and hesitant. *Maybe they'll get confused and shoot at each other.* It was an awful thought.

The rhythms of the trio were unusual compared to the others, so I focused on them. They were the closest and would remain so if they didn't move on. The more I studied them through the otherness, the more curious I became.

Their rhythms were more vibrant than the others. A chill crawled up my back. Were they some of the Youth Guard?

Pulse rising, I peered in earnest, trying to catch a glimpse. Would I know Selina, Ben, or Leslie through the otherness? The wind gusted through the trees, whipping the dried brush between us and the trio. A pale hand pressed a dark gray beret to a head. They were Youth Guards.

Blood pounded in my ears, and I rose to a crouch while Penny studied me, waiting for a sign. I rose until my head was among the splinters of the trunk, peering through them. The wind had eased, letting the bushes sway between us at full height.

Clouds had pulled in from the southeast, edging against the sun. It would storm soon.

Penny tugged at my coveralls, but I remained watching. Tyrell had said the Youth Guard would accompany the attacks, but who had he sent? I twitched when I thought of his full army somewhere behind me to the west and south. We had lost a lot of time this morning. Dean would worry, if he were awake.

The trio had nearly stopped, as if waiting. I searched around us. All of the soldiers had remained close to their positions. To the north at the far edge of my perception, I could sense another, perhaps one of those who had shot the Pahawan, creeping toward us.

"Could they be trying to corral us in?" I asked Penny.

"Get down," she said.

I needed to know who of the Youth Guard had come. Tyrell had said a special squad would go out that would have a medic healer like me or Eric. He had to have been lying; he didn't care.

Another gust rippled through the trees, carrying a scent that promised rain. When the branches dipped, tall Toni with her jet-black hair stood there holding her beret and watching me.

Her eyes widened before she yelled, "It's Caitlyn!"

As I dropped down behind the stump, the air around us roiled with the otherness. The rhythms were clear gray-white vibrations converging around me and Penny. Toni had returned from the Crèche. Her skill with fire was one of the best in the camp. Before she could draw heat to us, I pushed the otherness away in a frantic reaction.

A dome of heat centered around us burst into flame. We were safe on the inside, despite the sudden warmth. It lasted only a second, igniting dried brush and leaves. We had to go east to Vanya and Dean; I wouldn't take us any deeper west or south.

Grabbing the otherness and the already angry wind, I blasted the trio with a blunt gale. Their bodies rolled in the forest, one slamming against a thick oak. I didn't know if it were Toni or not. She'd always been fair with me, but we had to escape.

I jerked Penny up. "We're running for it."

She nodded, rifle in both hands. I didn't want her to shoot any of the Youth Guards, even if they weren't my friends anymore.

I ran into the woods the way we'd just come. Exhausted, I pulled a scream of the otherness as one of the fallen trio started to stand, and blew them deep into the woods. Through the otherness I could see two crawling while one appeared unconscious.

We were headed toward the tall, burned-out building where I'd killed a man with a tornado. Those soldiers had shot Wati, but I still tried not to think of the body I'd left in my wake. "We're going to make it." The road we'd traveled from Vinnie's should lay ahead. My heart raced, but my jaw was tight in determination.

The woods ended a couple dozen yards behind the house, leaving us to race through low brush. I focused on the trio. One had gained their footing, and I shot a weak gust to knock them back. We needed to survive and escape; nothing else mattered. We were gaining on the house, and I intended to cross the road and disappear into the thick woods on the opposite side.

The scent of rain in the wind grew stronger, then ozone tinged it as the otherness rushed toward us. My heart leaped. I flailed to push it away.

Lightning stretched down my leg, locking me into a crashing tumble with stiff limbs. Penny screamed in agony somewhere behind and to my left. Dirt and debris pressed into my nose and mouth. The world dimmed like the storm had swallowed the sun.

Chapter Twenty-Four

I dreamed of Dean chasing a motorcycle in his wolf form while it rained. The water came down in great drenching waves, and I gagged and sputtered, trying to breathe.

"Mercy is for the weak," the storm whispered in my ear.

I lost track of Dean and opened my eyes. Dark clouds rained onto me. The storm was Selina holding an upended canteen. She wore a hooded jacket, keeping the rain off her face.

Selina smiled, and a thin scar stretched at the right corner of her mouth and dug into her bottom lip. "How important is your new lover? She is still alive and will remain that way if you do not try anything."

I lay on the ground and tried to loll my head around, blinking against the rain. My wrists and ankles were bound. I was so weak I barely tested them. We were alone in the woods.

"We've got your girl secure. Don't worry. Is she with the Alliance? Are you scouts? What do they know?"

"Selina." My anger at her had diminished during my time hiding with Dean. She'd killed Eric. My lips started to snarl as buried feelings crawled back.

I sensed the otherness build, but too quick to stop it. A shock in the back of my neck snapped my head to the ground, and I nearly passed out again.

She laughed at my pain, then hardened her face. "Are you working with the Alliance? What do they know of our plans?"

Through the storm, I heard a motorcycle approach. There were other subtle noises behind the rain as well. I took a deep breath and began feeling the otherness around me. I'd gotten us captured. Just a few yards away in a circle around us were five people. Beyond that were three more. Soldiers and perhaps others from Camp Sparta were guards. None seemed to be Penny; I believed I could recognize her in the otherness. The motorcycle had two people on it and wound through the layers to us.

Selina watched, her cruel smile returning. She waited for me to react, so I didn't glance at the new arrivals. My heart did speed, though. Frantic, I reached farther with my senses, trying to find Penny.

A gruff man spoke as the engine turned off. "He's at least two hours out, but we've sent word to him."

Selina scowled and shook her head. With a brusque gesture, she called someone forward. I waited, unwilling to give her any reaction. My only goal was to escape and find Penny. Some part of me hoped that would include slamming Selina a dozen feet into the air.

I couldn't be sure I'd know Penny from any of the others. However, I didn't find a dying body or anyone prone. The people I could sense were standing alone, and they wouldn't let her do that. The man and the other arrival were only a few yards away. His passenger was a woman based on the rhythms, maybe even Youth Guard, if I gauged it right.

What Vanya had taught me, not much in truth, had

nearly saved us. She seemed to gain even more from the otherness. When we first met, she'd even guessed my skills. If I survived, I would spend a lot more time learning how to sense with the otherness.

"Always so much trouble, Caitlyn. So full of yourself." Selina's lips pulled back in a cruel smile. "Do you even think of what you've done to anyone else? Who you've left behind? The damage you caused? You can't be trusted. You are a traitor. I would kill you now, but they have other plans."

Footsteps approached, and another hooded figure came to face Selina. As much as I avoided being obvious, I peered at them. I could be sure they were Youth Guard. There was a certain rhythm to their otherness.

A young woman, confirmed from her fingers, reached into a belt pack. They trembled slightly, perhaps afraid of me or Selina. It took her a moment of fumbling to pry at something. From her zippered pouch, she produced a silver collar the diameter of a neck.

My breath hitched and I gasped. Selina grinned at my reaction. I'd worn one of these horrors at the lab for years. *Never again.*

In panic, I started to call the otherness, but Selina beat me to it and electricity snapped from my spine to the ground. My body trembled and all energy sapped from me. My throat thick, my mind started to drop into hysterical fog.

Selina refused the collar when the woman offered it. "The honor is yours."

The figure coughed and slowly turned to me until her face became visible.

Roxie was crying.

Chapter Twenty-Five

Like a gasping fish, my mouth hung open collecting cold rain. I blinked. "Roxie?" My voice was raw.

The otherness coalesced, then a sharp snap of electricity jolted my back. The world dimmed for a moment, and my grasp on the otherness dissipated. Ozone wafted in my nose before the wind tugged it away. My skin burned. It took a long moment before I could exhale.

Roxie's hands were shaking, and the silver collar wobbled in the air above me. She tried to speak, but the words melted into a sob. Her dark face hid as her head sagged forward and the hood shadowed her features.

"Do it," Selina barked, and I hated her most for terrifying my friend. We all knew the horror that collar provoked.

Despite a growing rage, I struggled to bring even my awareness of the otherness back. My limbs spasmed in random places, too weak to even move. My fear of the collar shriveled under my hate for Selina. Anything I had ever liked or loved about her vanished. My childhood friend was gone, replaced with this cold, cruel creature.

Roxie's hand dropped the collar, and it hit with a splash beside my head.

"Bitch," Selina swore. "You traitor. You lied."

"I can't," Roxie wailed.

The otherness welled, but around Roxie's legs this time. I tried to push at it, as I had with Toni's fire. Selina's magic shifted, but not enough.

The crack of electricity around Roxie's boots startled me. A second snap zapped the back of my neck. My vision swam as Roxie crumbled to the ground. Her toe kicked the side of my head as she dropped. The odor of plastic and burned flesh filled my next breath.

My lips moved, as if I wanted to say something, but I didn't know what. Roxie's gasping cries gave me some comfort; she was alive.

I flinched as metal touched my neck. Selina leaned close, her cruel expression visible even in the shadow of her hood. "I'd hoped you'd be out here. Prayed for it." The collar slid around my neck.

I died a little when it clicked closed. The metal pressed into my skin; it clasped so tight.

Selina grinned and stepped back. "Test it."

"No." My voice became a whimper, and I hated that.

As someone approached, I tried to gather the otherness, but I had no strength. Instead, I clenched my jaw and screwed my eyes shut.

The button clicked; an old hateful sound. An electric shock stabbed dots of light against my eyelids. My body locked.

I faded into blackness.

When I woke, my neck hurt. The rain still blustered in the wind, pelting my face. Voices murmured around me. My cheek lay in wet charred wood from the sharp musty smell. Hands tied behind my back, I touched rough brick as if from a wall. When I tried to shift, they tugged as if tethered to the ground.

Blackened wood blocked my view, so I tried to lift my head.

"She's awake," a man said. He wasn't very close.

"Good," said Selina. "Sit her straight so she can see, Ben."

Ben, a senior of the Hounds unit with a fuller mustache now, studied me nervously as he stepped into view. Grabbing my shoulders, he pivoted me into a sitting position, then quickly jumped back.

Weak, I managed to shift a knee to the side to rest against the wall, remaining upright. Penny and Roxie were bound at their wrists and ankles and staked three yards from me and a couple feet apart. Penny's eyes glared with burning rage while Roxie stared unfocused.

Selina stood behind them. Ben stood to one side of her, and a younger boy to her other side. He wore the coveralls of a Youth Guard, but I didn't recognize him, and his jacket covered his unit patch.

Three separate cracks sounded, and my heels burned with the shock. My leg spasmed, and I nearly slid back to the ground. Penny grimaced and Roxie shivered with her eyes closed.

Selina spoke with a smug tone and crooked smile. "I've honed my skill. Tyrell let me train with small animals and Roxie for a while, until he decided she'd learned her lesson. She obviously hasn't."

My face tightened. I wanted to kill her. When she'd put the collar on me, I could have. I just needed a touch. Why hadn't I thought of it?

Selina raised her right hand, and red lights played across Penny's brown head and Roxie's black curls. Bright red splashed into my eyes. When raindrops passed through them, I could see the lines coming from three different directions.

"You don't know what those are, but we have three snipers trained on all of you. If anything happens to me, then you lose your life and take your old girlfriend and new one with you." She lowered her hand and the lights disappeared. Two loud snaps jolted Penny and Roxie simultaneously. Their legs kicked uncontrollably and they both trembled.

"Stop." My voice was no more than a croak. I reached into the otherness to listen and see. There were three people hidden in the woods behind Selina, Ben, and the younger boy. Two more hid inside the house behind me. One of them might have the device that controlled my collar. Sensing out farther, I found what I believed were the snipers from where the red lines had pointed. The two who had targeted Penny and Roxie were to each side, while mine hid to the right in the woods. "Please."

"Oh, the mighty Caitlyn begs." Two more shocks cracked under Penny and Roxie. "Do you know what a mess you left?" Selina touched the scar at her lips. "Three other Youth Guards tried to leave after you did. They actually believed you were leading a rebellion. A hero for the oppressed. Idiots."

"I wasn't." I cleared my throat, but couldn't say more.

"Oh, we knew that, but they got it in their heads. Where is wolf boy? Did you have to put him down?"

I hoped Dean and Vanya were far from here. There were too many soldiers and Youth Guard for Dean to risk.

Penny cried out when the next set of shocks snapped under us. Roxie eyes were still unfocused.

"Answer me." Selina's face contorted. "Where is he?"

Rain poured down my face, but my throat scratched dry. "He ran off."

Three cracks sounded, and I nearly slid to the ground from the shock at the base of my spine. My hands tingled and my legs spasmed. The rain blurred, but I regained my hold of the otherness quickly. Penny or Roxie groaned. I refused to cry, though my skin burned like I held it in a flame.

Selina had refined her magic to a frightening extent. If I had the strength to block her like I had Toni, she'd likely have me shot with a wave of her hand. She hated me, and perhaps Roxie as well from her treatment of her. What had Roxie lied about, and what brought her here?

Our three tormentors glanced aside as a motorcycle rumbled close behind the burned building, then stopped. Footsteps splashed around the side, and a soldier dashed to Selina; she obviously controlled the Youth Guard, at least. Her betrayal of me at Camp Sparta had likely earned her a promotion.

"He's an hour out. He sent a message, 'Alive.' That was all."

Selina glared at me, then waved the soldier off. The otherness welled around me.

As the ground seemed to slam into my ass, blackness swallowed me, and I drifted away to the scent of ozone.

Chapter Twenty-Six

My first sight when I woke was of a lanky wisp of a boy maybe a year younger than me based on his slight size. He stood where Selina had been and wore a curious expression. The rain had lightened to a sprinkle, though the skies were still thick gray. Penny and Roxie were asleep or unconscious, each breathing with gentle rises from their chests. An engine rumbled in the front of the house.

It took me far too long to recognize my one visible guard as someone from the Sure Death unit; Andy had just turned senior rank before I ran away from Camp Sparta. He always wore his red hair nearly shaved, and freckles coated his nose and under his eyes.

Working my shoulders against brick and pushing with my heels, I sat and winced at electrical burns. Weak, I stretched out my sense of the otherness, searching for Selina. "Andy?"

An eager smile flashed across Andy's face before dying as he glanced at the side of the house guiltily. He straightened and locked an unreadable expression into place. At his side, under his wet jacket, he wore a holstered gun.

His momentary smile when I recognized him gave me

some hope. I quickly sensed not only the same ring of guards I'd had before, but a cluster of four people at the front of the building. Beyond them a thick line of people was marching past, as if on a road. Too many to register, it had to be the army itself.

My chest tightened. Vanya should have gotten Dean someplace safe. I wasn't sure if a god existed, but I prayed anyway. Prayers hadn't stopped the Sorrow.

Vanya thought the military would be traveling farther west. No wonder there had been so many scouts and the Youth Guard in this area. They would have traveled during the night, planning to clear out the Duathua scouts in the morning, long before they could warn the enclave. If Vanya and Dean survived, the Alliance would have an opportunity to prepare.

I'd lost all sense of time. "Is Roxie okay?" I asked Andy.

His eyes darted down to her, then snapped back to me. He worked his lips, but didn't speak. Andy had always been easygoing and generally fun, though we didn't hang out much. His strongest skill was fire, so we only practiced together with air on rare occasions.

Both Penny's and Roxie's rhythms were slow and gentle. Some of their skin along the ground was agitated and buzzing, probably burned like my own butt cheeks from Selina's shocks. The knowledge made my teeth grind and pulse pound. Water puddled around them.

I smiled at Andy while checking on the snipers farther out whose rhythms were low and calm. Killers waiting for a sign.

Three soldiers or Youth Guards crouched in the woods behind Andy, three snipers spread around us, two people sat right behind me in the house, four stood out front, and an entire army passed us by. Escape wasn't an option. Not for me. They might not chase Roxie or Penny. I sagged.

They would kill them without a thought. What did they want from me?

Selina had asked about Dean and the Alliance. I didn't know anything, really.

Too much longer lying on the cold, wet ground, and Roxie and Penny's temperatures would drop. I hoped for the sun to come out.

I stiffened. Tyrell intended to come here. Yes, he'd want information about the Alliance. Penny knew more than me, but he didn't know that.

My head turned when another motor grew closer, and Andy glanced south where I imagined he could see the road. Focusing my senses on the front, I scanned the rhythms of the four waiting there. Their hums pitched in a way that made me believe they were Youth Guards rather than regular soldiers. I smiled wistfully at Andy as I scanned him and the guards in the woods behind. There was a difference.

Two soldiers approached on a vehicle, and the rumbling of the engine grew louder, then stopped beside the four. One of the two men exited the vehicle and left the other behind. The four joined him as they circled the burned-out house, heading for me.

It had to be Tyrell. I drew in a deep breath of acrid, burned wood, and forced a smile at Andy.

Tall and muscular, Tyrell wore a thick vest and fatigues with an army cap sheltering his scowl from the rain. Droplets still clung to his mustache and sandy brown hair. "Caitlyn." He crouched a yard from me.

Pale Selina had her hood down, hanging on her back. She sneered as she took Andy's place, and he stepped back a couple paces. His expression seemed worried. Ben and two other male Youth Guards I didn't recognize surrounded Selina.

Tyrell brought back memories of Eric's death, so I just studied him without a response. He would let me know what he wanted.

"We heard you were out by the north marsh spying for the Alliance. We had Roxie there, as bait, but then you showed up here of all places." His tone remained conversational, but his sharp eyes studied my reaction when he mentioned Roxie.

"My plan is working, nonetheless," said Selina. "We have her. The werewolf will come."

I stiffened, and Tyrell noted my movement. "You did very well, Selina. Now, Caitlyn, why were you and the others here?"

When I didn't respond, Selina shocked my thigh long enough to make it spasm uncontrollably. My teeth clamped on the inside of my mouth, but I stayed silent.

"Where is the other one? They reported three of you."

He wouldn't believe me if I told him. Silent, I stared at his eyes and waited for Selina to shock me again.

"Where is Dean?"

Selina planned on Dean coming to rescue me. I couldn't stop that from happening, but in his present state and if Vanya hadn't alerted him, he might still be on his way to the enclave. The more I considered it, the less I believed he would allow that. *Don't come after me, Dean.*

"He ran away after your military butchered those families."

"Traitors," Tyrell corrected without the slightest concern. "They were working with the Duathua. The Alliance, as you know them. I'm not surprised you joined them. What do they think of Dean?" He stood and turned his back to me to study Roxie, then Penny.

"That's her new bitch, sir." said Selina.

Tyrell nodded, still with his back to me. "Caitlyn, what

were you doing out here?" He had to be afraid the Alliance knew of the army's path.

I shook my head and remained silent.

The barest shrug crossed his shoulders and Selina smiled, motioning to the younger Youth Guard who I didn't know. "We learned something from your antics at Camp Sparta, dear Caitlyn."

The man knelt by Penny. She was oblivious to his presence, her rhythms quiet. I tensed, but before I could say anything, he placed his thumb on her cheek.

Penny jolted awake, shrieking with pain. She fought against her bonds, splashing. Where the man had touched, raw skin oozed blood. I could sense the open wound and frantic rhythms.

"Stop!" I shouted. "Leave her alone." A sharp shock at the base of my back rocked me. The scene blurred.

Tyrell's voice carried over Penny's howls and curses. "Where is the third one we spotted with you?"

I forced words between ragged breaths. "She got away. We ran back to distract you — so she could leave. I swear. The truth."

"Hmm, I almost believe you."

Selina grinned as her shock bit my thigh and forced my leg to kick out.

There had been a time, even earlier in the day, when I couldn't conceive of harming one of the Youth Guard; now I wanted them to die. Penny growled as the man reached for her, but he grabbed her chin firmly in one hand. Her eyes widened as he placed his thumb on her forehead and held it as the flesh peeled open. I gasped a breath before Selina shocked me again.

My sense of the otherness faded. I was too weak. "Okay. Okay. We were — we were sent here."

Tyrell turned and studied me. "By whom?"

"A Duathua — named Halimay. She wanted us to bring Wati here and protect her. We did. Wati got away." I'd been taught to lie by Selina at an early age. She always said to sprinkle in as much truth as you could get away with.

Penny cried in pain, spitting out curses when she got enough breath. The monster who'd hurt her stayed close. Selina watched me. If they killed Penny and Roxie, I'd take her and as many of them with me as I could.

Tyrell knelt a good yard from my feet. "Very good, Caitlyn. Selina, have them taken to the front. Is everything else set?"

Anger flashed across her face before she composed it. "Yes, sir."

After they untied her bonds from a metal loop pinned into the ground, Roxie had to be carried away, unconscious. They wrangled Penny to her feet and forced her to walk. As tough as I'd always believed she was, she cursed them with nearly every step, as if her face weren't bleeding.

Unable to keep from glancing at me, Andy's eyes were wide as he helped them. Selina had burning glares for me and perhaps Tyrell as she followed the Youth Guard out of sight.

"You understand that if you attempt anything, you'll be shot?" He obviously knew of the guards. A smile flicked at his lips. "And there's the collar."

"Yes. Sir." Drawing in a tight breath, I played the beaten prisoner. My sense of the otherness stretched out. I hardly believed I could take all of them, but I needed to be prepared. There remained little likelihood of getting free at the moment, but I couldn't have them hurt Penny for no reason. Besides, there was still Dean to consider. At least I knew he hadn't been shot or captured; there would be no reason for a trap otherwise.

"What do you need to know?" I asked.

Chapter Twenty-Seven

I was cognizant of the tears that trickled down my cheek. He might notice them against my rain-wet skin. He needed to think of me as weak and willing to do anything for Penny. True, to a certain extent.

Tyrell tilted his head. "Why were you three sent here?"

I swallowed and spoke quietly. "Halimay thought you might bring the army down this road. They needed proof."

He gave no reaction except to nod. "Why was it important for this Wati to escape?"

"She's Duathua. Her flying is quicker than trekking back. We were supposed to lead you off and escape, then follow after her. Knowing your path will make all the difference." Did I expect him to just turn around?

"Perhaps." He didn't believe me fully. His eyes never left mine.

"Can't you just turn around and leave them alone?"

"Them," he said.

"I meant us."

"How long have you been working with *them?*" he asked.

"A few days after we escaped. They were helping us

survive until you came and killed those families." I truly didn't know the best lies to tell, but wanted to keep answering with something he might consider important. I might be able to heal what they had done to Penny's face if I got to her soon. Pushing down surges of rage, I held a chagrined expression, glancing down as if ashamed despite my accusation.

South of the front of the house, I heard the engine of a vehicle approaching.

"Where is Dean?"

"He's with the others, setting up the defense." I needed Tyrell and Selina not to expect him to come here attempting a rescue. The more I considered it, the more I knew he might. I blinked and searched, not just with my otherness, but with our unique connection. I didn't sense him, but he could find me. Their trap might work. My heart dropped.

"You expect me to believe they're working with a were-wolf? I know much of the Alliance. Love for werewolves is not within them."

"He doesn't shift," I said. Even trying, I couldn't get the fear of Dean trying to save me out of my voice.

Tyrell cocked his head slightly, wondering something. He believed enough of what I said to consider it.

Inside, I smiled. "They don't know," I lied in the most shameful voice I could muster. "We didn't have to tell them."

His eyes glittered, and I knew he believed me.

The hotter anger inside me had cooled, now that they weren't torturing Penny. I could sense most moving north, though not into the mass that was the army. I guessed Selina to be the lone Youth Guard remaining out of sight at the side of the house. I focused, trying to distinguish her from the others. Averting my eyes as if guilty, I peered in their direction. The brick house I leaned against blocked most of the view. Ahead lay a burned stretch of woods, just visible through the drizzle, and the large tower rising behind. We weren't far from where we'd been trying to escape. The huge field would be just on the other side of the woods.

I turned back, fighting to control a trembling lip. "What are you going to do with me?"

"Return you," he said with a harsh snap, then stood.

A shiver crawled up my spine. He could mean the labs or Camp Sparta; the former terrified me. Where my acting had been complacent and remorseful, panic fought to gain hold. Tears welled, and I gritted my teeth. Tyrell would never believe it if I played contrite and begged to go back to Camp Sparta. I could only hope another chance would come to free Penny and Roxie. I groaned inside when I thought about Dean; he might be too weak now, but he'd never give up.

"Selina. She's yours." Tyrell called out with a finality that chilled me worse.

Her blue eyes shone as she strode around the corner. A shock snapped at the base of my spine and dots flicked in my vision. "We'll catch him, sir. Does she know anything?"

"I doubt it. Though I do believe our element of surprise no longer exists. I predicted as much. We've got four hours until we arrive. They won't have their defenses moved in time." He gave me one last dismissive glance. "You're confident of the people you've selected to leave behind?"

She shrugged, and another shock went through my thigh, causing me to gasp for air. "The trap is set, sir. It would be easier if I could just kill him."

The sounds of more vehicles began to murmur down the road to the south. Thunder rumbled from the north.

Tyrell shook his head and began to walk away. "We

have interest in the werewolf. Attempt to take him alive. Wounded is acceptable if you need to."

"Bastard." Any semblance of my act crumbled away. "I wish I had killed you." My breath stopped at her next shock. The skin across my butt cheek blistered, and I started to slide to the ground, muscles betraying me. My face slapped into wet, charred wood, and I inhaled the acrid scent.

"My team can head out with you as soon as you're ready, sir." She sounded hopeful.

Tyrell's tone sounded nonchalant. "No need. Follow the mechanized infantry. Your teams will assault after we soften them."

Her face drew tight as he marched away, light splashes sounding under his boots. She cocked her head, and a shock snapped from my face to the ground. "Bitch. Why I can't just kill you and be done with it, I don't know." She made a motion in the air, and I waited for a sniper shot. "Did you know there is no Wolf Squad unit anymore? I don't even care; I made Section Leader and now Corporal." She lifted her jacket to show a new patch on her coveralls with simply a Camp Sparta design. "Idiots were making themselves honorary Wolf Squad. Even Yaz took up your imagined banner, but she's come into line. Eric became their martyr."

The otherness coalesced, too late and sluggish. The shock on my face caused me to bite my tongue. I could taste the blood. My pulse felt ragged from all the shocks. How long before one of them just stopped my heart? Maybe it would be for the best.

I croaked each syllable slowly. "If Eric — martyr — what does that make you?"

The crack sounded before my body locked, and I drifted into blackness.

Chapter Twenty-Eight

I woke, groggy from Selina's last shock, staring at lantern light dancing on the ceiling of a metal shed. Dank odors hung in the air. My arms and legs had been stretched to the sides, each wrist and ankle strapped to the floor by cold metal. Blisters dotted my skin.

From what I could tell, the rain had stopped. The rumble of passing vehicles was gone, and I could hear someone breathing nearby. It took a quick reflex not to lift my head and search the small building. They didn't need to know that I'd awoken.

My backside and legs were blistered, they'd taken Dean's jacket so my bones ached with cold, and I sorely had to pee. I swallowed what saliva I could down a thick throat. Reaching out to the otherness, I listened and stretched my senses.

The young man inside the shed had a nervous energy, certainly a Youth Guard. Just outside the shed walls were two prone people I assumed were Penny and Roxie, who were very much awake. Three more male Youth Guards sat sentry near them.

I sensed the air inside the shed. There was too little

mass to do more than bluster my guard's hair. Outside, I might be able to disable those who watched my friends, but they were likely tied and it would do little good.

Taking a gentle breath, I pushed out to the area surrounding my cell. If we were near the road, the army had moved on. We could, however, be somewhere else entirely.

I found one soldier at the far edge of my senses inside the border of some woods, and another barely registered, as the two were on opposite sides of me. How did they intend to trap Dean? My connection to the otherness didn't detail buildings or structures, as only the living had any kind of rhythm, unless they were metal and I was touching the surface. Then they vibrated lightly, such as the collar around my neck and the clamps pinning me to the floor.

I needed a plan before I started giving them any indication of what I could do. My exhausted state didn't help me think, but I didn't have time to wait for them to trap Dean. I had to have more information to tie an impossible set of actions together, and I didn't know if I had the energy to carry it out. "I'm thirsty," I said to my guard.

His humming rose, but his voice remained calm and quiet. "You'll survive."

"I haven't had any water all day." I lifted my head, viewing the inside of the shed. Small, ten or twelve feet square, it had one door directly behind a pimpled boy my age who sat on the floor. He held his gun on his thigh with his right hand. His other thumb rested on the button of the controller to my collar with a white-knuckled readiness.

"Sorry." He wasn't, but his rhythms were spiking.

"Please?" I asked. I preferred he open the metal door to go get me water, but his proximity to the door did offer opportunities. Hopefully, his skill didn't involve electricity; I'd become really tired of being shocked.

"No. Now, stay quiet or I'll —" He swallowed without finishing his statement.

"Shock me like they used to in the labs? You aren't from Camp Sparta, and probably not from the same lab I was in, but they're all the same, aren't they?" I didn't really need his sympathy, but the talking gave me time to rework my plan.

He didn't answer, but one of the Youth Guard outside stood and walked along the perimeter of the building. I'd really rather they wouldn't get too close with what I had in mind. They were all humming faster at the sound of my voice.

Someone drew in a roar of the otherness. My pulse raced, and I reacted, ready to push against whatever they threw at me. Heat, air, and certainly water would be difficult inside this enclosed space, but electricity didn't seem to care.

The attack happened outside, as two members of the Youth Guard began screaming. From the rhythms, I knew heat had been used. Their humming pitched higher along their chests, and I imagined skin blistering.

The third yelled, "Wolf Squad!" The voice could have been Andy's.

A smile lifted my lips as I melted the collar like I had the bullet inside Wati and the cage that held my drowning Dean. I hadn't hoped for help, but I'd take it.

I didn't hear the gunfire, but my benefactor, who I assumed was Andy, spun with a cry and dropped to the ground. His upper arm seethed with painful rhythms, and he cradled it quickly. It had to be from a bullet.

Penny started swearing. "Crap. Stay down." I couldn't be sure whether she spoke to me, Roxie, or the boy on the ground.

My guard stood, clicking the useless device before he raised his gun.

I had planned on taking out the snipers first, but I had an emergency. A blast of heavy, humid air slammed through the shed door at his back.

His gunshot cracked louder than the screeching metal and howling wind, then the pimple-faced boy flew over me. Flailing the distance to the far wall faster than I could see, his body crashed with a shriek of bending metal. I unclenched my teeth, scanned my body for holes, and turned my restraints into cold, soft goo.

Even as I scrambled to my knees, I formed dropping tornadoes above the soldiers in the woods. They weren't as strong as before, but I had to hope they'd give me time to find my guard's weapon and free Penny and Roxie, and maybe heal Andy if he'd been the one to help. I knew the pimple-faced boy was unconscious as I stood shakily. I grabbed his 9mm and headed for the open door in a crouch. My heart pounded, fast but steady.

"Roxie? Penny?" I spoke too low with my throat dry and raspy.

The Youth Guard and my friends were on the opposite side of the shed. Outside, a field stretched to a cluster of burned-out houses, with a small tornado tearing apart the woods at the side. The clouds were thin white with the sun brightly shining in between.

The two burned Youth Guards cried and writhed far behind me.

My faded gray shed sat in an open field where the closest tree had been blackened along with all the houses. A metal fence had been flattened around us, and the sod and grass had been ripped free in a wide swath that left raw soil. There was nowhere to hide.

A gunshot echoed at the same time a bullet ripped through the shed wall near the door at the height of my knees. My chest tightened. A second shot puckered the metal, and I dropped to the ground. Through my senses, I found three soldiers trotting toward us and two more at the edges of my perception.

"Run!" yelled Andy from behind the shed, his tone drenched in pain.

Penny and Roxie weren't hit yet, though they wriggled against their restraints. Roxie was using a dull growl of the otherness, but I couldn't be sure for what. Bullets screeched through the thin walls, and I winced as I crawled for the sunlight.

The tower lay to my left, so we hadn't been taken far. After the next two bullets sheared through the metal, I pressed my chin against mud between clumps of weeds and grass.

"Roxie?" I could barely hear myself; I didn't expect an answer.

I had crawled half out of the shed, dragging forward on my elbows, when a low shot nicked the concrete behind my boot. I flattened with a shiver and pressed my ear into mud to peer back. Inside, bright blood sprayed on the walls from where my pimple-faced guard had been hit. I hadn't wanted him hurt, just unconscious.

If the soldiers were willing to sacrifice Youth Guards in their hail of bullets, the soldiers would kill me on sight. Even as I resumed crawling, I found the closest of the snipers and unleashed a tornado on him.

A cloying smell, like that of burning plastic, hung in the air. I elbowed forward foot by foot, and bullets twanged through the shed. The image reminded me of the families who had died at the compound, caught inside their trailers. Roxie had shifted from where she'd been earlier. She had to be burning through the ropes from her renewed draw of the otherness.

Andy moaned something that could have been "Wolf Squad."

"Roxie?" I yelled. "Are you okay?"

Penny responded. "I'm effing okay, too. Thanks for asking. She's melting our ropes."

"Stay down." I scraped between two dried bushes, tilting them away with digs of my elbows.

"Yeah, I hadn't thought of that."

Tyrell wanted Dean alive; he'd said so. He'd left a lot of soldiers and Youth Guards to make sure. Why?

"You okay?" Penny's tone was softer.

"Good times. I haven't been hit."

Dean's jacket hung on the back of the shed. I could smell it, and they assumed so would he.

I unleashed another tornado on a soldier sitting at the fringe, noting some abatement in the gunfire. The problem came from the weakness of my call to the otherness. The strength proved enough to bring down a disturbance, but each of the men had been unharmed and resumed their position after the effects dissipated.

Worse, another had joined one of the first. I blinked, sensing something, but not through the otherness.

Dean had arrived. My love prowled toward me, his vibrations high pitched in his werewolf form, and I still didn't know their trap.

Chapter Twenty-Nine

I crawled to the side of the shed opposite the tower where Dean crept toward one of the firing soldiers. The nauseating scent of melted plastic stung my nose. I was just around the corner from Penny. Taking a deep breath, I drew on the otherness, found air, and sent a weak tornado onto the soldier closest to Dean.

A flash of the mangled soldier's body near the motorcycle made me wince, but I wasn't as repulsed from the idea as before. These people would kill their own to win. Selina had nearly begged to kill me.

"We're loose," Penny said. "Roxie is hurt."

Anger blossomed in my chest, and I crawled faster. Most of the shots came from the front of the building and the side I slithered past. The three men running toward us were deep in the woods in the direction I crept. We still had some time before I had to deal with them.

Dean attacked the man, and I felt no sympathy for the soldier.

I sensed Roxie. Her face had been bruised; it thrummed with a mix of dull and spiked rhythms. "What did they do to her?"

"Your friend didn't like one of her comments. Took a rifle stock to her face after she shocked her so bad — I thought she might have been dead already. Your ex is a tough girl."

Dean stalked off, leaving a corpse. I shivered, then sent down another wisp of a tornado on a soldier.

My elbow scraped against the edge of the concrete slab exposed at the corner of the shed. Penny lay flat on her back, staring at the sky. Roxie lay front down beside her, face to the side. I could see the purple bruising of her brown skin along the top of her cheek. Neither shifted. "Roxy, are you okay?"

"Mmhmm."

Sensing, I found the break in her jaw, humming a spike with each pulse. "I hate her." *Selina.*

As I crawled beside Penny's head, Andy mumbled. He lay on his back, wounded arm cradled across his chest and his coveralls dark with blood.

Penny tilted her head, studying me. "No new holes?" A weak grin flicked on her face. "I can't see why you ran away. Great friends."

I flinched, and Penny frowned, not understanding. Dean had just made his second kill. He headed slowly, inexorably toward me. I needed to know what they had set as a trap.

Healing Roxie filled the front of my mind, but we had to survive first. I pulled past them, scrabbling toward Andy. "We've got three soldiers heading for us." I gestured ahead toward the blackened woods just past a long field. "Andy, let me stop the blood."

He tried to smile, making his grimace appear as if he would start crying. "I —"

I laid flat as I stretched my hand over him, pressing into the soaked sleeve of his coveralls. The bullet had torn through the muscle of his upper arm just under the shoulder. The bleeding I could take care of at the moment. "Andy, what's the trap for Dean?"

"Hmm?" He barely held onto consciousness.

"Penny, did you see them set a trap?"

"After the bitch effing zapped me unconscious and I woke tied to a spike in the mud? Sorry, missed it." She grunted and started scraping across the ground toward me.

Dean had stopped hunting and headed directly for me. I had to know. Pausing from my healing, I sent a whirlwind onto the soldier who had the best opportunity to spot Dean, then resumed my healing.

The gunfire had slowed but continued at a steady rate. Dean had halved the number of people firing at us, until the others arrived.

The two other Youth Guards had dropped into unconsciousness; Andy had done a fearsome job on them. In fact, the level of burns on their chests might kill them if someone didn't heal them. I didn't have time. Healing required a lot less energy than using air, but time.

"He have a weapon?" Penny nodded toward Andy. "A rifle, preferably?"

Andy shifted his left arm up, exposing a holster at his side. I popped the strap, slid out the pistol, and shifted so I could see Penny and Roxie. Penny reached for the gun.

One of the other Youth Guards yelled, then coughed. They'd been shot in the side, and their lungs were pierced based on the raging rhythms there. A rib had shattered. They wouldn't last long.

I should have felt bad for them, but it just made me more concerned that a low shot would find one of us. Was this war? It had always seemed so clear cut when I read about it or when Tyrell preached about fighting the cryptids.

Penny took the gun. "How many, three? I'll take the guy in the middle. You two pick a side, left or right."

Summoning another whirlwind on one of the firing soldiers, I frowned. "Did you fight? The last time the army attacked?"

She took a deep breath. "Yeah, of course. Anybody with a gun. The Duathua are shit against weapons. They won't admit it. And, we don't have many like you. Vanya and them didn't really practice fighting."

"Did you kill?" I asked.

"Yeah." Penny didn't explain further.

Dean was nearly as close as the soldiers; in fact, they might see him first.

Penny crawled past me and Andy, heading in the direction of the oncoming soldiers. Roxie followed. Her swollen face set my teeth on edge. I had never wanted anyone to die before, but now I could only imagine what I might do to Selina. I despised her.

"Be careful," I said.

Penny scoffed. "I missed that option."

My healing of Andy had reversed the worst of the damage, and he had dropped off, unconscious or asleep. Either would do him well. He would live; at least the wound wouldn't kill him. I pulled my hand from his arm and resisted the urge to wake him. He had to know about the trap for Dean.

I rubbed mud off my lips and chin, then crawled around Andy to join Roxie. My muscles were weak and my brain foggy, but I had to try and heal her. Self-pity and grief jabbed at my stomach as I crawled to her. She had found a section where the ground dipped and lay with her head to the side watching me. The encircling ring of torn up soil and flattened fence gave us a low barrier two yards away.

"Keep your head down. I'll let you know when they are

close enough." The running soldiers were nearly at the wood's edge and would be visible in just minutes. Dean would arrive soon after that, and if the trap didn't get him, the soldiers might. The shed still took damage behind us. At some point, the more distant soldiers would either run out of ammunition or assume we were dead.

Penny had crawled over to the two burned Youth Guards. "Hah." She lifted the tip of a rifle in the air over her head. "Now, that's a weapon." It clicked as she worked it with two hands. "I'll keep the pistol too, if you two don't need it."

I might, considering how weak I felt. "Not yet." Reaching out, I put my hand on Roxie's face. A bullet dug into the ground beside us with a dull thud, and I shivered.

Bruises were hard to "heal" since the body brought extra resources to aid in the healing, and I couldn't remove it. I would repair the actual damage and the swelling would reduce quickly, just not immediately. The broken jawbone bothered me the most. I could do nothing about the two molars she was missing.

She studied me, then closed her eyes as I worked in the bone. It would hurt. The Roxie I'd left behind had been strong and dedicated to the rules of the Camp. She'd changed. I knew it from the moment she'd broken down when refusing to put the collar on me. I had left her in hell. The old Roxie would have never cried over that, and she likely wouldn't have agreed to it in the first place.

The soldiers would break out of the woods in a minute. "Ready? They're almost here." Whatever trap they had planned for Dean, I'd have to get him out of it after we took care of the closest threat.

Penny rested the rifle on the corpse's legs to aim. "It stopped."

Focused on healing Roxie, it took me a second. "They're

not firing." There had been pauses before, but the silence hung eerily long. I sensed out. "They're moving in toward us. We've got time."

"How?" Roxie spoke thick and slurring. She had to mean my ability to sense where they were through the otherness.

I removed my hand from her swollen cheek. "It's something Vanya showed me; I'll show you how, later."

She nodded and winced, then turned to focus ahead.

The fields hid the lower trunks of the trees, but motion showed in the shadows. "There, did you see that?"

"Yep. Effing middle one's mine."

The heads of the soldiers bobbed around blackened trunks. Roxie squinted, then tilted her head in careful nod. "Yes."

The sun lit the soldiers' caps as they charged across the field. I held my breath as I reached into the otherness. Roxie's call roared, and the ground around us vibrated in my vision.

"On three?" Penny asked.

The soldiers unleashed a hail of bullets like they had at the families' compound a few days before. Dirt spouted to the left of me, and the shed rang of bullets ripping through it.

"Eff that."

The soldier in the middle jerked back as sun-sparkled blood sprayed into the air. The one to the right stumbled and fell. In the otherness, I could see his throat and lungs humming erratically as he choked. Thin streams of muddy water glittered as they rose from the ground to his face.

Penny took a second shot and dropped the drowning man.

I knocked the last one back with the stiffest gale I could conjure. Penny finished him with her next shot, and the gunfire tearing up the shed ended. Taking a shaky breath, I croaked out a question, "Anybody hit?" My senses already told me that they hadn't been, but my mind lagged.

Penny answered as she rolled away from the body toward us. "All clear, boss." She smiled.

I couldn't find any happiness in the killing, but we had survived with only two left to worry about. My stomach churned. "Good. I need to figure out this trap." We were in an open field with waist-high, dry brush.

Dean ran in a haphazard lope, cutting to one side then the next. He had to know about the other two soldiers, or just expected someone to fire on him. I feared the trap was close to me. I'd been the bait.

Using the shed as a block from our last pursuers' sight, I rose on my knees, peering in Dean's direction.

Chapter Thirty

Thin, wispy clouds hung in the sky in Dean's direction. A light breeze stroked the winter-dead tan brush. The air would have smelled fresh after the rain were it not for the sharp odor of spent gunpowder from Penny's rifle.

She glowered at me from where she crawled on the ground. "Get down, you idiot."

"Dean is coming —"

Roxie yanked at the sleeve of my coveralls, but I remained partially risen. I could wave him off at the last minute, if he saw me. To the north, the forest closed in on the road, but through the otherness I found no one waiting there. The two soldiers approaching from the other direction were still cautious. Perhaps the trap had been the waiting Youth Guard and the soldiers. However, Tyrell had been explicit when he'd said "alive."

Shuffling to the far edge of the cover of the shed, I focused in Dean's direction. The best I could do would be to send him away from us, then we could deal with the last threat.

A gunshot cracked in the silence. I'd already forgotten

the maelstrom of sound we'd just experienced, and my shoulders jumped.

Penny got a grip on the back of my coveralls and yanked me to the ground. I landed sideways on my elbow, refusing to turn away from Dean. He bound like a lightning bolt through the brush, as if they'd been firing at him.

"You're effing going to get shot — over him."

I tugged forward. "I would."

"Effing idiot."

"Perhaps."

She grunted, but let go of me. The two who'd been approaching stopped, low to the ground. The field ahead gave no hint of Dean, but I knew how close he'd gotten. In seconds, he would break through the brush, leap over the trampled fence, and reach me.

A chill clawed at my neck. I rose, not just to my knees, but to my feet, staring at the torn ground just inside the fence. There appeared no reason they needed to till the soil. Yet, it seemed to have been purposefully dug into.

During the early years at Camp Sparta, we often found werewolf traps people dug near their homes. Some were pits with stakes, and others had sharp-toothed animal traps with heavy hinges. We'd been warned to keep an eye out for tilled ground in strange places.

"Dean, stay back!" I began flailing my arms in the air.

Sunlit, shining silver fur puffed out, and trotting low to the ground, he came bursting from the brush. His head swiveled in the direction of the last soldiers, ignoring me. Blood soaked his muzzle. In three steps, he changed his pace to a tightly wound gait as his rear legs prepared for the jump over the fence.

"Don't!" I yelled. "It's a trap!" I gathered the otherness in a bellowing roar, as if to blow him aside with wind.

I wouldn't have the strength, I could tell. Instead, I

reached instinctively toward something easier. Moving Wati had been as easy as healing, with almost no exertion. I'd also seen the weakened connections.

As Dean leaped, I began to float. With otherness, I reached into that strange place where I altered gravity. Penny yelped behind me and swore with a flapping of her jacket. My action threatened to expose us all, but I needed to save Dean.

A gunshot cracked out, and my flinch pitched my body slightly, in fear that Dean would be hit. He maintained his form even as his leap did not arc, but he remained flying forward.

The shed behind me groaned with shrieks of metal. Andy coughed and moaned.

A single loud snap sounded from somewhere to my right. Metal clanged against metal, then another followed with a cacophony of crackling traps on the far side of the shed.

I released the otherness, and weight dropped me an inch to the ground with a jolt. Dean landed, nearly atop the unconscious Youth Guard. He growled, shook, and studied me.

I pointed to the turned soil inside the fence. "It was a trap, for you."

He shook his head, silver hair fluffing like a mane, then sniffed the body.

"Don't," I pleaded. "They can't hurt us."

Roxie lay frozen on the ground, eyes locked on Dean. A gunshot fired, and a bullet ripped through the shed.

Penny swore. "Can you stop being an effing standing target now? Wolf boy is safe, as safe as any of us."

Andy groaned and coughed from the other edge of the shed. I grimaced. He appeared okay.

I dropped down beside her as a second bullet tore

through metal. The shed's roof had been flattened, as if pressed on, and the side buckled out. "I did that." I stated it, though it was more a question to myself.

"Your whole gravity gig needs some work." Penny pointed at the back of the shed. Bullet holes dotted it. "Where is the closest?" She gestured with her hand, side to side, waiting for me to respond. Her arm lined up with one of them.

"There."

Penny jammed the tip of her rifle into one of the lower holes, then pulled the pistol from her pocket. "Turn your head. Cover your ears." She blasted three times. "Clear."

She'd made a slightly larger hole to the left of where her rifle poked through. Lying on her side, she pushed me back with her shoulder and sighted down the barrel. "Ears."

The gunshot still made me flinch. The soldier's humming slowed. "You got him."

"Yeah, thanks for the update."

"Caitlyn?" Roxie's voice, still slurred, carried concern.

Dean had approached, tongue lolling, and lay low, close behind me.

"Focus," Penny said. "Where's the other one?"

Her voice was distant through the ringing in my ears. I pointed, arm stretched over her head and down the length of the rifle. "He's not moving."

"But," she said almost gleefully, "he's got a shiny scope."

A distant gunshot sounded, and a bullet tore through the shed near where her rifle poked into the hole. Penny grunted, then fired. "Eff you." She slowly rolled onto her back, right arm remaining on the rifle until the end to lay across her chest. Her arm just above the elbow bled.

"You've been hit." I reached for her arm.

"Brilliant perception. One of your magical skills?" Her voice strained.

The otherness growled at my command, and I felt the damage as her blood wet my palm. The shot had grazed the muscle, ripping mostly skin. "It's not deep."

"Yeah, that's what it feels like, just a scratch." Her grimace told me otherwise.

I smiled and stopped the bleeding, working the bit of torn muscle. "We're clear. I don't sense anyone else around. The pain will take a lot longer to go away, but you should be fine."

Penny nodded, then glanced behind me. "Dude, your junk. Please."

Dean crouched behind us in his human form. His voice rasped as he spoke. "Not a lot of options at the moment." He swiveled so his side faced us. It didn't hide everything. "Hey Roxie. Sorry about scaring you."

"I'm fine." Her voice was tight.

Penny winced as muscle knitted. "We need to go help the Alliance. They had thirty-five vehicles that I counted. A quarter of those had armor and weapons mounted on them. We fought four of them last time."

"We're hours behind them."

"Two, maybe three, so we need to start now." Penny glared at me. "Those are my people." She nodded to Roxie. "Your ex still has some juice left, and you've got the whole gravity thing. I've got a rifle. Dean seems better than this morning."

He cocked his head, unsure. "I'd rather take a nap. Somewhere safe."

I lifted my hand off her arm, and she stretched it, wincing. "Good as new. Thanks."

Her wound would be stiff and sore. I stood, wobbling slightly. "We do need to go, but first —"

"Dude." Penny waved at Dean, who had risen when I did.

I glanced and smiled, then reached for his hand.

Penny stood, slung the rifle over her shoulder, walked over to the corpse of the Youth Guard, and started to strip him. "It'll be a tight fit, but it beats waving that effing thing around."

I hugged Dean. "Are you okay?"

"Fell off the horse," he said. "To be fair, I'd been trying to get off. Vanya got a good ways away before I realized she'd left you behind."

I frowned and studied him with the otherness. "You seem okay."

"She did a patch job. Tried to get me to stick with her. She was sure you'd be back." He took a deep breath and glanced at Andy. "Where's Wati?"

Closing my eyes, I leaned my forehead against his shoulder. "I don't know. I tried to send her back to Denya. She'd been shot and we were surrounded. I don't know what I did."

Dean patted my shoulder. "I'm sure she's home." He nudged his chin toward Andy. "That one's awake."

"He helped us."

A pair of damp coveralls slapped onto our heads. "Button it up, wolf boy."

He grabbed the clothes before they slid to the ground. "When did she get so cheerful?" he asked me with a light grin.

"When that bitch hopped in a truck and left. Effing lightning." Penny moved to the unconscious Youth Guard, and I tensed. She dug through pockets and secured another pistol with its holster and a canteen of water that I considered enviously. At least she wasn't going to kill him. I kept an eye on her.

Dean climbed into the bottom half of the coveralls. "Anyone got a knife?"

I wanted to hold him, but his expression grew tight and serious.

Roxie shook her head, still appearing rather terrified of Dean. She kept her body squared to him, and stepped back rather than forward when she adjusted. If she had her usual staff, I imagined she'd have had it in a firm grip.

Andy lifted his good arm and waved weakly. "I've got a knife."

"We trust him?" Dean asked, even as he strode toward Andy.

"Yeah. He risked himself to help." I wasn't about to mention him shouting my old unit's name. Dean would laugh.

Andy sat up, wincing and paler than when we'd met. He didn't have enough body mass to lose so much blood. His freckles were sharp against his light skin. "You're Dean." He tugged a knife from a sheath, offering the handle. "You can control it, just like Tyrell said. I saw you shift back."

Dean took the knife and shrugged. "What about it?"

"He said some scary stuff about soldiers."

Standing between me and the men, but facing Dean, Roxie turned her head and caught my eyes. "Turning them, and healing them into special soldiers."

"Eff me. That would be an added nightmare." Penny waved the extra pistol in its holster. "Anybody want this?"

"Wait, is that why they wanted Dean?" I asked. "Alive?"

Roxie nodded and spoke slowly with some words slurring. "He found out how you'd been healed after getting infected by Dean. He wanted you as much. It's the whole reason they sent me out here."

Andy groaned and laid back down. "She was supposed to be bait to get you to come near, then they'd capture you with the collar." He lifted his head. "How'd you get rid of it?"

Roxie studied my neck as well.

"Hey, loving the Camp reunion," Dean interrupted. Having sawed off the top of his coveralls, he handed the knife back to Andy. "We should leave."

My head reeled at the idea of creating werewolf soldiers and had a hard time imagining Tyrell liking the idea. I wouldn't ask Roxie why she'd agreed to be bait, not in front of everyone else.

"I'm not leaving him to die." I pointed at the stripped Youth Guard with a blistered chest.

Penny stepped up to me, glaring. "You were bit?"

I'd kept the secret from her and the others, for good reason. "No," I said.

Dean grabbed his jacket from where it had fallen on the ground and tossed it over his shoulder. "I puked on her. Can we go?"

She didn't back down, her green eyes locked on mine. "What other secrets?"

"I'm sorry. You were already upset about Dean."

Penny growled and turned toward the Youth Guard. "I say shoot him, then leave."

My legs trembled as I slid around her to try and heal what I could of the Youth Guard. "We're bringing Andy with us." She could hate me for lying; I understood that. Penny liked her anger.

She steamed, staring north as I knelt by the boy and rested my palms on his tortured chest. I still had her blood on my hands. My legs were so weak I didn't know if I could stand when I finished. Tears welled in my eyes, and I tilted my head so they wouldn't see.

Tyrell was on his way to kill Penny's people. I had no doubt they'd be treated like the families at the compound.

We did have to stop it, and Andy would slow us down. I'd slow us down.

When I stood and swayed, Dean caught my arm, pulling me into a hug. "I love you," he said.

My throat thickened. "I love you. I — they set a trap for you. I can't lose you."

He kissed me, ignoring the others. When he released me, he moved toward Penny, pointing at the holster dangling from her fingertips. "I'll take that," Dean said.

She shoved it at him. "We're wasting time. We'll never reach the enclave to be any help. It'll take four hours to walk from here."

Holding his jacket between his knees, Dean strapped on the holster. "Lucky we don't have to walk. Anyone know how to drive?"

Chapter Thirty-One

I jerked to study Dean's smug grin, my hands still on the ruined chest of the Youth Guard. "What are you talking about?"

Roxie shrugged. "I can drive."

I gawked open mouthed at them. When had Roxie learned to drive? Only the military had vehicles. Dean grinned wider and nodded at Roxie's comment, as if that answered everything. Her face was still dark and swollen, but it had already started to reduce.

Andy rose up on his good elbow. "I can drive too." His eyes fluttered and he lay back down. "Maybe not."

My patient healed slowly, stinking of burned flesh. I focused not just on the layers of burned skin, but the taxed heart trying to repair the damage. "He needs water."

Penny snorted and walked around the shed.

Andy groaned and began removing a canteen from his belt, one-handed. "Here. I didn't want to kill him."

I nudged my chin toward Andy, and Dean grumbled, moving to help. He would have been likely to side with Penny and leave the man to die. My healing would forestall any immediate danger, but someone would come checking the shed. The military had to have some concern of their own.

Dean retrieved and handed me the canteen. "We really need to go."

I sensed around us, but no one new had entered the area. "Another minute."

He forced a smile. "You okay?"

"I'm having a hard time staying awake, but I'm not damaged." I glanced at the disturbed soil inside the fence. "The traps under the dirt are for you."

"A lot of soldiers and your people" — he gestured to the man I had healed — "just to get you and me. I feel sort of honored they wanted us so bad."

Penny circled the shed. "You set off a bunch of traps. I poked around with the rifle. I think we can get out there. Ready?"

I sighed, lifting my hands off the boy. Dean grabbed me under the arm and helped me up. "There's a vehicle?" I asked, and got a wink in reply.

In a couple minutes, with Dean carrying a protesting Andy over his shoulder, we crossed the road to a blackened house that had retained its roof. According to the name on it, a Jeep had been parked behind the building close to a crumbling porch. We fashioned a sling for Andy, though he would do fine without it. Roxie maintained her distance from Dean, and Penny did not have the most welcoming glance for me. She took the front passenger seat without a comment.

Dean settled Andy into the spacious rear seat and asked, "What's the plan, boss?"

Andy studied my face with too much interest. I shouldn't be in charge, but no one else replied. Stepping around to the driver's side rear door, I opened it and stared at Penny. "Penny, where can we be the most help?"

"Behind them, causing chaos." She watched Roxie hesitantly peering at the controls without getting into the seat.

"That might get us killed quick." Dean closed Andy's door.

"Might," said Penny. I couldn't tell how she meant the comment.

Military maneuvers were not something we had talked about at Camp Sparta. We were just weapons for Tyrell; I realized that now. "We need a plan." I wanted one, at least.

"Let's just get there and figure it out on the way." Penny prodded at the area in front of her, opening a small cabinet.

"Keys," said Roxie.

Penny leaned over and dug at an open container between the seats. "The little metal things?"

Dean sighed and tossed his jacket on the back seat. "Let me check the body." He'd killed a man near here, and he jogged in that direction toward the woods behind the house.

The interior smelled like sweat and food, a nauseating mix. We had plenty of room with a high ceiling, and the windows had a dark tint. As kids, we'd crawled inside some of the junked cars around Camp Sparta, but this appeared in better shape. Paper wrappers dotted the floor. I leaned over the back seat. "Hey, food. Ammo boxes. Water."

"I'm hungry," said Andy. He winced when he tried to turn around.

I climbed in, grabbed a canteen, and passed it to him. Then, I handed back paper-wrapped flatbread sandwiches. "Pass these up front, too." I greedily eyed a jar of canned peanut butter, and my appetite returned. I hit a stash of shelled pecans in a burlap bag and nearly squealed.

When Dean returned with the keys for Roxie, I slid next to Andy with two sandwiches in my lap while munching on a handful of precious pecans. My words were little more than a mumble when I handed him a sandwich. "Found food."

He raised his eyebrows, then leaned over the seat, returning with my hidden peanut butter stash. "Any cheese? Pie? I'd kill for those."

Roxie fidgeted in the front, glancing at me through the mirror. Her swollen face made it difficult to read her expression, but I thought she was nervous. Before I finished my pecans and eyed the peanut butter, the vehicle roared to life.

She shifted one of the knobs, and the Jeep lurched toward the house, then stopped abruptly. My wrapped sandwich hit the floor, but I clenched the pecans until they crumbled.

"Sorry," Roxie said. "Wrong direction."

Penny wiped her nose with the back of her hand. "This driving stuff. Have you done much of it?"

"I was trained." A hair of the old Roxie came through her tone.

After another shifting of controls, we moved backward in a curve and into the crumbling porch before we lurched to a stop again. Roxie put a hand up between herself and Penny. "Don't even."

Penny chuckled, tucked up her knees, and pressed her boots on the area in front of her. "Not a word."

After a couple more maneuvers, we slowly circled the house and reached the street. Roxie sighed and we drove onto the road, weaving for the first few yards.

I nearly choked when the vehicle started beeping. "What's wrong?"

Roxie gestured to Penny. "Seat belt." Then she plucked at something on her chest causing a strap to shake that rose over her shoulder and clamped to the metal between the front and back doors.

Tilting and searching, Penny found hers, then studied how Roxie's fastened. It took a while before metal clicked and she appeared satisfied. We passed a rusted truck that had pulled to the side of the road.

The sandwich contained slices of herb-roasted chicken that brought back memories of the kitchen at Camp Sparta. Roxie only ate it if she became really hungry, and her sandwich sat in the bin between the front seats. Both of her hands were tight on the wheel of the car, so I didn't offer pecans.

Little by little, the Jeep sped up as she became more accustomed to it. My energy started to return as my stomach filled, but the passing trees made me queasy if I tried to watch out the window. I leaned against Dean's shoulder and plucked out a finger of honey-sweetened peanut butter.

"Thanks," Andy said to me.

I assumed he meant for the food, and I offered him the jar, but he didn't take any. I capped it and tucked it safely between me and Dean.

"For helping Derek, the guy I burned. I've never killed anything — anyone. Me and him were from Camp Morea and just arrived at Camp Sparta last week. That was cool, because we'd heard so much about you and the Wolf Squad."

I blushed slightly, remembering Selina's comments. "No problem." Hoping the conversation ended, I snuggled against Dean.

"There are plenty of us who want to rebel, just like you did." Andy said the last part with a whispered reverence and I cringed.

I closed my eyes, wanting Andy to stop. Dean chuckled slightly but didn't comment, or I would have punched him.

"There are those who believe you'll come liberate us." His tone ended too dramatically, and Dean laughed.

The conversation ended there. I didn't want to be their symbol or hero.

I woke later, with my head leaned against Dean's shoulder. He snorted, and we both straightened. Andy continued to snore quietly beside me.

The bumpy road had turned pitted and black beside one of the large, rounded trucks. Most of the vehicles we had passed were rusted, but some were burned. This one had been burst apart, and black scorched every part of it. An acrid scent wafted through the Jeep. The buildings around were burned, some to the ground.

"I fell asleep," I said, almost guiltily. My butt was stiff, but I felt worlds better.

"Dean snores worse than you," Penny said in offhand manner. She turned back to us and flashed a quick smile.

"How long were we asleep?"

She shrugged and tapped numbers on one of the instruments between herself and Roxie. "This had 1:16 on it when I noticed it." It had 3:38 displayed on it now. "More than two hours." She pointed at the houses. "We're close to the enclave. Southeast of it. An hour's walk."

I had no idea what the enclave really was, or where the fighting would take place. "Did the army come this way?"

Roxie flicked her eyes to mine in the mirror. "I believe so. They let me in on all their meetings at the end. Tyrell and Selina expected me to believe they trusted me and wanted me with the Youth Guard. I studied everything, like a fool." She spoke more clearly, and I wanted to believe some of the bruising had eased from my healing.

The sun had lowered far enough to my left that it flickered through the tinted window. It would be sunset in a couple hours. Sleepiness had faded, and my chest tightened at what lay before us. "When were they supposed to attack?"

Roxie swallowed. "They weren't sure when they'd meet the first resistance, but about now."

Penny straightened in her chair. "Can't you go faster?"

"I could." Her voice tight, Roxie focused out the front window. "I'm doing twenty now and want to keep us on the road. Any faster, I might lose control. I tried, remember?"

"Yeah. Still." Penny leaned forward. "You're doing better. You should try it again."

I guessed I'd been asleep, gratefully, during whatever they were referencing. We passed Dollar General with a fire-singed sign. The Jeep began to accelerate, and I rested against Dean instead of watching the outside pass by. His skin smelled like chicken, wood, and his leather jacket.

We wove at one point and slowed down, forcing me to close my eyes.

"Does the road curve up there?" Roxie asked, and the Jeep slowed again.

I didn't open my eyes and regretted eating so much. Dean shifted forward, disturbing my nest. "There's someone up there, on the right."

"Crap, crap. We're going to the left. Don't stop."

I sensed into the otherness as I opened my eyes. A Jeep, similar to our own, was parked at the entrance to a road branching off from ours. Woods surrounded both roads. Two men were scrambling down from the roof of their vehicle, rifles slung over their shoulders.

"They might fire on us," Roxie said. Her knuckles were pale on the wheel she had in an iron grip. "Slouch down. I'm in uniform."

Penny complied, knees to her chin. "Faster."

"It's a curve."

The men appeared confused. We were obviously in one

of their vehicles. They started walking from their road into ours. I hesitated, holding my breath as they stepped nearly in front of us, as if expecting us to stop.

"Don't," growled Roxie.

When it became clear we weren't stopping, they stepped back hurriedly. Just as we passed, they unslung their weapons.

"Go, go." Penny rose in her seat.

The road curved sharply in the direction of arrows on faded yellow signs. My head swiveled as I followed the soldiers. They still aimed their weapons, but they appeared to be arguing.

We were a dozen yards away when they aimed in unison.

"Shit," Dean said.

I started pulling in the otherness in a belated roar, but we weaved suddenly and I slid into Dean. The back window and the side window at the rear behind me cracked as a bullet tore through. Dean folded me down as Roxie yanked the wheel back. The Jeep sped as it whipped in a different direction.

Gunshots cracked behind us, and suddenly the Jeep careened wildly. First it turned one way, then the other, slowing all the time. A thudding sounded from underneath. I slapped into Dean and swayed toward Andy two wild swerves later, then the Jeep tilted to the right side.

Penny swore just before we crashed into something and jerked to a stop.

Chapter Thirty-Two

I was wedged between the two front seats, stopped only by the slight angle and my right knee. Dazed, I watched as Penny fumbled with the catch of her belt, her swearing growing louder. A burning scent wafted in the air. A door opened behind me, and I pushed back, righting myself as best I could in the slant.

Dean had jumped out.

Andy's eyes were wide, and his head snapped about. He'd awakened to chaos.

"Get out," I told him, then turned to follow Dean.

A bullet twanged off the top of the Jeep, and gunfire echoed dully in the forest. Dean's return shot cracked much louder, then the gunfire began in earnest. I paused at the opening of the door. Live oak and pine shaded the road. Dean had disappeared.

The glass on his door cracked with a gunshot, and I whipped around, peering from Penny to Andy. Both were trying to open their doors, to no avail. The front window had shattered, and I remembered once crawling over the front of a car's hood to the roof, only to have my foot fall through glass similarly broken.

"Penny, Roxie, push on the front window." I had to yell over Dean's return fire. He moved away from us.

Penny quickly jabbed her rifle muzzle, and it slid through. In three quick thrusts, she had a small opening cleared. Roxie had wormed around to the center and pushed a larger adjoining chunk with both hands. Bullets were clanging off the top of the vehicle, and my muscles clenched tighter with each one.

As Penny crawled out, I reached out with my otherness and sensed the two men far behind us, where they'd moved to the trees on the opposite side of the road. A bullet sung past me and tore a hole in the left side of Roxie's seat. It cracked into the instruments, but she had already squirmed into the middle between the two seats.

I shivered, blinking as she began to follow Penny, then gestured to Andy. "Go."

"Not until you go first." His lips formed a firm flat line, but he trembled, as pale as when I first healed him.

Opening my mouth to argue, I realized we'd be sitting targets while I flexed my protective instinct and his chivalry, or whatever drove him. I nearly bumped Roxie's feet as I crawled out of the Jeep. Glass poked into the knees of my coveralls, but didn't cut. Falling off the front nearly on top of her, I leaped up and reached for Andy; he appeared grateful as he stretched out his good hand. Less so when I whipped him across the hood toward me and over the edge.

"Grab him," I yelled to Roxie. Together we eased him to the ground.

Steam and a burning odor rose from the front of the Jeep. A tree tilted from where we'd crashed into it. Penny was already worming up the incline to the asphalt, her rifle ready.

I shifted to the forest side of the vehicle. Dean was

standing behind a tree far from the vehicle, dipping out to take a shot, then hiding as splinters flicked off the trunk.

The two soldiers were close to each other, barely six feet apart in my senses. "I'm going to distract them." My energy had recovered, but I didn't trust it fully. "Let me know when you're ready." I meant the latter for Penny.

"Alright, wait." Dean dropped down and moved closer to the men, creeping through brush in a crouch. I could see he was aiming for a rise around a large oak's roots.

Penny's voice was dead calm. "Ready."

I watched Dean and drew in a groan of the otherness; I wouldn't need much for what I planned, and the moist air would be easy to manipulate. My distraction would begin about twenty yards behind the men. Those of us who had skill with air had often used it to tease the younger kids at the camp. The two soldiers shifted and vibrated. They might wonder if we'd run away, or run out of ammunition.

Dean scrambled up the roots, two feet higher than he'd been before, and in a completely different place than where he'd been firing from. He saw me watching, smiled, and nodded.

Bundling air in a tight wad nestled among the leaves, I called out, "Now" I drew it through the debris and shrubs toward the men. For them, something would sound like it was rushing them from behind.

Penny rose to her knees, rifle cracking almost immediately. Dean fired two shots from my left before Penny got off her second shot. I could sense the vibrations from one of the men lessen as he tumbled to the ground. His partner burned with a vibrancy that told me he was wounded and not dead. Dean and Penny each took another shot before her weapon clicked empty.

She dropped to the ground cursing. Dean leaned

against his tree, sighting down his weapon, but he'd stopped firing.

The soldier crawled away through the brush.

Dean sprung off the roots, running in a crouch for the road. My heart leaped in my throat. "No, he's leaving."

Andy's call to the otherness roared behind me. The air chilled, then the rain-damp woods where the soldiers had been burst into flames. I sensed the vibrations of heat ahead and Andy's drawing in of the otherness behind. The wood and leaves did not burn, only the air itself.

Glaring back at us as if cheated, Dean turned and loped toward the Jeep. "Grab the ammo. Penny, better hope they have some for you. The guy stationed near the Jeep fired the same weapon."

She moved quicker than Roxie or me. Andy finally released the otherness with a weak gasp, the inferno vanished, and only a few random flames remained. The soldier had taken to his feet and was running away.

Roxie grabbed Andy's bad shoulder as he started to buckle, and the pain brought him up sharp. His nerves were still raw from the wound, but she couldn't cause any actual damage.

"I'm sorry," she said, wincing and pulling back. "Are you okay?"

Dean rummaged in the back, calling through the ruined vehicle. "Chat later. If anyone heard that gunfire, they're on their way."

I stretched out my senses as I moved for the Jeep. Nothing showed within range other than small animals. The pecans tempted me, but I climbed in and grabbed two nearly empty canteens while Penny and Dean rifled through ammo in the back. They were unaffected that we'd killed another man. I couldn't act with the same coolness, but Penny's people were in danger, and the fighting wouldn't end soon. I donned Dean's jacket even though the air wasn't cold yet.

There would be no more driving to the battle. I scanned the road ahead and swallowed my nervousness.

"This is the road," Roxie said from the front. "I'm sure of it. Instead of attacking from the south where the Alliance expects, Tyrell wanted to circle around to the west."

"Where the human families are," snarled Penny. "His little spy had to have told him that. Vanya better have gotten to them so they could evacuate." She replaced her magazine and tucked the spares into her pockets. Pointing her gun back toward where the soldiers had been, she continued, "That crossing is always guarded by Pahawan; it leads over one of the waterways that border the enclave. Werewolves don't like water."

I hadn't seen any water there, but we'd been busy trying to avoid bullets and find a tree to crash into. Dean shrugged, stuffing ammo into his coveralls pockets. "I like water."

She gave him a questioning glance, then walked up to the road. "If they've taken this road, they'll hit the farms, then the first houses. We have to hurry. The sun will be down in two hours."

I searched for the sun on the other side of the road where it burned through the upper canopy of the woods. "How long will it take to get to the houses?"

Penny frowned at Andy. "Half an hour walking. Can you run?"

"I'll try."

Roxie still steadied him. "No. He shouldn't."

The two locked eyes, then Penny snapped away and focused on Dean at the back of the Jeep. "You ready?"

He grinned as he held up two steel balls. "These are grenades."

"Christmas is early." Penny's droll response turned sharp. "If you're going to carry those, keep away from me."

I frowned. They were explosives; I knew that much. Beyond that, I didn't know how they worked.

Dean marched toward us, stuffing the steel balls in side pockets at his knees. "Might come in handy."

Penny took the lead with a brisk step that formed a gap, Roxie and I walked on either side of Andy, and Dean trailed two paces behind us. The woods were thick, untouched by fire. The asphalt had crumbled and pitted as all roads had, but we kept a decent pace. However, no matter how fast Andy strode, Penny always scowled back at us. These were her people.

Andy shivered on occasion, and his face remained pale.

Roxie kept checking with him. "How are you doing?"

"I'm good. Tired, but I can do this." He glanced at me and nodded.

My focus on the otherness peaked when we found the first Pahawan dead on the side of the road near a tiny rusted car pulled nearly into the woods. Their armor had been cracked, and pieces had shattered off from too many bullets. Penny whispered a name when she knelt over them, then growled and marched forward before we reached the body. She had a dozen paces on us.

Curious, I stopped to pick up a shattered piece of armor, tapping into the otherness. Layers of hardened air expanded and contracted with my magic. The formation was simple, though I could not determine what made it hard. Blustering shields that we learned at Camp Sparta seemed a thin sheet compared to this steel. Tired, I let go, and air blew my hair back as it exploded into its natural density.

Andy coughed and pointed to an angry Penny twenty paces ahead, facing us with her legs in a wide stance.

Roxie spoke quietly. "Her family is there?"

I strode for the road. "She doesn't have any family like that, from what I understand."

In the pale blue sky, a smudge of smoke drifted ahead and to our left. The breeze carried it quickly before it could rise too high, but we could see it where the leafless branches broke through the live oak and pine.

"Looks like we're late to the party," Dean said. His tone carried no humor. He always tried to make light of situations, even the worst ones.

"Do you think that's from the Youth Guard?" I asked.

Roxie and Andy both agreed, and she added, "Andy's not the only one included for his abilities with heat. They are the bulk of Tyrell's support squads, from what I could tell."

"Last time there was more gunfire from snipers and others in the woods. He planned on us burning out nests, as he called them." He spoke with a huff at each pause, and I let the conversation end.

Only minutes later, a second Pahawan lay in the distance, and Penny jogged up to them. We were getting close to the fighting. I barely sensed any animals around. Cringing as I passed the corpse, I wondered if the Duathua had any chance against the armed soldiers. This might be a slaughter we couldn't hope to stop.

"Is that how the Alliance repelled the last attack, by attacking from the woods?" The trees thinned ahead to the right. I swore I heard dull gunfire.

Andy nodded. "Mostly. The humans had barricades as well. The Duathua don't do well against gunfire or magic. After we had to reposition, they attacked the sides, according to the reports."

Roxie scanned the woods around us, then tugged on her coveralls. "I hope they figure out we're here to help."

"There's no one around us," I said.

"Yeah, how does that work? You seemed to know where they would come from." She never liked not knowing anything.

I drew in a tight breath, thinking of Vanya and her training. "I learned how to sense through the otherness. People, or anything living, are easy to find within a certain range. I'm getting better at it."

Andy giggled. "Othersense? That is way too cool."

I smiled at him, but felt no mirth. People were dying. "Yeah. It is."

Penny ran toward another fallen Pahawan, and my hopes dwindled. We had to try. From what Roxie described, Tyrell intended to attack the Alliance's families as quickly as he could, rather than just their defenders. She took longer than I expected, then began stalking toward us, searching the woods.

"It might have been a dog, but something has been ripping at the body." We met, and she didn't slow, turning in step with us. "With the guards retreating to the enclave, werewolves could have gotten through."

My senses bristled, but found nothing. "I don't find even a dog."

She pointed past the open fields ahead to the right. "That's the old salvage yard where we get our metal." A sign and drive angled off the road. The farms are just ahead." Her face tightened. "We'll be in the open if we stick to the road."

Dean grunted. "You lead. We'll follow. You know the area."

A wire fence, mangled in many sections, surrounded the salvage area containing rusted sheds, trucks, and massive containers. A breeze brought the scent of smoke and the reminder of the battle ahead. Weeds grew heavily where a drive had circled through it, but Penny strode through them as if they weren't there on her way toward the woods at the back.

"There's a dirt road we'll cross ahead, then cut through houses we don't use, just south of the outer farms." She gestured toward the road. "It'll keep us parallel, though we need to keep a sharp eye out."

I focused on the otherness ahead — my othersense, and reached out as far forward as I could. "We're clear."

Andy stumbled often, especially navigating the flattened fence in the back, so Roxie and I stayed by his side. Dean passed us and joined Penny a few yards ahead. The dirt road became clear from the lack of life in the otherness and a thin patch in the trees. Heavier smoke rose into the sky from multiple locations. Between our noisy steps, I caught muffled gunfire. My pulse rose, and I imagined smelling the fires.

Penny reached the road, glancing first one direction, then the next. I sensed nothing except one fading body at the far edge of my othersense. Taking deep breaths, I tried to calm myself. I needed to be alert, not panicked. The attacking guards had rattled my nerves, and the bodies of the Pahawan had left me fighting hopelessness. Penny's people, maybe Dean's and my people, needed our help.

A crunch sounded behind me, and I spun to the right as Andy stumbled forward. Roxie whirled as well. It took us both a moment to catch the spotty gray coat of a werewolf racing toward us.

Chapter Thirty-Three

The otherness howled from both of us. Roxie's magic hit the werewolf first, bursting it into flames before my gust slammed into it. It cried out as it flew, fire coating its skin before the hairs themselves ignited. The scent of burning flesh reached us. As the wolf arced into the air, a second raced in at Roxie's side.

"Roxie!" I pulled in a shriek of the otherness and blasted air toward it. My impromptu magic was too weak to blast it away, but the wind slowed it as Roxie stepped back and turned to face it.

Dean's gun blasted and the cryptid jerked aside, toppling into the brush. Penny fired before it rolled once.

I didn't see the one that attacked from behind. My othersense had been so focused ahead of us that I left us exposed from the rear.

Teeth clamped into my right forearm, barely piercing Dean's leather jacket, but tearing with weight and momentum as it dragged me to the ground. Pain shocked me, and the woods spun with Roxie's angry features as I fell to my back. Gunpowder, burned flesh and hair, and the musty scent of the werewolf filled my nostrils.

My head turned to the creature as it released my arm. Sharp teeth remained exposed as it turned toward my face and neck. Muscles in its jaw and shoulders rippled with movement.

A bellow of the otherness swelled inside its head, and the air beside my face turned freezing cold. The rhythms of the cryptid's brain and even eyes spiked as heat steamed from it. Its tongue swelled and twitched as the body locked. Andy was doing this. I could tell the difference between his magic and Roxie's.

I rolled away, wincing as my body pinned my arm for a moment.

"Caitlyn." Roxie leaped over the falling body, nearly landing on me. "How bad?"

Lying on my back, I didn't send otherness to the wound first, but to the surrounding area. "I'm sorry."

Roxie leaned over me and pulled aside my braid that had wound about my neck. Andy shifted into view, sitting upright. In seconds, Dean and Penny were there.

No other werewolves; nothing hid around us. "We're clear. I was focused on the area ahead of us. Never checked behind."

Penny's expression remained tight. She focused on my arm. "You've been bit. Again."

I lifted my hand with a grimace. The holes in the leather were barely visible, but blood had trickled out and down my fingers, staining them. "I'll be okay."

Dean knelt opposite Roxie.

Resting my arm on my chest, I focused healing to my blood. Expecting the same infection, I grew surprised when I found my own body rejecting and destroying altered blood. Still aiding it with healing, any residue disappeared within a minute, and I worked on closing torn flesh and the damaged muscle. "I think I might be immune."

Roxie flashed a weak smile, as if unsure what to believe. From Penny's tilting head and set jaw, she wasn't assured in the least. I expected a comment, but she just took a deep breath, scanned the woods, and stepped away toward the dirt road. "Someone had to have heard the gunshots. If you can walk, we should get going."

Dean snarled. "Give her a second." If it had been someone else, he'd have likely said the same. Reaching over with my left hand, I held it out for him. He took it quickly and squeezed.

The last werewolf had died gruesomely, but I didn't feel any regret, just disgust. Andy's magic had been timely and efficient, and I appreciated not having a flaming wolf that close to me. Leaning up, I let Dean pull me to my feet. My arm throbbed, but it had been healed. "Thank you," I said to him as we both stood.

Andy beamed. "Wolf Squad."

Dean chuckled, but I just smiled. "Wolf Squad," I said with slightly less enthusiasm than Andy. Eric had been part of the unit, and the name reminded me of losing him. The only one I had left to care about from that time was Roxie, and she was with me, if not safe.

She touched my shoulder lightly. "Wolf Squad."

Penny had reached the road again, peering up and down. She avoided my eyes when she glared back at us and gestured sharply for us to follow. "Effing clear."

I kept a lopsided hold on the othersense, with most of the focus ahead and to the sides, but not all. The dirt still had puddles and mud. A pair of tracks had crossed our path, back and forth since the rain, leaving clear prints. It seemed more a driveway leading to a low house that I watched. The road we had been traveling on lay to our right, barely visible past a group of rusted cars.

The smoke plumed thick now, hazing the sun. We all

looked to the right as we padded across a damp yard easily visible from the main road. Rust colored the old siding on the two houses across the road. Penny headed there, jogging across the asphalt. The muffled gunfire sharpened on occasion at the whimsy of the wind.

I spoke just loud enough that Penny could hear. "I sense someone dying off to the right, perhaps on the far side of the road."

She didn't respond, leading us into the woods behind the houses and keeping us within sight of the road, but in the shadows with the sun so low. We had one short metal fence to climb behind the third house, before the woods ended at the edge of a deep field with low uniform brush and only the occasional tree to break the view. We'd be easy to spot.

"Wait." I focused the othersense into the woods beyond and found faint vibrations. The rhythms were too low to be alive. "There's someone dead ahead of us." I pushed to my right, to the far side of the road and found even more. "There too." I gestured.

Penny nodded, watching my arm, not my eyes. "That's it?"

I returned my focus to include a distance behind us. "Yes."

"We likely took our first stand here at the outer farms." She climbed over a white fence and dashed for the first tree in the field.

As I followed, I caught a glimpse of flame down the main road. Trees and houses blocked it all but a flicker. I pointed it out to Roxie and Andy and inhaled the sharp scent of burning wood. We were close.

After we crossed the massive field and climbed another white fence, we passed the bodies of two Alliance humans, but I could sense so many more in the woods around us.

The metallic odor of blood mixed with spent guns and distant burning wood.

Penny murmured names as we passed but didn't stop. Dean took a rifle from one and dug in pockets for extra ammo, earning him a momentary glare from her, but she said nothing while she waited.

Within a minute of entering the woods, there was no doubt of the fires. Smoke hazed our view, and flames rose from the trees ahead of us. Gunfire cracked clear and continuous.

Penny stopped, holding her jacket against her nose. "If those fires stretch too far to the south, we might get bogged down in the marsh and rivers. It'll take us a long time to circle around to the join the fight."

I pointed ahead and to the right, where a smaller fire burned. "That's where the fighting is." If we were going to do this, I wanted to cause some damage. "We might be able to create more of a distraction from behind. I don't think they heard us with the werewolves, or I'd have sensed men on the main road."

Penny finally met my eyes. "It's risky."

Andy spoke quietly, but with pride. "Wolf Squad."

I flicked a hand to silence him. He wasn't helping with that. "I can pinpoint where they are. We should find a place where we can pick them off. The smoke will help." It might hinder too.

She searched each of our faces, then nodded. Her deadpan expression almost broke when she said, "Wolf Squad."

I groaned, but smiled. If we did draw some of them off, we could retreat east, I hoped.

She marched us toward the road in a crouch. There we found asphalt, smoke, and bodies. Soldiers dotted the road-sides. Flames flicked from the woods on each side of the road ahead. The fire on the right raged closer; the one on the other side burned far enough back that we only saw the tops of engulfed trees. Gunfire snapped and echoed, dull and sharp.

We all jogged in a ragged line behind Penny, with Dean taking the rear. There were no bodies on this section of the road to stare at me as I passed. The heat from the fire to our right warmed the air. It engulfed a house as well as trees and threatened a second house beside fields. Smoke hazed the area, but I caught my first sense of a person ahead of us.

"Wait." I dropped to a low crouch, and Penny did the same. I pointed straight down the road. "One person, as if standing guard."

Penny peered ahead. "I wish you could effing aim."

"Roxie's good with a rifle."

"She can't othersense them like you can. Should we have you try?"

"It would just warn them." It might also be one of the Youth Guard. We should be sure.

Besides the fire immediately behind us, the forest to our left had a larger area with raging flames, just deep enough in that it didn't pose an immediate threat. On the opposite side of the road, two smaller fires kindled in spots beyond the fields behind the house. Between was just smoke. I pointed where I sensed the person. "The woods to the right we can reach without getting too close to those other fires."

She nodded, gesturing to the field of short, dried brush. "Let's cut behind the woods and see what kind of havoc we can stir."

"Yeah."

We trotted as a group, and within a few steps I caught a second person. "They're not alone."

"How close?" Penny asked through her sleeve.

"Fifteen yards." We hadn't gone that far before I started

to slow. "Make that fourteen. They appear to be guarding the area." I recognized the rhythms of one who appeared to be using the otherness. "One's a Youth Guard." A chill crawled up my neck as I noted Penny's rifle ready in her hand. She would shoot them without hesitation. Killing a werewolf was one thing, maybe even a soldier, but one of my kind felt different. "Roxie, Andy, do you have a way to disable them without killing them?"

Squinting, Penny darted a quick frown back at me. Dean stepped up to me and laid his hand on my shoulder. I expected his expression to be hard, but he appeared pained, as if understanding my plight.

"I don't want to kill them," I said to Dean, though they all could hear. "Any of them."

Penny spun, stepping close to me. "Those assholes are murdering people I love and care about. We just killed half a dozen soldiers to escape. Do my people deserve to die, now that we are free?"

Dean squeezed my shoulder. "It is easier when we're defending. However, a few days ago, when the soldiers were slaughtering those families, I would have killed them. It is no different now."

In the heat of the moment, I might have agreed. I winced, realizing what was different, and it felt selfish. "Some of those soldiers — are Youth Guard."

Snorting, Penny turned away from us. "I should have effing known when it came to —"

"Some of them would join the Wolf Squad." Andy interrupted with a confidence I didn't feel.

Roxie nodded with a tilt of her head as if agreeing, but not as confidently. "Selina and Tyrell weeded through a lot of them, but some of those present might have reservations, like Emery and Kim. If I can get close enough, I'll burn them enough to keep them from being able to focus."

Roxie's suggestion would put herself at risk, and I balked internally at that idea. Penny was right. I picked and chose who to protect, and I hadn't committed to her people as I had to my own. In truth, I couldn't easily make the decision who to protect or harm. In my othersense, a third person joined the other two. The sounds of gunfire hadn't abated.

"There's a third." I peered into Dean's eyes. Moonjir had said I should search there if I had a difficult decision. "I want to help, but don't want to kill the Youth Guard if I can help it."

"If we help, playing safe won't always be an option. I'd say they chose their side, now we choose ours." He nudged his chin toward Penny. "Tyrell and his army are the wrong side. Penny and her people need our help. Seems simple."

A fourth, wielding the otherness, clustered just at the edge of my awareness. We had a chance to disturb the attack against the Alliance, and it *was* the right side to be on. "There's a fourth. All in the same area. Let's go."

Chapter Thirty-Four

Penny and Dean took the lead, crouching as they jogged toward the smoky woods ahead. Each breath of acrid air threatened to choke me. Gunfire barked ahead and farther away to the right. The damp brush crunched under our feet.

The scattered group I sensed in the otherness increased as someone ran in from the north. "Five now." I coughed, and my throat tightened as I took a breath.

Fires burned in trees to the right of us, competing with the brightness of the sun dangling at the top of the tree line. The people we were about to ambush were in an opening, possibly the curving road. The sun might be in our eyes.

Within a few steps into the sparse, sunlit woods, my othersense picked up a large group of combatants to the north. The wind from the south brought drifts of smoke from the heavy fires there. "Wait," I called just loud enough for Dean and Penny to catch. Gesturing along what I believed was the road ahead of us, I spoke. "There's a much larger group there."

I could make out the otherness swelling and roaring as the Youth Guard worked magic where I indicated. Gunfire was a random cacophony in the air that seemed to come from a wide arc ahead. Bodies, soldiers and Pahawan, littered the ground and asphalt. Directly ahead were larger shapes in the smoke that had to be vehicles.

"How many?" asked Dean.

"Too many to count." There were wounded and dying among them. My othersense resisted definition of the rhythms. "They're mostly Youth Guard."

Andy peered directly ahead. "We were supposed to keep behind the soldiers."

"Those houses up there, a couple are — were populated."

I pulled in the otherness and added to the breeze, clearing some of the smoke. The sun glared bright and gold, but four bulky army Jeeps of various designs were spaced along the road leading north. The carnage of a battle left corpses strewn everywhere. We were forty yards away from the closest and largest vehicle. A soldier stood guard between that Jeep and the next in line, his back to us. Everyone else I sensed was on the far side, closer to the battle. The sole Youth Guard worked with the otherness at the farthest vehicle.

Dean gestured to the scanty shelter of the woods around us. "If we could draw them this way, we could pick off a few. Might disrupt their position."

Penny moved to a heavy fallen log and kicked it. "Pretty rotted. Not much cover. I'd rather use those metal vehicles for cover. They look effing solid, especially that last one."

"Pop the back one, draw the small guard in, and clear the area. We can use cover and smoke to keep hidden." Dean shrugged.

Roxie knelt beside me. "I can't reach those trucks with heat. They're like forty yards out or more. Water I could do."

Dean hefted one of the steel ball grenades. "Yeah, I need to get closer too."

I wasn't sure what his weapon could do, but it was worth a try. "No, you don't. I can push them with air."

He bounced it in his palm, making me nervous. "They're heavy. Don't want to make a mistake."

Pushing down a reflexive panic tightening my chest, I put out my hand. They were heavy. "No problem. Throw it as far as you can; I'll just need to push from behind, not really lift. Aim high."

He smiled. "No regrets." Taking a step beyond the tree trunk closest to us, he pulled a pin from the top and launched it into the air.

I drew a tight gust behind the steel ball and propelled it forward, which turned out to be more difficult than I'd believed. It wobbled in flight, and I shifted to keep it aimed at the closest vehicle. I had seen the damage of exploded vehicles, but these were military vehicles.

Focusing, I fought to keep the ball high enough, hoping to break a window. Interacting with my othersense gave me a tight connection to the nuances of my air magic. Even as it lost some momentum, I had excellent control at the end.

The grenade bounced against the window without breaking it. It never reached the ground, exploding with a flash near the front tire. The soldier ahead screamed as he went down. The vehicle tilted as the tire shredded, but otherwise remained intact. I had imagined a bigger explosion. The windows didn't even crack.

Dean didn't give me a warning when he threw the second grenade. The otherness roared as I pulled it in and gathered air. This time I aimed to get under the rear end. I'd seen how much of the explosion had pushed upward when the last one flashed.

Two of the four people nearby were heading toward the damaged vehicle and soldier. "Two are coming toward us."

Penny and Dean both dropped to a crouch, leaving me feeling exposed. I refused to lose my focus and only needed a couple more seconds. The acrid smoke took some of my breath, but I held my ground. A small group, three people, were approaching from a quiet area of the woods to the right. I'd worry about them in a moment.

As I pushed the steel ball artfully toward the rear tire and underside, Tyrell rounded the front, kneeling to check on the downed soldier. I blinked in surprise while the grenade smoothly bounced under the vehicle. The immediate explosion rocked the metal body and tore tires.

Tyrell caught some of the blast shooting from underneath the front bumper. I winced as the soldier spiked with new injuries.

Tyrell's rhythms vibrated in damage and pain all along his right leg. He rolled away from the seemingly undamaged vehicle, jumped to a staggering stance, and limped toward the battle, leaving the dying soldier.

My shoulders flinched to my ears when Penny and Dean fired in unison. I thought at first they were shooting at Tyrell, but a uniformed officer buckled at the far end of the line of vehicles. His gun fired belatedly. Penny put a second shot into him, and he dropped flat.

"Caitlyn." Roxie pushed down on my shoulder, reminding me to hide.

In the othersense, I tracked Tyrell, limping toward the larger mass of Youth Guards. A soldier raced to join him, seeming to cover his escape. The remaining Youth Guard stalked toward the line of vehicles as otherness gathered in a massive swell along our little section of trees. The massive span of it circled ten yards in diameter.

"Watch out." I pushed into the area of otherness around us, diverting a small dome of three yards.

Lightning hummed around us, then crashed up from the ground, sizzling through puddles and the dead bodies into the clouds above. Trees cracked behind me. Andy cried out in pain.

My hair rose in the onslaught, but a chill ran up my spine. I assumed it was Selina.

"Where?" Roxie whispered beside me.

Fixed on Selina through the othersense, I pointed at the third army vehicle. "Six yards past that truck."

As the lightning died off, the otherness roared from Roxie. Flames consumed the air behind the vehicle. I squinted as the blast knocked a pale-skinned Selina backward. As it extinguished, I was left with the afterimage.

"She's farther back," I said, unsure if I truly wanted Roxie to kill Selina.

"I don't have the range."

Selina rolled to her feet, fired a revolver in our general direction, and raced after Tyrell. He'd reached the larger group and blended into it. The trio far to the right were trying to steal in our direction through woods.

"We've got three over there." I gestured without a glance.

Penny rose slightly. "We should use that truck at the end for cover."

Dean led the way, and I turned to find Andy. His coveralls steamed on his good arm, but he was up and ready to follow. He'd been the farthest behind us. Trees and ground smoked, but nothing had ignited from Selina's lightning.

"You okay?" I asked Andy.

He smiled but obviously favored his already sore arm. "I'm in. A little stunned, that's all."

I grabbed his good arm and steadied him to follow the

others. Leaving him in the woods might have been a good idea, but we might have company come in from behind, and he wouldn't know it until it became too late. We had to stay together.

"You almost took out Tyrell," he said. His tone pitched with excitement; that was more emotion than I felt.

"The lightning came from Selina." I coughed from the smoke.

"Yeah, she's the strongest and has a wicked range. They've lost their command center, though." He beamed at me.

I didn't know what that would mean to the army's attack, but it seemed important. Penny and Dean had reached the vehicle we'd blasted with grenades and positioned themselves to fire. The soldier was dead, his rhythms beyond faded. We passed ten bodies of soldiers and a Pahawan to reach the asphalt and vehicle. The sun burned orange through the smoke.

Roxie watched me. "Where is everyone?" She gestured toward the woods where the trio stalked, and ahead to the larger mass.

Whatever response we'd expected from the Youth Guard ahead hadn't happened yet. The three were getting close, but with the thick haze of acrid smoke, neither of us would spot the other until we were on top of each other.

"We are a good sixty yards from the main group. Tyrell and Selina are there, somewhere." I frowned. The trio were altering their path, directly toward us. Focusing, my eyebrows shot up and my head swiveled to peer into the smoke. "Vanya. She's with two others."

Penny did not relinquish her cover, but her tone was harsh and worried. "Where?"

"North, northeast of us. She must know we're here." Of

course she did. If I'd been paying attention, her rhythms were obviously unique.

"How'd she effing end up behind the lines?" Penny asked. We both knew I couldn't answer that.

I focused down the road and noted the changing mass. "They're spreading out." The Youth Guard buzzed with the otherness as their earlier clusters around what I assumed were more vehicles pushed out at the sides. If they continued too far to my right, they might find Vanya and the others who were moving too slowly. She would sense them, though. "I think they mean to form a front aimed at us."

Penny grimaced. "Good. Then they'll ease up on the Alliance."

"We're talking twenty Youth Guards," I said.

"Tell me when to start firing."

That would give our location away. I nudged Andy closer to the others. I would have to protect them when all hell broke loose. "Roxie, Andy, how far can you send your fire?" Burning air had not been a thing when I was at Camp Sparta.

"Thirty yards, effectively," said Roxie.

Andy smiled. "Maybe forty."

"They're maybe fifty yards plus, still spreading themselves out."

"Vanya?" asked Penny.

"The same, and in no hurry." I took in a deep breath and regretted it. Coughing, I fought drawing the otherness in an attempt to clear the air. At varying distances, fire raged nearly all around us, though only a glimpse or two of flame showed through the haze at any one moment depending on the shifting winds.

Whatever disturbance we'd created with attacking Tyrell, it hadn't affected the constant gunfire. The larger mass had shifted into the line, curving as if to encircle us, though it hadn't reached halfway around.

"Where are they?" Andy asked.

I gestured the breadth of the present arc the Youth Guard formed. "Not moving closer yet." The left side proved nearer. "I think they're centered on the woods where Selina attacked. Maybe they didn't realize we moved." They wouldn't have. My breath hitched, and I choked. "Soldiers. To the left. They're about eighty yards out and moving fast in our direction. Maybe thirty of them." My pulse sped. I couldn't stop bullets.

I pulled in the otherness, and Roxie frowned at me. Holding my hand out, I pulled the air into a thick mass. At Camp Sparta, we made wind shields, but they moved. I was trying to make something similar to Kudara, just thicker. It didn't reach the hardness level and taxed my energy. Shrugging to Roxie, I focused on the othersense, trying to determine where all the players were on the field in front of us, and Vanya and her people to the side. I didn't forget to check behind us either. The werewolf attack had taught me that.

I sighed, relaxing slightly. "Vanya's shifting away from the Youth Guard."

She had turned her group in a sharp angle and sped up to a slight jog. It led to the area behind us, between where we'd first attacked Tyrell and our present position. My biggest concern came from the charging soldiers from the west. The sun hung over their location, and smoke fully covered any sign of them except in my othersense.

A group of Youth Guards had spaced themselves about three yards apart and turned, so I murmured a warning. "The Youth Guard is approaching now."

"Tell me when to light up the left side," Andy said. His

voice was too eager. "We'll let them know the Wolf Squad is here."

Penny scoffed, but she'd repositioned toward the sun, ready for the quicker threat. Dean had taken a new position on the ground, aiming through the thin space under the vehicle left by the ruined tires.

My eyes flicked in one direction, then the next, until I finally took Vanya's advice and closed my eyes. It gave me the most cohesive view in the othersense. What she'd taught me might save all our lives. Roxie and Andy's fire appearing unseen might give the Youth Guard something to worry about. Some might break before they ended up scorched. I'd have to thank Vanya properly, especially after being such a grumpy student.

Far behind the Youth Guard, along what I assumed was the road, tight clusters of people were moving too fast to be on foot. Six vehicles were racing up behind the line of Youth Guards. "We've got more soldiers coming in vehicles. North, from the north."

Penny swore. "Pull back. I'll stall them."

"No regrets," Dean said at my feet.

The otherness swelled, but not around us. Behind us, toward the area we'd been hiding previously, it grew, preparing to strike. Vanya and her two people were jogging right into it.

"No," I whispered. My push did nothing except affect only the closest edge four yards away. I drew in a panicked breath, and some of the otherness deserted Selina's control to stream into me, but not enough.

Chapter Thirty-Five

My eyes were closed when the lightning hit. Lines of light burned through anyway. In the othersense, I saw the strike that killed Vanya. My pulse thudded in my chest as my knees weakened.

Her rhythms flared and burned out in a moment, along with those of her companions. Puddles steamed, and the corpses twitched. My eyes opened in the aftermath, and I made out Vanya's falling body by the tuft of flame climbing her dress. Lightning left twisted lines in my teary vision, saving me from the full image of her mangled body.

"Vanya." My throat thickened and barely squeaked out her name. I had known her days and owed her so much. She would never know how grateful I was.

Andy's pull of the otherness roared in my ears, but I didn't turn. The smoke weaving between me and Vanya glowed orange with his fire.

Dean, legs stretched toward the scorched ground and Vanya's body, called me back to the maelstrom. "How close are the soldiers?"

When I turned, Andy's fire flickered out, giving way to the smoke. The Youth Guards closest on the left had stalled, with some pulling back. The soldiers were undeterred, racing toward us.

Penny had tears on her cheeks, but faced the threat, not our losses.

"Sixty yards, plus."

The otherness formed in the air high above me, and I drew it in, teeth clenched. Somehow I knew it wasn't Selina's. The air heated six feet over us but never ignited.

The line of vehicles was still behind the semi-circle of Youth Guards but gaining quickly. My mind numb with Vanya's death, I rattled off what I could glean from the othersense. "The six vehicles have between four and six soldiers each. The Youth Guard have pulled back on the left side but are closing to fifty yards at the center and the right."

Selina's otherness pushed closer to us, and I drew it in with a snarl. It seemed to well up inside me, begging to be let out. As lightning crackled weakly behind me, I drew a fierce tornado down the path of thirty soldiers. Badly aimed, it scooped up three near the front, toppled a handful more, but the bulk swarmed around it.

I felt the shift of gravity stir around us.

"Don't." Penny whipped a glare at me. It would only debilitate us, and I doubted I could reach that far afield to hamper them.

A bullet clanged off one of the vehicles toward the middle. Then more pinged in streams as the soldiers avoided my tornado. Andy roared with otherness again, and this time I squinted against the flare of burning air just under the dim sun. It fell far short of the oncoming soldiers but caused them to spread out. The Youth Guard started to pull back, unwilling to run into the flames.

"The soldiers are still a dozen yards and spreading out." My voice grew dull, cold. I wanted them dead and hated it.

A double twang of bullets against metal glanced off our cover then sprayed across the next vehicle. Roxie edged closer to Penny at the back of the vehicle, and Andy neared Dean, leaving me at the corner just behind the ruined wheel.

One of the Youth Guard in the middle had slowed, pulling out of formation. As the otherness concentrated around us, I knew it was Selina. I drew it in like guzzling water and felt how tired I became as it filled me. The air crackled and my hair puffed, but no lightning formed.

"How close?" asked Andy.

I focused on Selina and barely heard the torrent of bullets raining against the vehicles. Windows crackled. Unlike the beast of a truck we hid behind that reminded me of a heavy-duty Jeep, the other three parked on the road were plain Jeeps like the one we'd crashed. The bullets tore into them while ricocheting off ours. The sharp smell of petroleum drifted in the breeze.

I sensed otherness building from behind as I pushed through my weariness to form a maelstrom high above Selina. The air behind us ignited in a flash that reflected on the window of our cover. Heat melted some of my hairs with a sharp, noxious stench as the blast slammed my chest into the corner of the vehicle, and I grabbed warm metal with both hands.

The tornado I had dropped on Selina proved badly aimed. It threw her a few yards, then churned uselessly across the ground and puddles.

Andy stopped waiting for me to respond and unleashed a fury of flame toward the soldiers approaching from the west.

"Too short." My voice croaked after inhaling so much smoke. We would never be able to stop the two groups of soldiers and the Youth Guard descending on us. Our little distraction would likely not help the Alliance, and we would die here. Andy's fire had forced a few soldiers to pause, but they were moving again, and the bullets hadn't stopped. One of their shots would find us.

"How close?" Andy repeated. His voice was low, and he sounded as tired as I was.

"I'd guess forty yards; so are the closest Youth Guard to the north." Their group stretched over the road. They were near the last vehicle in the line. The soldiers in the military trucks would reach us before then.

"Do you smell the fuel?" Penny asked. I could barely hear her over the gunfire. "Where is it coming from?"

"The other Jeeps in our line." I gestured north up the road, but she remained focused to the west. The only scent I could make out came from the melted ends of my hair and smoke.

"Tell me when they're close to the farthest Jeep," Roxie said quietly. It lay about thirty yards away.

A fresh hail of bullets forced Penny to press against the back of the vehicle. Numbed by Vanya's death, I didn't flinch; instead, I ground my teeth. "The other soldiers will be here before then. They look like they're heading behind us."

A swelling of otherness, not Selina's, grew above and just behind us, and I drained it. Even that effort taxed my energy, but I squashed the magic before it started. From the amount of otherness that swelled inside me, threatening to burst through my weary control, it could have been several attacks that I drew in.

The two groups of soldiers seemed ready to converge upon us nearly simultaneously. I wanted Roxie and Andy to burn them. The Youth Guard at either end of their line had slowed, letting the center near Selina march forward. I was disabling the occasional bouts of magic, but too much more, and something might get through. A concentrated fire or lightning would be disastrous as tightly packed around the vehicle as we were.

"Get ready, Andy." I leaned against the metal. The soldiers from the west were spread out; he wouldn't be able to succeed in a concentrated attack since he'd grown tired as well.

The line of army trucks never paused when they passed the arc of Youth Guard. They mowed down one of them and kept plowing through, scattering the others. They were filing close to the woods where Vanya and her people had come through. They would be behind us, a scant ten yards from our vehicles. I had to try and stop them.

Using the otherness and air thick with smoke, I formed a maelstrom of spinning wind in their path just three yards ahead of the leading vehicle. Six soldiers piled in a knot inside or on top; I couldn't untangle their rhythms clearly. My storm shifted the last Jeep in our line. When the first truck in the soldiers' column hit my storm, the front lifted up as if climbing a steep hill. In the moment after, it flipped backward.

The second of their vehicles slammed into the first, spilling some of the passengers and bringing them both to a crashing halt.

"Now, Andy!" I didn't feel any remorse as the rhythms of passengers spiked in pain. The third vehicle joined the pile of two toppled trucks while the three remaining veered wildly and stopped. A remote part of othersense noted Andy's flames tearing through the middle of the western soldiers. Their rhythms spiked in pain and the comrades at either side of the fire rolled to safety. My voice became a dull monotone. "You hit them in the center." My legs shook, threatening to buckle.

Andy placed his hand against the Jeep by mine, sagging visibly. Still, the otherness roared in him again.

It almost drowned the swell gathering on top of the vehicle. A moment late, I drained the otherness, still not Selina's, and almost stopped the crackling electricity that raced to it. A single snap sounded from the metal to the ground before the shock tossed me onto my back.

Andy landed beside me quietly. The world had gone silent except for a ringing in my ears. Dean's heel kicked in the air from his position under the oversized Jeep.

"Dean." I pushed an elbow into the rough asphalt to lift myself up, stopping only to draw a growing surge of otherness directly above us.

My vision blurred, but no flames exploded in the air. I forced my othersense back into focus. Dean wasn't hurt any more than Andy and I were. His rhythms were agitated, but not spiking or fading. As I rolled to my side, then knees, I had to draw in another draught of otherness forming near us. The smoke had become too thick to see anything but flickering glimpses of fires around us like blinking hateful eyes and the low orange sun dying in the west.

Roxie pulled at my arm and helped me stand. Eyes tight with concern, her lips moved but only dull murmurs worked through the ringing. Penny kept glancing back to check on me. I shook my head pointing to my ears.

Another flash of flame lit under the sun, and Andy took down two more soldiers, scattering those who had resumed their attack. The approaching Youth Guards had mostly come to a stop except for two creeping figures directly ahead. Selina stood close to where I had thrown her.

"Roxy, now." I couldn't really hear my own words, and I might have shouted.

The soldiers to the north had abandoned their vehicles and reformed into knots of four or five advancing toward us, except for six who were dying or injured. The closest group came within Roxie's range. The scream of otherness she gathered drowned out the ringing.

When the blast of fire spread in the north, it swallowed the last vehicle and slammed back two of the clusters of soldiers. I could feel the heat and see the smoke swirling toward us. Youth Guards nearby scampered back, though they had to be ten yards from the flames.

The Jeep at the end of the line exploded, and I could hear it. The vehicle behind it rocked and skid back a few inches. A black shape cut through the smoke, winging just two feet overhead.

The north soldiers scattered away from the fire and into the woods.

Andy's rhythms spiked with pain, even as he lay in the road. His hand gripped his leg where the damage was worst. My pulse quickened, fighting through the numb anger that had absorbed me since Vanya's death.

"Andy!" Dropping to my knees, I felt the shard of metal sticking out of his thigh. My healing felt the depth of his injuries and were readying the muscles and flesh as I pushed away his trembling fingers.

An inch of curved metal wound down into his muscles. A tiny artery had been severed, which I worked on with healing while simultaneously liquefying the shrapnel and oozing it out. Blood flowed heavily until I sealed the worst.

The distant thuds and clangs of bullets worked through the ringing in my ears. "A quick patch. We don't have time. Don't stand." Torn muscles would rip worse if he put weight on it.

The Youth Guard had recovered from the explosion, and a well of otherness formed nearly on top of my head. I swayed as I poured it into me. The action reminded me to refocus on my othersense. The northern soldiers were spread out and inching forward. Some of those in the front would hit us if they fired in our direction.

I pointed without turning up. "There, Roxie. Now."

Her call to the otherness screamed behind me. The resulting flames highlighted the blood soaked through Andy's coveralls and the stains of it on my hands. In the othersense, the northern soldiers drove deeper into the woods as flames engulfed two of them and blasted into the trees. Darkness returned as our cover blocked the setting sun from that side of Andy.

A splash to my right caused me to turn up. The dull thrum of gunfire had worked its way past the ringing, but it wasn't until now that I knew the soldiers who Roxie had firebombed had a clear shot to me and Andy.

"Help me," I called out to Roxie. "Pull him to the vehicle." It would hurt, but less so than getting shot.

She understood and grabbed both his ankles. I could hear his groan, or it might have been a scream, and I lifted and shoved his shoulders until we were closer to the corner of the vehicle. We crowded in Penny, who had pulled back to avoid the bullets from the west. Roxie squeezed in close behind, nearly standing on Andy's legs. We were exposed to both directions.

Reaching into the air with the otherness, I tried to mimic what I'd felt of the Kudara armor. It took no real effort. I could make a shield, perhaps. Smoky gray air thickened, but it extended out about a yard from where I wanted it, and certainly wasn't the same as the hard glossy Duathua armor.

The ground trembled, and I released my hold on the shield, expecting some new attack.

Penny smacked me, murmuring something. She waved toward the northwest, so I leaned back for a view around our cover.

Despite the haze, an explosion on the horizon blossomed like a bubble of orange flame. It had to be deep in the Alliance enclave considering how far away it was. From her earlier comment, her people were there.

Two white lights, like evil eyes, soared to the right of it.

Chapter Thirty-Six

I gawked at the sight, trying to make some sense of it. Even as I watched, a tongue of flame lit from below the eyes, then they were hidden by another explosion, closer and rivaling the first.

"God, the helicopter." Roxie's head beside mine, I could hear her words.

I'd heard of aircraft, though hadn't believed in them. I could affect it from here. In a moment, the white eyes returned, appearing to be focused on us.

As an otherness gathered behind me, I had no time to watch. Drawing in the otherness, I fell to my knees. The need to release the store I'd built up pressed against my eyeballs. The little I'd used to patch Andy together wasn't enough. My closest targets were the soldiers creeping in behind us, and the men in the woods took my full fury.

Unleashing a whirling gale into the midst of the closest group sent one flying and forced three more to fall aside and, in one case, cling to a trunk. The effort darkened my vision, and I was nearly puking when it ended.

Seven soldiers continued to approach from the west, some Youth Guards had stopped forty yards from us, and thirteen men were scattered in the woods to the north. I couldn't see well enough to know what the helicopter attacked. My hearing had returned enough to recognize the bullets ricocheting off our stalwart Jeep. The noxious fumes from the burning Jeep at the head of our line caught the breeze from the south and clogged our air.

"Roxie, over there." I weakly gestured toward the seven, the closest to us now. Before I dropped my hand, a swell of otherness began to form around us, and I drained it, nearly falling atop Andy.

I heard her call to the otherness but never saw the flames. Far behind Selina, a new force raced toward us. They were spread out as if on foot, but they'd arrive eventually. There were dozens of them. Too many. I was too weak. The seven were now five, but running toward us. Penny and Dean would shoot when they came in sight, and by doing so, give themselves and our location away. I didn't think I could stir a breeze. We'd distracted Tyrell's forces but hadn't counted on the helicopter.

"I can't," I said more to myself than anyone.

"Wolf Squad can," Andy responded.

A resentment rose, but I didn't have the energy to snap at him. Besides, another swell of otherness formed, and I had to draw it in.

A bullet ricocheted on the asphalt where Andy had lain a minute before. Dean's legs, Andy's head, and nearly my whole body were exposed. Pure luck would hit one of us.

I ignored the otherness swelling far behind us, and Selina's lightning crashed into the woods where Vanya had died. Light flashed through the smoke, reflecting off the vehicles. My pulse sped. For those seconds, I might have been visible.

"Roxie, there." I pointed toward the northeast woods

where two soldiers had broken from the deeper section and were within her range.

"Got it." Her voice had grown tired, drained, but the screech of otherness built from her.

Roxie screamed. Falling to her knees at my left side, her hand covered her ear. The othersense showed the pain and injury, and for a moment, my heart dropped, thinking they'd shot her in the head. My hand reached for her, even as I drained another swell of otherness from an attack by the Youth Guard. Her fingers were wet and sticky with blood as I pushed them aside. She cried in pain, but we didn't have time. Her upper ear had been notched; it couldn't be restored, but I forced the flesh to heal and the blood to coagulate. I hated that it hurt her.

Penny had dropped lower and stared in the direction of the explosions. They had become no more than red haze in the smoke.

"Shit." My hand drifted from Roxie's head. The two evil lights crested the lip of our vehicle, shining dully through the smoke covered windows. Tiny circular cracks had formed in the glass that I hadn't seen until now.

Ignoring the bullets thudding off our cover, I drew closer to the edge by Penny and stared at the aircraft. It was moving too fast and heading directly toward us. My heart pounded in my ears. The sharp smell of blood, acrid smoke, and the noxious fumes from the burning Jeep caught in my throat. Transfixed, I watched the lights get closer.

Blades spun above a black box that had sharp angles like a jutting chin where the bright lights were located. Below it, the smoke billowed away and revealed the soldiers running. Even they glanced up at it. If it fired one of those explosions on us, our cover wouldn't matter.

The otherness inside growled. I tried to call the air to push against it, but I was too weak. The blades let out a muffled thudding, and the helicopter moved air quicker than I could. My attempt dispersed like I'd spit into a storm.

Dean yelled something as he began backing out from under the cover of the vehicle. Penny dropped to her knees nearly under me. I had to do something.

In the othersense, I focused on the rhythms and then the bonds. Before when I'd altered gravity, I'd succeed in saving Dean, and then failed miserably to the point of nearly crushing Andy, but I could think of nothing else to try. The connecting threads strung from me in dozens of directions, many toward Tyrell's Youth Guard.

Like a spider's web, we all had connections leading to each other and out into the smoke. I couldn't know what the lack of gravity might do to this aircraft, but air didn't appear to work. My focus reached far around us, and I pushed in the same way I had to save Dean from the trap.

"We need to run," he said. He squirmed, but hadn't cleared the vehicle.

Even as I felt the first sense of lessening weight, the helicopter spun easily, positioning itself to point back toward the Alliance as if it ignored the othersense. Through the haze between, a red light at its tail gave me some sense of the design beyond a bulky black shape. The orange sun flashed off a dark window where I could just make out a soldier inside through the othersense.

"Caitlyn?" Roxie grabbed my leg, probably feeling the effect from the gravity.

The magic had shifted me, and the toes of my boots dragged on asphalt. I rose up, threatening to lose the cover of the oversized Jeep.

Flashes lit from the front of the helicopter as it unleashed a torrent of bullets at the trees marking the northwest horizon. I couldn't sense anyone at this distance, but guessed the defenders of the Alliance were there.

The vehicles next to us began to groan, but I couldn't be distracted. I focused only on the aircraft. My chest tightened, and I didn't breathe.

Andy flailed as he lifted, tapping me. Roxie's hand kept me steady.

The helicopter tilted oddly, spraying bullets onto its own soldiers who were running toward us. It stopped firing almost immediately, angling first to the left, then to the right. The aircraft drifted away from me, reaching the far edge of my othersense as if trying to escape.

"Caitlyn." Roxie's hand tightened on my leg, but I remained too focused on trying to keep my effect spread to its limits.

The helicopter jerked forward, flipping so that its nose pointed down. Its sharp angles were backed by the spinning blades on the far side of the craft that whipped smoke around it. I thought for sure it had escaped me when it suddenly whirled so that the tail sparked against the metal below it.

In one quick second, it rotated tail over nose, skidding farther away. Out of control, the deadly machine crashed into the ground beyond the edge of my othersense. A fireball blossomed like an angry mushroom.

I blinked in surprise. The flames carried high into the sky, lighting the trees around it with a dull red. The next explosion blasted to the sides, visible through the smoky glass of the Jeep. I wouldn't have been able to see as well were it not for my body drifting higher.

My heart drummed in my chest, and a smile tucked at the edges of my lips. I'd destroyed the aircraft. It wouldn't be attacking the Alliance anymore.

I turned to see Roxie's reaction, but she'd been pinned to the ground, at least on her left side. She grimaced in pain, barely able to extend the one arm locked on my leg.

Penny lay face down, fingers pressing against the asphalt as if trying to rise.

I drew in a shaky breath, and let go of my magic. My feet settled easily to the ground with my heels barely an inch in the air. Andy dropped with a thud. The vehicle in front of me groaned and rose visibly.

Dean. I gasped. In the othersense, his rhythms were dull and muted as if dying. Nearly stumbling over Andy, I fell to Dean's side. He'd made it out as far as his waist, with his chest still under the vehicle and one limp left hand extended.

"Dean." My voice rasped a croak from all the smoke and a thickening throat. He wasn't dead, but when I put my hand on his bare back, I could feel only a weak pulse through my healing. Tears blurred my vision, but I put my left hand on the massive vehicle and called in a roar of the otherness to add to what I already held inside.

Metal softened and moved at my command, but other substances resisted my magic. Liquids oozed out, and plastic rings stuck halfway embedded. I choked back a sob as the overall mass pulled back enough to create a cavity and expose Dean's reddened, marked skin with the imprint of the metal I had pressed on top of him. He wasn't breathing. Healing wouldn't work. I hadn't paid enough attention in our CPR class at Camp. My hands trembled.

"Dean, Dean!" I yanked at his hips, trying to drag him toward me, but he weighed too much. He couldn't die. I'd risked what truly mattered to me.

Thin little Andy wedged beside me and with his good arm, got a grip on Dean's elbow. Together, we shifted him an inch.

"He's not breathing." My voice became a choked whine, and I could barely see through the tears. I'd done this to him. I should have been paying attention. The attempt at the shed had proved I had no control.

"Eff me," Penny growled behind me, and suddenly Dean's leg lifted and jerked with her pull. His second leg rose as Roxie joined in.

The four of us dragged him across the asphalt, clear of the metal cave I'd formed. Andy grabbed Dean's opposite shoulder, trying to roll him over. I jumped to the far side and helped push Dean's limp body while Roxie and Penny joined Andy, and we flipped Dean onto his back.

His beautiful, olive-skinned face was scratched and bleeding down the right side from forehead to chin; the whole front of his body had bleeding gouges from dragging him. Crumbling asphalt had left tiny, pockmarked indentations on his chest.

Andy paused, staring at the blood, his hands drifting off Dean. "I —"

Werewolf blood. I inhaled, throat thick and my body trembling. "I breathe in his mouth, and push on his chest, right?" I barely recognized my harsh, dry voice.

"Pinch his nose." He nodded almost frantically, and pointed to a spot on Dean's chest, careful not to touch him.

The gunfire near us had disappeared during my alteration of gravity, leaving only the more distant background battle. I jumped when one of the soldiers recovered enough to begin firing again from the west. The Jeep next to us thudded with bullets.

Keeping one hand on Dean's chest to check his heart with healing, I pinched his nose with the other. "I love you. You said you wouldn't leave me." My voice trembled with a whisper.

Lips locked over his, I blew everything from my lungs into his. He appeared pale as I pulled back and drew my own breath. His sticky blood covered my hands when I pressed down on his chest.

The others had drawn back, wide-eyed and rhythms racing. All around us, the enemy moved again; some of the Youth Guards were pulling away. More soldiers resumed firing at us.

Dean coughed, and I started laughing, then joined him, choking on acrid smoke. Sobbing with my nose touching his, I left one hand on his chest and moved the other to his torn cheek. I healed what I could, speeding oxygen into the blood and knitting the scrapes. His eyes fluttered open as he dragged in a ragged breath. He was bruised across his torso, but no bones were broken. I could have crushed him. He would have died if I hadn't stopped my magic when I did. We had to get safe.

Something smacked my back, bouncing my face off Dean's. I blinked, then sought out a pain growing there. My skin was torn, and my rib vibrated with damage as well.

I'd been shot.

Chapter Thirty-Seven

As pain seared across my back, I fumbled to heal the bleeding. My muscles were torn, and the bone ached enough to make my next breath painful.

Dean was trying to rise, but I pushed him down with a wince. I barely reacted when Selina's otherness swelled overhead. Even as I drew it in, a second Youth Guard began an attack. They knew where we were hiding now; Selina's earlier lightning had given us away to at least some of them. Otherness swelled in me as I drank in the next attack.

The soldiers to the north had easy shots, as most of them had a line of sight around the other Jeeps, even if the haze still hid us somewhat.

"Roxie, there." I gestured behind me to the trees where the closest soldier had crept within twenty-five yards of us. He'd be able to see us through the smoke soon. Even as I spoke, a bullet ricocheted overhead off the mangled metal of the Jeep.

Even my flinching hurt. Kneeling beside Dean, I tried to shelter him from a shot with my body while I healed both of us. He kept trying to rise, but I could sense his rhythms flare with the attempt before I pushed him gently down.

His ribs were bruised badly, and his body had been without oxygen.

My world was Dean. I had tried to cure him, but failed. Now I would lose all of him.

"We — need — to — leave." I could tell each word pained him.

We were almost surrounded. Roxie's flames weren't as strong, and her last blast had just toppled a lone soldier.

I drank in the otherness of another attack by a Youth Guard. Those who remained kept their distance, but we had over a dozen active soldiers firing and advancing. The larger force behind Selina was regrouping against the Duathua, though the misfiring helicopter and the explosions afterward appeared to have rattled their momentum.

Eventually, another bullet would find one of us hidden in the smoke, or too many Youth Guards would attack for me to stop their fire or lightning. Roxie and Andy were as weak as I was. I had to try something different, something that would let us retreat and disappear into the haze. Even Penny would have to agree that we'd done what we could to disrupt Tyrell's army. I had killed a helicopter.

Dean shouldn't move yet, and my back still felt like someone had taken a club to it.

A bullet flicked through my singed braid, tugging it over my shoulder. Maybe they could already see us. I released the healing and called the air into a thick, smoky, quasi-Kudara shield to protect us from the soldiers there. It might not stop a bullet.

A string of shots from the north clanged off the front of our mangled vehicle, and two of the bullets embedded into my shield. They hung in the thick air about a yard away from me. My eyebrows raised, hopeful. I winced as I shifted. Pouring all of my otherness into the shield, I called it roaring to me and made it denser. I could feel the effort, but it wasn't like creating wind.

A spray of bullets from the west caused me to squint at the red ball of a sun, just touching the trees. Penny dropped down, back to the still-recognizable rear end of the vehicle. Roxie knelt beside her, facing me. I nudged my head toward the trees. "Same place."

She nodded wearily, and we both called a roar of the otherness.

Mine I used to create a second shield on the other side. Immediately it took a bullet and held it two feet from Penny. She stared at it, swallowing. "Eff me." It had traveled through most of my shield with barely an inch left.

"Get Roxie and Andy out of here." They couldn't carry Dean out. I'd have to wait for him to gain some strength.

Andy shook his head. "Wolf Squad." He sat awkwardly, favoring his arm and partially healed leg.

I snapped at Andy. "Stop that." He hadn't been part of the Wolf Squad unit. None of us belonged anymore. That group had died with Eric. Otherness formed overhead. They knew exactly where we were hiding. I drained it, adding it to both shields with a single thought. "Please, get Roxie out of here for me." I coughed. My throat was thick and dry.

"I can move," Dean said. He pushed up onto his elbow, grimacing. His rhythms shot with pain.

Bullets dug into my shields and clanged off metal. The northern soldiers had almost cut off any escape. "Roxie, do you have anything left?"

Andy smiled grimly. "I do."

I pointed. "Twenty yards. In the woods."

Reaching with my othersense, I found a smaller group of soldiers who had remained behind Selina, but they were advancing again. I couldn't hold these shields forever. My friends had to leave, or I had to draw the fire to me.

As I stood, the loose healing on my back ripped open, and I began to bleed. It would stop in a minute or two without my aid, so I focused on stretching my shields higher, calling on more of the otherness.

"What are you doing?" asked Dean. He tried again to raise himself before his eyes fluttered and he sagged back to the ground.

Bullets poured into my shield. One pierced it, bouncing to the asphalt behind us a few feet away. Piercing didn't appear to weaken the condensed air. I frowned and reached through my creation, liquefying the trapped bullets. They dispersed like the smoke particles trapped inside.

Two swells of otherness formed, weak, but dangerous. I drew them in, adding to my shield so that it covered two sides from the ground to my head. Stepping over Dean, I put a foot on the bumper. Metal softened and reformed into a flat step. I stood on it while drawing in more otherness, then carefully extended the shield to protect my new height, including an arc in front of my face. Barely more than a consideration formed the metal into a series of steps to the roof, even ledges between the back and the rear side window.

"Caitlyn, don't." Dean's voice grew frantic, but I couldn't have him shifting now. He'd charge off into them.

"Trust me, Dean." I lied to him with a smile. Once he could actually stand, I'd have to convince him to leave me. Not just my beloved, but all my friends. I had strength enough for that. Already, the newest trail of bullets were trained on my head. Blond hair stands out.

Roxie shook her head. "Don't."

I drained another Youth Guard attack, adding the otherness to my shields as I absorbed the latest collection of bullets. The shield almost glowed with white smoke and metal. "Stay down until you can move, Dean, then we'll leave."

Andy shook his head, then hardened. "Where?"

I pointed left where one of the soldiers had come closer, edging south to circle us. "Twenty-five yards." On my next step up, my legs wobbled, nearly letting my clumsiness topple me. My head above the top of the vehicle brought a torrent of bullets ricocheting off the roof and embedding into my shields. Hot bullets fell through some places, one blistering my cheek as it bounced off. The others rained dangerously close to Dean.

Andy's flame burned small, but dead-on target; the soldier screamed and rolled as he burned. It slowed the few remaining from advancing, but it didn't stop them from shooting at me.

The Youth Guard were too far away to see me, but I'd definitely drawn the attention of some of the soldiers. The next gathering of the otherness lay two yards behind me and took an effort to draw in. I extended my shield to the roof and adjusted it along the sides of the vehicle, keeping everyone protected.

"This is suicide." Dean managed to get to one elbow, swaying when he tried to roll to his knees.

I knew it as well, but shook my head. "When you can get up and run, I'll be right behind you." My foot could barely lift to the next step I'd created. The wound on my back had stopped bleeding, but the pain flared with every move.

Roxie's voice was near a sob; she knew as well. "Where?"

I pointed west. "Twenty yards." If I could give them one direction to run, it would be south, then east back where we'd entered the battle; the western soldiers were infringing on that option. Her weak flame barely lit an area three yards in diameter, but it lay close enough to send two soldiers running back.

Selina attempted another attack, but even she'd grown weak. I drained it, then took the final step to the roof, draping the shield a foot in front of me, then down the sides to protect my friends. All the bullets seemed for me. I'd automatically started adding them to my shield as they embedded. Only a few clattered down to the vehicle and the others. Penny cursed when one hit her. She hadn't tried to stop me. They had one chance to survive.

Dean managed to get to his knees. His oxygen levels were still likely weak, with all the smoke in the air. "Dean, I'm waiting on you."

"You're lying," he said. His voice weak, he gagged as he said the words.

"I'm going to try," I said. I would, though I doubted the hailstorm of bullets would give me a chance. In truth, I was so weak, I couldn't be sure my shield wouldn't fall. If he saw me die, he would likely shift. I had to hold on.

The closest soldiers to the north had stopped their advance, probably just firing on me. The red sun seemed to glow against my shield. More of Tyrell's army were joining them.

Andy spoke, but I couldn't hear. "What?" I asked. My physical vision dimmed. When a new swell of otherness formed nearly on top of me, I drained it, sagging as I added it to my shields. I could see the passing smoke drawn in with the air.

He didn't answer, but he called the otherness.

A shiver ran up my back.

Well beyond the edges of my shield, fire formed around my sides and behind me in a bright half shell. The air chilled so much around me that my breath fogged. I stood ringed in flame at the rear of the battle with only my shield in front of me. Exposed, I drew in a breath as the firelight lit some of the Youth Guards. Andy had done this. *No.* Andy had betrayed me.

Roxie called in the otherness and wind sucked in around me, clearing the smoke ahead.

Andy bellowed, voice carried by wind above the gunfire toward the Youth Guard, "Wolf Squad! Wolf Squad!"

I stood as the flaming martyr. Bullets doubled in my shield and rained on the metal roof at my feet. I had chosen this.

Dean climbed nearly to his feet.

My breath barely formed words. "Run. South."

Andy's fire dimmed, even as Roxie fed it air. They were both near exhaustion.

I grew near my end as well. "Run," I begged them. A well of otherness formed, nearly inside my shields, and I drained it, pushing what I could into my shields to extend the side, giving them a little extra shelter to escape.

As Dean stood, none of them moved. My mouth opened, but I didn't have the energy to say anything. In the othersense, I vaguely noted a well of otherness, but it wasn't near me; it gathered at Selina.

Curiosity alone kept me upright.

The attack hadn't been strong, but someone tried to set her on fire. Her rhythms spiked in pain as she dove for the ground, rolling. In the next second, lightning struck the closest Youth Guard to her.

A dim call rose above the gunfire from a Youth Guard who ran toward me. "Wolf Squad!" A woman's voice.

Another echoed her, then a third. The Youth Guards began to split in my othersense, some running for us, and some away. Eight, nearly half, appeared to be approaching to help us. The rest backed away.

Fire, lightning, and wind battled between the divided groups. White stabbed from the sky. Red flowered near Youth Guards on both sides. Distant sounds cracked and echoed, but my mind couldn't place from where or who. I stood without moving; afraid I would topple if I did. One or two attacks came near us, but I snuffed them out as if taking a quick breath.

Our side was gaining. Many lay dead or dying along with other Youth Guards. An hour earlier these had been comrades.

Selina's forces bolted for the north. Shocked, I nearly dropped the shield.

One of the Youth Guard lit the forest near the northern soldiers, and a second sent lightning in to follow it. The combination set two trees on fire, bright at this distance.

"Where?" asked Andy. His flame behind me had extinguished.

My legs finally gave, and I dropped to kneel on the roof. I managed a hand to point to the west, directly at the angry red sun half embedded in the trees. "Twenty yards."

Andy's weak blossom of flame caught a soldier in the back. From one of the Youth Guards, a larger, longer lasting crescent of fire caught two of the soldiers fully, sending their rhythms spiking in pain.

I blinked, barely able to take in the mayhem in front of me as otherness swelled, burst, crackled, and killed. Andy had saved us. The Youth Guards were joining us as he'd promised. *Wolf Squad.* Those running to us were alight in the othersense.

My vision dimmed again. The bullets had stopped. My shield vaporized in a gush of expanding air.

When I slid backward off the roof, I landed in Dean's arms, and we both went down.

Chapter Thirty-Eight

I awakened on my stomach on a mattress that smelled like pine needles. There was no bed frame, so a wooden floor stretched from nearly my nose, under the legs of an upholstered chair, to an empty mattress beside a pale green wall. Birds chirped and a horse snorted somewhere outside a curtained window with a beam of light squeezing through to highlight a few specks of floating dust.

Except for underwear, my clothes were gone, and I had a smooth sheet draped over me. A blanket weighted down my lower half. I lifted my head and sucked in a breath from the pain in my ribs. The room smelled lightly of a cooking fire.

Two familiar boots dropped down from the chair. "Seyir Udal says you're still going to be in some pain. Bones or some shit." Penny's voice rose as she leaned down and placed a canteen next to me. "She also wants you to drink all this, then I'm supposed to get you some juice. Before you go whining and pining, Dean's okay. Better than you."

I smiled. "Anything else?" Dean rested close, somewhere to my left.

"She doesn't want me to shoot you right away if you

show any symptoms. I'm taking that as merely a suggestion. But, drink."

Wincing, I rolled gingerly to my side and sat up. My hair had been unbraided, even brushed. It felt like someone had hammered a nail in my back. Parched and starving, I swiveled my head slowly. The small room had just the two beds, one window, a closed door, and the chair. I wrapped the sheet around me against the chill. "What happened, after I — fell?" Shivering, I opened the canteen.

Penny had on her usual black coat, but no rifle. Her short brown hair had been cut even more, until it barely came halfway down her ears. She felt my forehead before speaking. "All hell broke loose for a while. A bunch of your unit mates or whatever they're called came to Andy's rally. Fire and shit, but the real trouble for us came when the army evacuated. We, well Dean, had to drag you back toward the outer farms to avoid them."

I stopped guzzling. "Vanya's body."

"Recovered along with the others, afterward. Some wounded, including the enemy. You've been out for about seventeen hours."

A chill gripped my neck. "Others? Where's Roxie? Andy?"

She pointed at the canteen. "Drink. They're fine. Well, about the same as before you took your nap. Some of your other friends survived. I don't remember their names."

I glanced at the door. "Where is everyone?"

"We're keeping them away from you." She pointed at the scar on my arm from the werewolf bite. "You might be confident you're immune, and even Seyir Udal might think you're safe, but the rest of us are enforcing the twenty-four hours, despite your Wolf Squad bitching."

Frowning, I handed her the empty canteen. "You've got a gun?"

Her smile quirked to one side. "Figured it might not be much use against you. There's a Pahawan stationed in the kitchen and a sniper outside. Please don't get all cranky and try to go out there."

I raised an eyebrow. "Did you just say please?"

Penny chuckled and rolled her eyes. "Shit, don't tell anyone." She stood. "Stay. Let me get some juice. Seyir Udal will want to check on you."

"I'm starving."

She shrugged and shut the door behind her, and I focused the othersense around me. A horse snorted outside, I assumed Bella, with Odie sitting beside her. Inside the house, only the Duathua and Penny stood in the other room. There was a distance before I could find another human in the woods, who I assumed guarded against me turning wolf. Beyond that, a bustle of activity seethed all around us. Humans mostly, they were humming from activity and moving in clusters. There were too many for me to guess which of the rhythms were Dean and the others.

After Penny met with the Duathua, they ran out the front door while she brought me a mug.

"No food?" I asked.

"Seyir Udal first. She'll be here soon."

I took the mug. "Bella and Odie are okay." I nodded in their direction.

Penny stared down at her hands and sat on the opposite mattress, coat draping around her. "Yeah, Vanya brought them here first."

The juice proved to be a sweet blend that I couldn't identify, though it tasted like berries. Thinking of Vanya's death soured any enjoyment. "How? Why was she out there?"

"Evacuating the farms. The army that raided the air

force base had cut off her coming in from the north, I guess. I don't know how she ended up near us."

I sagged, staring into the dark liquid. "She was coming to me; she sensed me."

"Don't let your head get all swelled. What makes you think it wasn't me?" Penny forced a smile.

She could be right, but it didn't remove the guilt or pain. I drank another sip. Beyond peach juice, we rarely had any at the camp. "What happened at the air force base?" Three Duathua were jogging, maybe flying toward the house.

"A group of the army went there and collected some weapons. Big stuff we didn't even know had been there, in underground tunnels or something. The Pahawan are going to torch the whole place before we leave." She turned as footsteps sounded on wood at the front.

"Leave?" I asked.

Penny nodded. "Drink your damn juice."

I finished it, grimacing at the pulp on the bottom. The losses and cruelty from the previous day weighted with the uncertainty, and my stomach churned. The little house on the outskirts of the enclave no longer appeared an opportunity. I sagged, and the chill air crept through the sheet. Dean and I had a quiet life a few days ago, even if we were only eating fish.

Nur opened the door, dressed in only her skirt and no tunic. She smiled. "I am pleased to see you up, Caitlyn."

Behind her, an even taller Duathua stooped to enter the doorway. Their face was creased with hard lines on pale gray skin. Over their shoulders they wore a knitted yellow shawl that draped past the top of their skirt, clasped at the front with a design of metal with blue highlights. "She's got more pink to her cheeks. No temperature either." Their voice was high pitched and rasping. "Breathing fine?"

"Yes, are you Udal?"

"Call me grandmother." She leaned down, placed cool hands on my cheeks, and peered into my eyes. "Yes. Much better. Your lungs have worried me. All of you were brought to me in rough shape."

Penny's voice was respectful when she spoke. "She's hungry."

Udal closed her eyes, and in the othersense she glowed with vibration as her power hummed. "As she should be. Fill her lightly. I think you should fetch her some stew."

I was surprised when Penny stood so quickly. "Yes, grandmother."

"Can I see my friends?" I asked studying Udal, then Nur.

Udal sighed, eyes still closed and fingers on my face. "The others require some more hours to prove what I already know."

Penny bared her teeth at me in a parody of a werewolf.

Nur chuckled and waved Penny toward the door. "A few more hours to wait. Sunset should be sufficient time to judge your condition. That will be the time for you to join your friends. The six of them are as impatient as you presently are."

I frowned, my features moving under Udal's fingertips. "Six?" Penny had confirmed Dean, Roxie, and Andy were okay, but there had been more than three Youth Guards who crossed the line to join us. "Who?"

She tilted her head, her expression appearing sad despite the rigidity of her skin. "I apologize that I do not know all their names for all they have done in our aid. The one named Fawn has been helping us with healing the wounded. The Alliance owes you and your friends many lives for bringing down the airship, as it turned the battle for us."

I blinked. "It did?"

"A most destructive weapon your humans created. The explosions it wrought upon our enclave killed so many. The bullets it fired forced our last defenses to retreat with so much loss." She nodded toward me. "Its destruction caused many of their automobiles to burn when it crashed. The reports tell that the human troops attacking were disrupted and began to retreat. I have not seen the battlefield, as the fires still burn on the other side of the river."

Udal lifted her hands from my face and opened her eyes. "Your lungs are fit. I want you to eat and rest until sunset. You must sleep well tonight, as tomorrow will be a taxing day."

"Tomorrow?" I asked. My chest hollowed, knowing her comment connected to Penny's about leaving.

"All of the able-bodied will be heading to the city of Columbia to join the Alliance there. We had hoped this need would not arise." Udal exchanged a knowing glance with Nur. "The assumption has been that you and your friends would accompany us."

Nur knelt, dropping her closer to eye level. "Dean's condition has been discussed, and the two of you are welcome to join the Alliance. The offer is extended cautiously with an assumption of his continued control."

My heart lightened and I smiled. Dean would likely accept the offer, on my behalf if nothing else. I just wanted someplace safe where we could live. It might be Columbia.

Before I could respond, Udal chuckled. "Your trick with Wati might have had something to do with the decision."

A chill washed over me. "We didn't really have a lot of choices. They would have —"

Nur nodded. "Penny explained. Did you truly send her back?"

My pulse lurched. "I don't know. I really don't. I didn't want to, but she begged me, and —" Tyrell's people would have taken her. We'd been captured afterward anyway, but it would have been sooner with Wati unable to move. They might have killed her on the spot, or sent her directly to the labs.

Closing her eyes, Nur nodded. "I feared as much. Do not worry."

"Don't be surprised when the others request the same." Udal stood, crouching slightly.

I swayed. "Why would they? I can't know where they might go."

She shrugged. "They are young and have much to return to. If my wife remains on Denya, she would understand why I must stay here with our people."

Nur rose. "We will discuss this topic and more. Rest."

As they left, I dragged the blanket up around my shoulders, but it didn't stop me from shivering. Would all the Duathua expect me to push them from Earth? I could be sending them someplace worse, or be killing them.

When Penny returned, she carried a small pot made of Kudara with a wire handle and my folded coveralls under her arm. The brown stew inside had two different beans and vegetables, including carrots, sloshing about. She dropped my clothes on the mattress and placed the pot in front of me. "Let me refill your canteen, unless you want more juice?" She pulled a spoon from her pocket and placed in by the pot.

"Water," I said, plucking at my coveralls. My stomach churned, still thinking of Wati. "Is that Halimay, guarding the other room?"

Penny's face dropped. "She didn't make it. She died at the first barricade. We might have passed her body on the way in. There were so many . . ." She grabbed my mug and canteen and left, obviously not wanting to discuss Halimay's death.

I unfolded my coveralls; they'd been cleaned and had the scent of fresh pine. Someone had embroidered colorful flowers in yellow and red with some green leaves to mend all the tears. The rip along the shoulder had been patched with a thick green fabric, and the yellow flowers there were sewn into an intertwining vine. My Wolf Squad unit patch that had been threatening to peel off had been secured with a wreath of tiny red buds.

Standing shakily, I was halfway in them when Penny returned. "Don't plan on heading out."

"I'm not. It's cold."

She frowned, putting the canteen by my stew and then placing her hand on my head. "Still no fever."

I forced a smile. "Don't sound disappointed." My mood had fluctuated since waking, but the reality was that the Alliance was mourning their losses, and I hadn't been able to find a cure for Dean. If there had been a real chance, it would have been with Nur and Vanya's help.

We lapsed into silence as I ate. The food was hearty and spicy, but I had no passion for it.

Hours later, at sunset, Dean brought my boots and his jacket. He poked his finger through the hole in the leather where I'd been shot and wiggled it at me. "How you feel?" His bare chest was ridged with bruises from my experiment with gravity. He caught my glance and waved it off.

"Okay. How about you?" I carefully touched his chest. "I'm so sorry."

"I love you, even when you try to break my heart." He handed me the jacket and shrugged. "Doesn't hurt. Fawn did some healing on both of us while you were unconscious. Then the Amazon Duathua came out and checked us all over. Did you know they don't really stop growing?" Angling his head down, he smiled at Penny. "Makes you kind of wish, doesn't it?"

Penny cocked her head and frowned at him. She wasn't that short, only a couple inches below me. I took my boots.

"I love you. I should have been more careful." I dropped into Penny's chair to pull on my boots. My foolishness could have killed him. It also might have saved the Alliance. If I'd got him out from under the vehicle first, I might still have taken down the helicopter. "Where's Roxie? Andy?"

Dean jerked a thumb over his shoulder. "Outside. We've got a place for the night we'll take you to. We've got room for Penny too, since she's babysitting you."

I glanced at the other mattress. She'd only left to get me food and take care of Bella once. "Thank you," I said to her.

His jacket made me feel warm, and safer somehow. I winced as I walked to the door. The Pahawan in the kitchen had left when Dean arrived, and the dim light of the sunset exposed little more than a table and chair near the kitchen. "Do we know if Vinnie was attacked?" I asked Penny.

"No. Iandil and her people will check in with everyone; let them know we're evacuating."

Outside, the scent of a forest fire laced the air, though I didn't see any actual smoke. Lanky Andy beamed at the front of the group, with Roxie just a step behind him. Her ear had white tape on it. She relaxed when she saw me.

Behind her stood Ben with his almost mustache. I would never have guessed he'd leave Camp Sparta, but he had been friends with Eric. Beside Ben was a tall, bright-eyed teenager with light brown skin and long black hair. She smiled when I glanced at her.

As Penny headed to the side of the house, Odie ran out to sniff me and nuzzle Dean's hand.

Andy favored his leg when he stepped forward. "I knew you'd be okay. You had to be. We still have to rescue the other Wolf Squad."

I gawked at him. "What?"

He gestured to Ben and the others. "There's more who didn't come with Tyrell. They'll expect us to come free them. We all did."

Dean chuckled and knelt down to pet Odie. "Nice."

"I, we if you want, are heading to the city of Columbia." I stepped forward and winced at Roxie's ear. "Does it hurt?"

She gave me a hug. "Yeah. It'll look cool though."

Ben scraped his hand through his hair. He turned his eyes down when he spoke. "Tyrell will bring the whole army to Columbia."

Had Tyrell survived? "Hey, Ben." I didn't let go of Roxie.

He lifted his head and flashed a smile. "Hey, Caitlyn. Glad you're okay." His eyes flicked to Dean, then he busied himself digging in his coveralls. He pulled out a Wolf Squad patch. "This was Eric's. I thought you might want it. I've been carrying it around for a while."

I swallowed and released Roxie. "How?"

"Stole it. I needed something to remember him by." Ben's Hounds patch was gone, leaving a discolored circle.

My hand twitched, but I didn't reach out. "You keep it." I swallowed down the lump in my throat.

Ben pushed the patch into my hand and nudged his chin to his side. "Yatika embroiders. If it's okay with you, she'll make us patches."

I took Eric's patch, running my thumb across the threads. "Of course, Wolf Squad." My old unit's name felt awkward, and I swallowed again, refusing to tear up over Eric in front of them. "Hi, Yatika."

She beamed and shot out a hand. "I've always wanted to meet you."

Choking down a half laugh and half sob, I took her hand, then pulled her into a hug. "Thank you both — for saving us last night."

Her voice cracked when she spoke near my ear. "I wish Damian had made it."

Blood drained from my face, but I held her shoulders when we separated. "He was there last night?"

She nodded, eyes wet. "Damian, Terry, Jasmine, Emery, and Kim."

"I'm sorry." I would ask about those names again, and not forget them. Eric was first on the list. "Did Selina survive?"

"Last I saw she was running north after she killed Emery," Ben said. "When the army came back through was when we lost Terry, Damian, and Jasmine. We were just trying to hide, so I don't know if Selina was with them or not. I can hope she died in a fire." His voice had turned dark and vengeful.

He went slightly stiff when I hugged him. Later, I would ask for details about how the others died.

Andy managed to hug the wound on my ribs when his long arms wrapped around me in a surprising bear hug. I stifled my cry.

Bella snorted as Penny led her to us. "Getting dark. Let's go." She had two rifles strapped to the saddle and packed bags.

"Did Tyrell make it?"

Penny shrugged.

Ben nodded. "I'm betting so. He and Selina came and got us. We didn't know it was you until you stood up and started glowing."

"Then we heard the call." Yatika smiled.

I slipped Eric's patch in my pocket. "Thank you." I pointed to the flowers.

Her skin darkened with a blush, but she beamed. "My mother taught me when I was young. It's what I have of her."

Penny led Bella toward the setting sun. "C'mon kids."

Dean chuckled. "Said the shortest."

She didn't glance back. "Roxie's shorter. I measured."

Roxie laced her arm in mine, walking with me. "They lied to us about the Duathua."

"Yeah."

"Have you seen what their Seyir can do, besides heal?"

I thought of Vanya's teachings. We'd all learn the othersense. "Some, not much. I didn't really get this far."

"They make armor, buildings, and containers out of air."

"Kudara."

"Yes. They can make plants grow, like healing but something else." She sounded excited. "They're so free."

"Don't you miss the rules?" I smirked.

Roxie's skin flushed. "I like order, but I was just trying . . ."

"To be the perfect soldier."

"I don't want that now." She squeezed closer to me. "I'll figure out what I do want."

Andy kept up as best he could, still limping. Yakita and Ben hung to the back, while Dean walked on my other side scanning the thin line of trees ahead.

A lamp burned in the window of the brick house we approached, and a tendril of smoke drifted out of the chimney. Despite all my sleeping, I was a little tired. We'd get a good night's sleep, then walk to Columbia for our new life.

Cutting through a yard on our right, two Duathua just a little taller than Dean, carried wooden crates in their arms. Their path would nearly intersect ours, and Penny waved. They smiled at her, then spotted me and spoke in a hurried whisper in their high-pitched language. They curved, obviously intercepting us.

One of them had small breasts under a beige tunic. Both

wore the classic skirts I'd grown used to. I had begun to assume from Wati that the Duathua laid eggs and did not breast feed, and that was why none of the women I'd been introduced to had any. Assumptions were proving difficult with their species.

Penny stopped Bella and stepped ahead to introduce us. "This is Manu; he's a forging Seyir."

I swallowed, trying to understand, but Dean cocked his head by my ear. "He's got breasts."

Manu answered with a smile, and appeared to address me, rather than Dean. "Yes, the eggs are mine to carry. It is a pleasure to meet you, Miss Caitlyn. We have heard so much about you."

Mind spinning, I forced a weak smile. "Just Caitlyn. Nice to meet you." Glancing at the two large crates, I did not ask if they were full of eggs.

"And this is Alana; he works at the forge." Penny gestured to the other Duathua.

He hefted the crate, as if it held meaning to his work. "Worked. We will not know what Columbia holds for me. I look forward to speaking with you again, Caitlyn."

They both smiled before continuing behind the houses.

Penny clicked her tongue to Bella, then smiled at me conspiratorially. She leaned over, but spoke loud enough for any of us to hear. "Two penises. Each."

We were quiet, perhaps stunned and awkwardly embarrassed. Upon entering the house, the scent of roasted chicken drenched us. I found a waking woman rising from a mattress near an open fireplace. She had shaved one side of her head and left a bit of short brown hair on the other. Her eyes were dark, and from her height and build, I would have assumed her a year older than me.

"Fawn, this is Caitlyn." Andy seemed to spring to her side, offering a hand for her to get up.

She swiveled to a cross-legged position on the mattress and cocked her head to study me. "You look better. I wasn't sure you were going to wake up for a while. Then they'd told me you'd been bit."

"Thank you. I heard you helped heal us."

"Patched you up and dragged you through the brush is more like it. Lucky we didn't get shot. Again." She pointed toward the lamp on the table. "Can we eat now, Andy?"

"Yeah, I just thought —" He motioned toward me.

Dean laughed. "Is she supposed to bless the food?"

I couldn't help but grin. They were treating me like something special, and I wasn't.

When we finally did sit down to eat, Andy of course made it uncomfortable. He lifted his mug in a toast. "Wolf Squad."

The others joined in vigorously, and I couldn't help but say it. "Wolf Squad."

We spent a little while in conversation during and after the meal. With Penny's urging for an early night and a sunrise start on our trip, our little group settled down to sleep. She handed Dean the nub of a candle and a box of matches, then pointed to a grayed white door. "You and Dean got that room. Mattress and blankets. There's a pack in there we found for you."

Dean leaned to my neck as I opened the door. "A romantic candle and a mattress, love." His breath gave me chills.

I smiled and opened the door wide. The lantern light from the main room leaked into a small worn room with a thin mattress in the corner. The sky was black outside the windows and kept us in the dark as I closed the door. "I love you so much."

The scratch of the match was followed by a blossom of light, and I yelped.

Moonjir lay sprawled across the bed on his side. "Shh," he said, "you'll wake the others."

"What the hell?" Dean growled, swore, then lit the candle.

"That's no way to greet a friend," Moonjir said. "Then again, I did say you were direct and bold." His blue and pink-tinged fur remained colorful despite the dim yellow flame.

I sagged. "What are you here to tell me?"

He raised both hands in the air and his tail swept up the wall. "I wanted to congratulate you."

"On what?" I asked.

"Everything." He slid up to stand on the mattress, and floated a couple inches above it. "You learn remarkably quickly. People admire you. These people might have been decimated had you not stepped in." He dropped to the mattress with a light thud. "I can only imagine what you will achieve." He held up a finger as I started to respond. "I would caution you from pushing people around. It could lead to disaster."

A chill crawled up my neck. "Is Wati okay?"

Moonjir paced toward the end of the mattress, bouncing slightly. He didn't reply until he had done one lap. "I really shouldn't encourage you, but yes. She's home on Denya, for what it's worth."

I let out a long breath. "Thank you."

He smirked. "Do I get a patch? They're all the rage, I hear."

My lips pursed, but before I could answer, a breeze blew out the candle. Dean cursed and the box of matches rattled. "He'll be gone you know, when I light this."

Moonjir giggled. "That would be just like me."

He was.

Dean placed the candle carefully on the floor and began

working his boots off. "I got the secondhand story about Wati, and I'll have to agree with Moonjir on this one. Don't try sending the Duathua back."

I dropped onto the mattress and peeled off Dean's jacket. "I won't. The situation — I didn't have a choice." I touched Eric's patch in my pocket. "You seem okay with heading to Columbia."

He shrugged, and helped me with my boots. "Tahiti's packed this time of year."

"Tahiti?" I grabbed the blanket and laid back on the mattress. My back still hurt.

"Some island. Read it in a couple books." Dean slid down on the bed. "Penny says they have some books here. Who knows what we'll find in Columbia."

I stared at the ceiling where paint had peeled into interesting shapes, highlighted by the flickering candle. We had helped the Alliance, and maybe found some people of our own. I doubted it would be easy, but I hadn't had fish for dinner. Roxie was safe. Well, safer than at the camp, and Andy had escaped with some of the others who wanted to. I couldn't save them all.

I rolled my head over to study Dean's face. The scratches were healed, but like any healing, they'd left light scars. "I'm sorry I never found a cure." I ached to have all of him.

Dean lifted his body to face me and cupped my neck, shrugging with one shoulder. "Nothing is easy. I love you. And we survived." He leaned in and kissed gently, kindling a burning passion inside me. I sighed when he pulled back to speak. "I'm getting better at holding it in."

My body warmed. I didn't dare hope, but I wanted him in every way. My lips wanted his hot chest under them, and I wanted his mouth across every part of my body. Pressing into a kiss, I stroked across the muscle of his chest and trailed fingers down his side. With my thumb, I traced along the edge of his jeans to his hard abdomen. I wanted more, and my fingers scratched lightly across the denim, searching.

He pulled back from our kiss, but not my touch. "We've got a lot of company out there. If I turn —"

I dug my thumb inside his jeans, pushing down. "If you do, don't howl."

We'd love your review on Amazon, Goodreads, or wherever!

Afterword

We've left Caitlyn, Dean, and the Wolf Squad with new allies. The army of the Savannah Charter has been defeated, for the moment.

However, everything is not perfect. Dean is still infected. Tyrell and Selina have survived.

Home of Fire and Tempest is the adventure-packed conclusion to the Sorrowborn Trilogy.

Acknowledgments

Our common passion for Brandon Sanderson's work led to a love of characters who persevere despite their personal failings.

We appreciate everyone who supported and encouraged our project. Editors, critique partners, and beta readers have all been there for us.

Special thanks go out to Heather Norris who gave us our first review in her beta read, "I loved this book. The story was fantastic, and I love the characters. . . . I got attached to them enough that I cried . . .."

About the Authors

April Davis owns a bookstore in rural Florida, runs bookclubs, edits novels, cosplays, and reads a wide variety of genres.

Kevin A Davis travels nearly every month to convention and events as a speaker, vendor, and even staff.

Find us at
Sorrowborn.com

Also by April Davis & Kevin A Davis

The Sorrowborn Trilogy

Path of Sorrow and Wind

Alliance of Bonds and Storm

Home of Fire and Tempest

Sorrowborn.com

Grab some free short stories from Dean, Caitlyn, and Roxie set just before the trilogy begins.

Join the newsletter with the download of Dean's short story *Never Give Up*

https://dl.bookfunnel.com/d8rkbkphxt

or get Dean's story without a newsletter signup

https://dl.bookfunnel.com/v7szegjy27

Follow the links at the end of the story to download Caitlyn's story, then Roxie's

Also by Inkd Pub

The DRC Files A fantasy series by Kevin A Davis

The Khimmer Chronicles A fantasy series by Kevin A Davis

Spooky, horror, fantasy, science fiction, LGBTQ+, mystery, and explicit romance anthologies. Find them at InkdPub.com